DIE NEXT

DIE
NEXT

JONATHAN STONE

GRAND
CENTRAL
PUBLISHING

New York Boston

Copyright © 2020 by Jonathan Stone

Cover design by Alex Camlin
Cover copyright © 2020 by Hachette Book Group, Inc.

Grand Central Publishing
Hachette Book Group
1290 Avenue of the Americas, New York, NY 10104
grandcentralpublishing.com
twitter.com/grandcentralpub

First Edition: April 2020

Grand Central Publishing is a division of Hachette Book Group, Inc. The Grand Central Publishing name and logo is a trademark of Hachette Book Group, Inc.

The publisher is not responsible for websites (or their content) that are not owned by the publisher.

The Hachette Speakers Bureau provides a wide range of authors for speaking events. To find out more, go to www.hachettespeakersbureau.com or call (866) 376-6591.

Library of Congress Cataloging-in-Publication Data
Names: Stone, Jonathan, 1956- author.
Title: Die next / Jonathan Stone.
Description: First edition. | New York : Grand Central Publishing, 2020.
Identifiers: LCCN 2019054643 | ISBN 9781538733226 (trade paperback) |
    ISBN 9781538733233 (ebook)
Subjects: GSAFD: Suspense fiction.
Classification: LCC PS3569.T64132 D54 2020 | DDC 813/.54--dc23
LC record available at https://lccn.loc.gov/2019054643

ISBNs: 978-1-5387-3322-6 (trade paperback), 978-1-5387-3323-3 (ebook)

Printed in the United States of America

LSC-C

10 9 8 7 6 5 4 3 2 1

This book is dedicated to CoCoBuYa, the long-running, endlessly entertaining group text that has kept my family connected for years.

Sometimes technology is wonderful.

But sometimes…

1.

AT A CROWDED downtown GreenGirl Coffee, Zack threads his way through tables of patrons in their own little worlds. Hunched over laptops, earbuds in, *Times* or *Journal* or work files spread out around them, checking their smartphones obsessively.

Zack finds an empty stool at the counter by the window and sets down his muffin and his Americano Grande. The cute Latina barista had flirted with him a little as she took his order. "I'm calling you Red," she said with an impish smile, writing it on his cup before he could give his actual name. No mystery there. His wildly curly red hair. His calling card all his life. Along with a warm, unguarded smile, which he deploys at the barista in return.

Zack takes a deep sip and looks out, waiting for his pal Steve, due in about twenty minutes.

Snippets of conversation rise above the GreenGirl din. A girl behind him gushing to her friend about her date last night. Two bearded techies discussing coding—like switching

1

between English and a foreign language. Zack watches the businessman on the stool next to his dialing his cell phone to make a call and then turning his back to keep the conversation private.

When the businessman ends his brief call and sets his phone down by his newspaper, Zack sees that he has the same phone Zack does. A black iPhone. Same gray cover. Thousands in this city, Zack figures. He double-checks his own phone, there on the counter next to him, and sees no new texts while he sugars his coffee a little more, puts his napkin in his lap, and breaks his muffin in two.

He digs in. *Mmmm.* He's soon so deep into its cranberries and chocolate chips—a surprisingly tasty combo the barista had persuaded him to try—he is barely aware of the businessman slipping out, but he does notice and welcome the sudden extra space on the counter beside him to spread out a little himself.

He reaches to shift his iPhone over.

It's not there.

He looks where the businessman was sitting. The businessman's iPhone is still on the counter.

Christ! No! Guy took the wrong phone!

Zack jumps up and runs to the door to try to catch the businessman. No one there.

He looks back. His muffin is on the floor, knocked over when he jumped up.

He goes back to the counter and picks up the guy's iPhone. Yeah. Identical to his.

But without the guy's four-digit password, this one's pretty useless.

Except for one thing. One crazy, ridiculous thing.

He knows the guy's four-digit code.

Jesus. He knows the guy's code!

Because Zack happened to see him enter it when he made his call.

2 5 8 0

Because at that moment, seeing him stab in the code and being kind of a numbers guy, Zack had the passing thought that it's the only four-digit all-number code you can enter in a straight line down. He'd had the thought—vague, passing—that maybe the guy couldn't remember numbers? Had cognitive issues? So that's what you'd do, just make it visual, a row going straight down.

Zack wouldn't have caught the code otherwise. He'd thought no more about it because it wasn't his phone.

But now, temporarily, maybe it is.

The businessman, wherever he's heading, is getting farther away from the GreenGirl every second.

Straight down, Zack thinks.

He punches in each digit.

2

5

8

0

He's suddenly looking at the home screen.

All those familiar colorful icons.

Holy shit. I'm in!

He's giddy.

A flush of victory.

Only for a moment.

3

Zack takes a deep breath. He dials his own phone. Luckily you don't need a passcode to answer a phone; if the businessman hears it ring, he can just swipe and talk.

"Hello?"

All right!

Zack can tell by the quick answer. The guy doesn't yet realize it's not his phone.

"Hello, sir, my name is Zack Yellin...Uh, were you just at the GreenGirl at Cross Street?"

The businessman is silent. Careful. Then, "Do I know you?"

"Sir, we swapped phones. By mistake. You've got mine, and I've got yours."

Silence. A pause. The businessman obviously trying to process this. Maybe holding Zack's phone out in front of him to look at it, seeing it's indeed identical. "But...you're not calling from *my* phone, are you?" the businessman asks. Still confused. "You'd...you'd have to know my code."

Zack feels a flash of shame. The impulse to hide. To simply hang up right now.

He sees no alternative but to tell him.

"Look, sir, I..." No way around it. "I happened to see you enter it." He doesn't say how dumb it is to use that code. How easy to see. Or all his passing thoughts about cognitive issues, memory problems, or just the arrogance, the sense of invulnerability, in using that code. Zack keeps all that to himself.

More silence on the other end. Alarm? Fury at being spied on? A silence Zack feels compelled to jump into, to push past the moment. "But...look...I mean, now we can each get our phones back, right? Sir, I'm still at the GreenGirl. I can come meet you with it somewhere if that helps—"

4

The businessman cuts Zack off. "No. Stay there. I can be back there in…twenty minutes. Maybe less."

"I can wait. No problem."

"Just sit tight," says the guy. Kind of aggressively, Zack notices. Then, sounding suddenly a little warmer and more appreciative—or at least trying to be—"And, hey, if I get delayed or have some problem, what's your code so I can call you?"

Zack pauses for a moment. But what's really on his phone that's so private or important? Goofy texts from his new girlfriend and his old pals. Dumb pictures of him and his friends you can see on Facebook anyway. Nothing so special. And they've got each other's phones anyway. It's a moment of human trust, of common humanity, human connection. Each other's phones, each other's private lives, that they're returning to each other in twenty minutes. The guy is just some straight-laced New York businessman, after all, who only wants to get his phone back.

So Zack gives his own code. "Oh, and hey, what's your name?" Zack asks.

"Oh, don't worry about that. See you soon."

Click.

So Zack has about twenty minutes to cool his heels before the businessman gets back to the GreenGirl. No big deal. He's waiting for Steve anyway. Who's always late.

What's he gonna do while he waits?

Twenty minutes to kill.

Hmmm.

Zack feels naked without his own phone.

Of course, he's got this guy's phone, to fill up the time a little.

He knows he shouldn't really look around in it. But what's the harm? A quick little peek at a stranger's life. What's the big deal? Who's it hurting? He scrolls through a few of the guy's texts. Not very chatty. Just some street addresses and rendezvous: 12th and Broadway. Apartment 3C. Southwest corner. Some addresses and meeting places in different cities. Super businesslike. Not a lot of fun in this guy's life. Or not on his phone anyway.

So Zack goes a little further, where he told himself he wouldn't, but now he's more curious based on texts that tell him nothing.

He starts to look at the photos. Organized into folders with just a single name on each.

Huh. Not a single selfie.

Huh. Photos of buildings. Some photos of random streets. Almost like planning a route or something.

Some shots of people on the street. Who don't know he's taking their picture. A little creepy, thinks Zack.

And then a series of photos that changes everything. That makes him grab suddenly at the counter, to steady himself there in the GreenGirl. That makes him feel instantly dizzy. Close to retching.

A lifeless body on the sidewalk. Photographed from *close up*.

Several photos of different bodies, photographed from various angles. And something in him knows—instantly, instinctively—what a series of photos like this must be.

Documentation.

Verification.

Proof.

Proof of what?

But something in him already has the answer.

He suddenly understands what the other photos are. Street corners. Buildings.

It's research.

Research before a hit.

Holy shit.

His heart is drumming hard against his chest. He blinks repeatedly to try to steady himself. To clear his mind a little.

Twenty minutes until the "businessman" gets here.

He can stay here with the guy's phone and pretend he hasn't seen any of it and innocently, cheerfully, hand the phone back to the guy.

But a guy like this—is he gonna take that risk? A professional killer, who knows that a kid who's nosy enough to watch him entering his passcode has been sitting here with his dead-body-filled phone for twenty minutes? Suddenly the kid's not nosy? Come on.

And by now the guy might know a lot about Zack. He might have used *his* twenty minutes and Zack's phone to learn a lot about Zack, and his friends, and the details of Zack's life.

Should Zack use the twenty minutes to race to a police station? Try to get to someone of authority and in a rush try explaining this crazy turn of events of the last half hour? A story about switching phones with a killer? Just by chance seeing the killer's passcode? They'd never believe him. They'd think it's some kind of prank.

And Zack also realizes that all this evidence, all this proof, will be gone in twenty minutes, gone forever when he hands the phone back to this guy. And no one will ever believe him. And the guy will never be caught. And when and if anything happens to Zack after he returns it, no one will ever know why.

Zack's no hero.

But he knows what he's got in his hands.

He looks at the phone. He sees his own hand holding it actually start to tremble.

The trusty little black device he knows so well. Suddenly transformed. Suddenly something entirely different.

It's not an iPhone.

It's a diePhone.

2.

AS JOEY RIDES the subway back to the GreenGirl, the fury in him is so explosive, so uncontained, he feels like shooting someone.

Anyone.

That stupid-looking cow of a nurse across from him with all her blue veins mapping her fat white legs. Those two skinny kids with glasses and buck teeth coming from some fancy school uptown. That gray-bearded black janitor, sweating like a pig.

Pop. Pop. Pull the Glock with the Evolution suppressor out from under his coat, a couple of pops, and hop off at the next stop, feeling much better, calmer, more relaxed. Joey is surprised at how close he feels to doing it. How out of control he feels. And that makes him even madder. Even more pissed at the world and at himself.

You're supposed to be in control in this job. And he always has been. But look how easily he gets *out* of control. Look what it takes. Just one smart-alecky phone call from one smart-alecky kid. *Hey, dude, you left your phone.*

Yeah, he feels like killing someone right here.

Someone else, that is. Someone additional.

He is so pissed at himself. How could he leave the god-damn phone at the coffee shop? What was he thinking? Well, he was thinking about some big stuff. Important stuff. Job stuff. It makes sense that he was a little distracted. But still, part of doing this is the care, the planning, with every step.

He's pissed at himself. But he's more pissed at this kid. Why couldn't the kid notice it a minute or two sooner? Catch up to him before he got in the subway? A kid who saw Joey enter his code—his dumbass code. He knows how dumbass it is but what can he do? Couldn't the kid see it was the wrong phone just a little sooner? Or did the kid not come running out *on purpose?* He saw Joey enter the code, right? So did he wait a few minutes just so he could look around in Joey's phone? Have a little fun. Not knowing what kind of "fun" he would discover.

If the kid hadn't seen the code, that would have been a lot better, of course. Just a useless piece of hardware. Tossed into a landfill somewhere. The phone would be forever dead. Instead of it now having to make more people dead.

And even though Joey's pissed—pissed at and focused on this kid—he also knows the deeper reality of the problem. And the deeper reality is that he's a fuckup. He's always been a fuckup. Whenever he has everything going right, running smoothly, that's when he throws something in to fuck it up. That's the pattern he's noticed about himself. How he always undercuts himself at the worst moment. Something in him wants to fuck it up. *Likes* to fuck it up. Something in him, some weird, dumb, fuckup part of him, didn't turn his phone away from some kid sitting right next to him, just a second or two sooner, when he entered his code.

As he rides the subway back to the GreenGirl, Joey starts to cruise around the kid's cell phone. It's exactly what he knew he would find from the kid's happy, upbeat voice. He didn't even need to look in the phone to know. Lots of photos of friends. Fun parties. There's the kid in these selfies, obviously. Big smile. Curly red hair. Zack, he said his name was, Zack something or other. Good-looking. Surrounded by people. Look at all these text conversations. Let's meet here. Let's meet there. Not a care in the world. *Until now,* thinks Joey. *Until now.*

Let's see, got a girlfriend? That's got to be her, right there, in the most recent photos. Pretty cute. I wouldn't mind a piece of that. Maybe I might get me a piece of that.

And this kid here. This little runt. Lots of pictures of him too. Must be a best friend.

Joey doesn't have a best friend. Or a worst friend. Or any friend, really.

Joey feels the rage rise in him again, boiling up, just glimpsing this kid's life. Zack. Looks like everyone loves Zack.

He's still not sure what he's going to do about Zack when he sees him at the GreenGirl. He tries to calm down and think clearly. The kid is such a Boy Scout, calling him to return his phone. Maybe he's enough of a Boy Scout that he didn't look in Joey's phone.

But Joey realizes he can't risk it. The phone is too full of darkness. Of evidence. Unfortunately for this kid Zack and for Joey, he just can't risk the fact that the kid may have seen what's on the phone. The problem being, there's not a lot on that phone so if he's seen *anything* on it—an address, a text, a photo—he's seen too much.

What a fuckup. The rage rises in him again.

He has to control it.

Sometimes he can't.

No, he doesn't know yet what he'll do about this Zack kid.

But he knows there's nothing he *won't* do.

Story of my life, thinks Joey cynically.

Calming down a little.

Getting ready to deal with this. This little problem. This kid Zack.

3.

ZACK SCURRIES DOWN the crowded street. An assassin's cell phone in his hand.

Not wanting to draw attention by breaking into a full run. But wanting to. Wanting to run. With no idea where to run to.

He's moving fast.

His brain is moving faster.

He wants to throw it away. Toss it in a trash can. Just get rid of the thing. Get away from it. Why not? The guy doesn't really know who he is or what he looks like. Well, yes, he does. He's seen him in pictures by now. He knows Zack's whole life by now. If he's a professional assassin, he has almost certainly looked around Zack's phone, figuring out who and what he's dealing with.

Normally if your phone is taken, you'd get to a computer, log into your iCloud account, go to Find My iPhone to see where it is, and wipe all your data. But Zack had been so excited about using his new iPhone—downloading Facebook,

Instagram, all the fun apps—he never activated Find My iPhone. It was just some security app.

And normally your phone isn't taken by a professional assassin, who has probably already been exploring Zack's phone, taking mental notes, maybe even copying contacts and data in case Zack does try to wipe it.

And as for discovering his own phone's location—well, he'd only want to know it in order to stay as far from it as he can, considering who's carrying it and what would happen if Zack "found" it. The reverse of what the app was meant for, Zack realizes—keeping the phone as far away as possible.

But wait. Couldn't this guy use Find My iPhone to see where Zack is? So maybe he *should* just toss it in the trash, get away from it.

But even if Zack tosses the phone in the trash, and even if Zack tells the "businessman" what trash can it's in, where to find it, it won't matter. Because now Zack knows what's on that phone. And that's not going to be acceptable to a businessman like this.

Zack no longer cares if he gets his own cell phone back. But this guy cares very much, intensely, if he gets *his* phone back.

Zack hurries down the block. Walking as fast as he can. A block he knows so well. A block where everything suddenly looks different. Strange. Tilted.

His brain is spinning. Has he misread the situation entirely? Is he just overthinking it somehow, overreacting, overly alert? The same over-alertness that got him into this guy's phone in the first place—was it now just going into overdrive? It seems absurd that there even is such a thing as an assassin for hire.

Doubly absurd that he has photos of victims on his cell phone. Triply absurd that he's hanging around at a GreenGirl—what, between appointments?

Zack has learned to trust his instincts, but this time maybe he shouldn't. Maybe this time he should trust logic, not instincts. Logic says the odds against accidentally swapping cell phones with an assassin in a coffee shop are astronomically high. Against all reason. So maybe Zack is wrong about something here. Maybe there's something he's missed.

Those photos. Maybe the guy is just a death fetishist. Listens to the police radio and gets to crime scenes before the police do. Sells the photos online in some sick little club. Maybe this guy's not the assassin. Maybe he just takes the proof pictures and doesn't actually commit the murders. So maybe he needs his cell phone back because, if he doesn't get it back, he *himself* could be killed. That would change things, wouldn't it? *Hey, I'm just the photographer. Please, please give it back, or I'll be killed. The assassin I work for doesn't have to know.* That would be an ingenious ploy on the part of the businessman, wouldn't it, saying something like that, to get Zack to come back to the coffee shop? So ingenious that Zack can tell it's only his own ingenious imagination working overtime. *I'm just the photographer.* Wishful thinking. No basis in reality.

Maybe the photos are all staged. Some kind of weird, dark performance art project thing. Maybe once the photos are snapped, the victim gets up, brushes off, and peers over the photographer's shoulder to see what they got. Maybe the photos are an exhibit in some edgy downtown gallery Zack's never heard of. Hey, it's New York.

Maybe he should turn around, go back to the coffee shop,

and tell this guy that he knows it's performance art. Or that it's a perverse hobby. *Hey, to each his own. Here you go. Here's your phone back, you weirdo. There's a lot of weird hobbies and perversions out there. I'm not judging. And I'm not saying anything to anyone. See you later. Have a good day. Let's forget this little phone exchange ever took place.* Would the businessman buy that? Would he risk that?

Zack can tell that he's looking for any excuse, any story, to make this not what it is. To turn it into anything else.

Maybe he should delete all the photos. Delete them all and then call his own phone, let the guy know he's deleted all the photos. But he has no idea if that would make the situation better or worse. And his instincts tell him worse.

Zack can tell already, with those same instincts, that if this is a professional killer, these photos might exist only on this phone. They're probably not backed up to the Cloud or anywhere else. Because the killer can't risk them somehow ending up elsewhere. It's this phone, and this phone only.

The problem for the "businessman," Zack realizes, isn't really the existence of the photos. It's the fact that Zack has *seen* the photos.

The guy's problem isn't the existence of the phone.

The guy's problem is the existence of Zack.

Zack's instincts told him what he was seeing. And his instincts got confirmed in the brief conversation with the guy—he had a toughness, a lack of education, at odds with his business clothing. Something immediately wasn't right. Zack had noticed the tattoo on the back of the guy's hand when he reached for his coffee. A youthful exuberance before joining the workforce, Zack figured. *No, stay there, I'll come to you. My name? Oh, let's not worry about that.* The guy wanting to control the situation. *Needing* to control the situation.

The formula forms in Zack's mind in a dark math, a bleak, deadly calculation: the longer he keeps the phone, the longer he stays alive, because the guy needs to get it back from him. But the longer Zack keeps the phone, the angrier the guy is going to be.

The phone in Zack's pocket.

It's his bargaining chip.

It's his death warrant.

Without thinking, Zack heads toward his apartment. As he tries to picture his contact list, he realizes, with a little beat of thanks, of momentary lift and elation, that his own name isn't anywhere on the contact list. Zack did say his full name when he called the guy, trying to be forthright, polite, project honesty, and now he might pay the price for his politeness. But maybe the guy missed Zack's last name in the confusion of that first call—lots of people miss a name the first time—or maybe this is a guy who doesn't miss anything.

And yes, sure, lots of photos, to know exactly what Zack looks like, and sure some of the old texts from his friends might say "Zack," but his full name is nowhere on that phone, and without a full name, there's no finding his apartment, and his apartment should be safe.

Zack slows down. Realizing, he moans aloud. No, his phone's contact list doesn't say his own last name but it's got all the Yellins of his family listed—his parents, his grandparents, his uncle Saul and aunt Jenna. If you look down that contact list, it's pretty obvious what his last name is. Yellins all over the place.

And as far as his address, all you have to do is go to his Google Maps app or his Uber app, look at his previous destinations, and you'll see his home address stored there, and pretty obvious. That nice, convenient little one-button home address, to help navigate subway lines or road trips—now giving him away.

But wait. It gives the street address. Not the apartment number. Two hundred apartments in his building. Can he head over there safely? Slip into the building, tell the doorman not to say what apartment he's in if a businessman in a trench coat shows up and asks for him.

And then his heart sinks again. Because he thinks of the new text messages on his phone that say his apartment number, that weren't there a few weeks ago.

Texts with Emily. Who he's just meeting. Just getting to know. Just falling in love with.

What apartment are you in?

> 15H. Come on up.
> You'll love the views.

I love the views even
without the windows. ☺

> Haha. Can't wait to see you.

There in ten.

He'd saved it. Looked back at it several times since then.

Just like the businessman could be doing now.

Dammit. His whole life is on that phone. For whoever is smart enough to explore it. And you don't have to be all that smart.

He thinks with a new panic, new fear: Is *Emily's* last name on there? On any of those texts?

Is her address on there?

No. He doesn't think so. But he's not sure.

'Cause this guy could definitely stumble into that lovey-dovey text trail and know immediately he has some leverage. Easily sense Zack's budding relationship. Drag Emily in as a bargaining chip...or worse...unthinkably worse...if the guy can find her.

Zack stands at the corner. Assessing.

He can't risk going home.

He can't risk going to Emily's. Can't risk dragging her into this, getting her involved.

He doesn't want to make any calls from this phone anyway. Doesn't want the record of them on here for the guy to have eventually.

Or *does* he want the record? Does he want to add to the evidence? Start his own trail of evidence? So someone can find that trail someday...

He doesn't know what to do.

And amid his swirl of panic, confusion, paralysis...

Shit! He forgot about Steve!

He's so caught up, so terrified, he forgot about meeting Steve at the GreenGirl. The whole reason he was there. Because Steve wanted to get together, wanted to talk through some life issue in person with him.

Steve is his oldest friend. They'd met at sleepaway camp as kids, Steve the nerdy misfit in the bunk above him, unathletic, socially awkward, gloomy, grumpy. Zack's total opposite, with nothing in common, but that's what they came to like about each other. That's what they both eventually thought was special about the friendship. He hadn't seen Steve in months but they talked and texted, would always be close. Their friendship was a fact of life.

Should he just…text him?

Dude, it's Zack, texting from another number, lost my cell phone, long story, had to cut out of GreenGirl before you got there…

But putting a text to Steve on this phone—won't that put Steve at risk along with Zack? Because what if this guy thinks Zack has told his pal Steve about the photos, about what he found? *Dude, you can't believe what happened to me.*

Okay, so send Steve the text and delete it right after he sends it. But doesn't Steve's number stay stored in the phone's memory, even if he deletes the text?

Stop. Think. He's going too fast. Maybe it's better not to text Steve just yet. Maybe it's better to leave him standing there at the GreenGirl, not knowing anything—annoyed, waiting, out of the loop—until Zack figures this out.

4.

JOEY WALKS INTO the GreenGirl.

Looks around quickly, fully, expertly.

He knows immediately. Zack isn't there.

And if that do-gooding, Boy-Scout-sounding kid is not there when he said he would wait, it makes it pretty clear: the kid must have looked at the phone.

He was nosy enough to see Joey enter his code. So why would he suddenly stop being nosy?

The rage rises again. He feels the Glock under his trench coat. The rage starts to pound, generating heat and itch beneath the trench coat, beating against the inside of his skull.

Well, at least now there's no guessing about what he's got to do. He's got to get rid of the kid. 'Cause looking around Joey's phone even a little means seeing way too much.

Joey turns and is about to ask the barista—skinny Puerto Rican bitch about twenty-five—if she happened to see a red-haired kid sitting at the counter over there. Joey is pulling

Zack's phone out to show the barista a picture when someone steps in front of him to ask the barista something.

"Hey, did you happen to see a curly red-haired kid here about twenty minutes ago?"

The exact question Joey was about to ask.

Joey drops back a step. Turns his face away. Turns back just enough to see who's asking the barista.

A short little guy.

Who Joey recognizes immediately from the pictures on Zack's phone. The little runt. The best friend.

Joey drops back another few steps. Makes himself a little more invisible, as he is expert at doing.

The barista smiles. "Yeah, I know who you mean. He was definitely here," she says, still smiling, "but he left a while ago."

"Damn," says the short guy. "Okay."

And Joey sees the short guy take out his cell phone and begin pressing buttons.

Joey quickly shuts off the ringer on Zack's phone and slips it into his pocket. Moves away a little more.

He sees the short guy texting something on his phone.

Joey feels the buzz of the text arriving in his pocket.

He doesn't even have to look. He knows the gist of what it says:

Hey Zack, Steve here. I'm at GreenGirl but they said you left. Where are you man? Lmk.

The short guy puts away his phone and leaves the coffee shop.

Joey is right behind him.

5.

ZACK STOPS. TRIES to gather his thoughts.

He sits down on a bench.

The assassin has his phone. Maybe is looking through it thoroughly.

So Zack starts to look more closely through the guy's phone.

It's such a contrast to his own. His own phone filled with fun, dumb messages, jokes, rendezvous, all the silliness of his life. He'd hate to face his maker and give an accounting of his life with only his phone to show.

But this phone has nothing on it. Those pictures. A few terse texts.

The phone's not new. Same vintage as Zack's, a couple years old. So for its contents to be so thin, it seems to Zack that, once some jobs are done, the guy must delete the relevant texts and photos. Very orderly. Very neat and businesslike. No fooling around. No evidence of a life beyond his business. A business phone. In the worst possible sense. For the worst possible business.

But it probably means that anything that's still on the phone is active, current, important. Too important to delete.

Zack checks the list of recent calls.

He notices immediately. There are several recent calls to the same number.

Obviously a currently important number.

Okay, he could call that number. That's not adding anything personal to the phone. That number is already on it.

And maybe he can call that number and tell whoever answers it, *Hey, I found this phone, and found your number on it*, and whoever answers it can be an intermediary and get the phone back to the businessman, which would be a gesture of good faith, right? *Hey, I don't want your phone. I don't want anything to do with it. You can have it back, here you go. And my own phone? Hey, toss it. I'm fine with that...*

He's got nothing to lose calling this number.

He takes a breath. He calls.

"Hello?" It's the first surprise. A woman's voice. He'd expected it to be a male, based on the dark world he'd been imagining. A woman's voice. A little tentative-sounding. A little nervous. "Joey?"

So the guy's name is Joey. And yes, she's a little afraid-sounding. Maybe someone as afraid of the guy as Zack is. Maybe someone to bond with.

And then: "Everything go okay?" the woman asks. "It's all done?"

Suddenly Zack has a sinking, sickening sense of where the "businessman" was for those twenty minutes he had asked Zack to wait at the GreenGirl for him. *"No. Stay there. I can be back in…twenty minutes."* Zack realizes what business might have been transacted in those twenty minutes.

He is suddenly speechless. Doesn't know what to do or say. He does all he can think to do. He hangs up.

Stares at the diePhone.

Which seems, at the moment, very much alive.

6.

EMILY JUMPS OUT of the shower, getting ready for work, and dresses, feeling lively, chipper, cheerful.

She hates her job. So why is she suddenly looking forward to the day? Why is she so suddenly upbeat?

She smiles to herself. She knows why. It's this guy she just met. Zack Yellin.

She knows it's ridiculous to feel so upbeat. To feel so good. She knows the odds are it's not going anywhere.

She knows he's kind of a slacker. Doesn't really know what he's doing in life, hangs around different GreenGirls with his friends, is *kind of* looking for work, trying to figure it out.

She knows it's ridiculous of her. But she knows how he makes her feel. She knows what happens when they look at each other.

She can't help smiling. She sees herself smiling as she looks in the mirror, checking her outfit, adjusting her brunette ponytail, and that just makes her smile even more.

She knows plenty about the reality of relationships, how

they fail, why they fail, when they fail. She's had plenty of experience, for better and for worse.

And she also knows this one feels different. More open. More lift. More energy.

Part of her knows it's not going anywhere.

And part of her feels, deep down in a place she's always been able to trust, that this one really *is* going somewhere.

She's been here before.

She's never been here before. Not exactly.

It feels—she laughs out loud—ex*ZACK*tly right, for whatever crazy reasons, as she floats out the door.

7.

AS ZACK SITS there dumbfounded on the bench, the phone in his hands suddenly rings.

He jumps. A little freaked out to feel the assassin's phone come alive in his hands like that.

He looks at the number.

It's his own.

Is he going to answer?

It's his only choice. He can't just run forever. Maybe there's a chance to resolve this. To do more than just run.

"Hello?"

"Hello, Zack."

The voice of the businessman again. But now, something different in it. A shift to a darker hue. Zack senses a strange new intimacy. Even in the silence that hangs for a moment between them.

"You shouldn't have run, Zack. That just tells me you looked in the phone. If you had just stayed there, handed back the phone, acted happy and dumb, that might have worked. I might have bought it."

"No, you wouldn't," says Zack. "I couldn't risk it. 'Cause I knew you wouldn't risk it."

There's a beat. During which Zack feels Joey is assessing his intelligence. "Well, maybe you're right, Zack. But now you leave me no choice. Now, I need that phone back."

Zack can feel his hand trembling, holding Joey's phone against his ear. "Hey, I'm willing to give your phone back and forget everything," Zack says. "But I know you're not going to do that. You're not going to forgive and forget. That's not how guys like you work." And then he maybe goes a little too far. "That's not how people succeed in your business."

A grim silence at the other end. Zack can feel the guy assessing. Irritated.

"You're going to make this hard on yourself, aren't you, Zack? Hey, I'm good with hard. Hard is what I know." A long, menacing pause. "You got a lot of friends, don't you, Zack? Wow, look at 'em all. Looks like your life is a lot of fun. Now who's this one here? She's particularly cute. Emily. Such lovey-dovey texts between you two. Maybe you'll be sending her one more lovey-dovey text right now. Hey Em, let's get together. Beautiful day. See you in a few minutes."

"Leave her alone! She's not involved!" It comes out of him, unbidden, instinctively protective. He immediately regrets it.

"They're all involved, Zack. They're all on your phone. They're all fair game."

"So what are you gonna do, shoot them all? Is that the best way to get your phone back? Shoot everyone?"

The irritation bubbles over. "How 'bout you shut the fuck up and listen to my instructions, you nosy smart aleck, and maybe no one gets shot. Just bring me back my phone."

"And what happens to me?"

A pause. As if the businessman is thinking it through, to make it sound reasonable, reassuring, to phrase it exactly right. "Look, you seem like a smart enough kid. Smart enough to remember the code you saw, when you saw that we swapped phones. So maybe you're smart enough to not say anything to anyone. Smart enough to forget all this. Smart enough to go on with your happy life with Emily. Are you?"

"Yeah. Yeah, I'm smart enough for that."

But, Joey, are you smart enough to believe me?

"There's a diner," Joey instructs him. "Aldo's. Back table. Fifteen minutes."

Some haunt of Joey's? Enemy turf? "Look, how 'bout just a street corner somewhere?"

An explosion of anger. "This ain't a fuckin' negotiation! Aldo's, fifteen minutes. Aldo's in fifteen, or Emily and I go on a little date."

A first date. A last date.

It hangs unsaid between them.

Zack swallows. "Okay. Aldo's."

If Zack goes to Aldo's, he doesn't know exactly what will happen to him. But he has a pretty good idea.

Aldo's is suicide.

And not going may buy him a little time.

When Zack doesn't show up at Aldo's, it's going to make the guy even madder, Zack knows. But as long as Zack still has the phone, there's still a reason for him to be alive, because the guy needs Zack in order to get his phone back. It's a bleak logic—and the only logic he's got to work with. Until he can somehow manipulate that logic. Rework it. Make it change somehow.

And what difference does it make if the guy gets even madder? What difference does it make at this point whether the guy is furious or calm, if he's going to pull a trigger either way? Because pulling a trigger is obviously pretty easy for this guy. Does it every day. Including today, apparently. Right after a nice coffee.

Now of course there's no choice.

He has to warn Emily.

He hates to drag her into this.

He can't believe he has to do this.

He knows enough about relationships, about their fragility, to know this will be the end of it. Maybe he'll survive this, somehow. Maybe she'll survive it. But the relationship sure won't. No decent girl likes to get involved with a guy who's being chased by an assassin.

They're in the honeymoon phase. Getting to know each other, enjoying each other. Long talks and moonlight and long kisses and wondrous sex. Getting to know each other's brains and bodies and joys and likes and dreams.

Talk about the honeymoon being over. Coming to a crashing halt.

But there's no choice. He has to protect her. And the first part of protecting her is warning her.

He takes out the phone, lifts it to his ear, preparing in

his head what he's going to say to her. *How* he's going to say it to her.

And then, suddenly, he realizes.

Shit. He doesn't know her phone number.

He can remember the words of his text exchanges with Emily. Whole sentences come back to him. But he can't think of her phone number, because he's never known it. It's a dating custom, a little moment of promise, of intimacy—you hand your phone to the other person, and they put in their number for you. So he's never actually dialed it.

No one knows anyone's phone number anymore.

And at that little rented office space where she works, where she does freelance work, producing and delivering "content" for several websites, there's no general number. It's just a shared workspace filled with independent contractors. That's the way of the world now. So he can't reach her there either.

The panic rises in him.

Jesus, and all that thinking and worrying about Steve. He can't reach Steve anyway because he doesn't know *his* number. He can't reach any of his friends. Not without his phone. He tries to think of Steve's number. Summon it up out of the past. Not even close. The mindless convenience of technology. It's fucked him!

Okay. Think. How to get a message to her. He can get on the Internet from this phone. He can't email her, doesn't know her email address; they've only talked and texted and of course connected on social media. He checks the phone's icons again. No Facebook or Instagram but he can download the apps by going into the iPhone's settings to get the guy's Apple ID. Or would he need the guy's Apple password too? But then he'd be stuck anyway, because he doesn't know his own Facebook or Instagram passwords; they've been on his phone since he got it so he hasn't had to log in for years.

Think, think. Okay, just open new Facebook and Insta-gram accounts. Authentication will go to his Gmail account, and he does remember that password, *Pebbles123.* His dog, growing up.

But if he does all that, will she even see a message he sends? She keeps her Facebook and Instagram notifications off while she's at work. What about Twitter? If she's even on Twitter, and if she doesn't use a photo of herself, and assuming she uses her own name and not just a handle, he'd have to send a public message to all twenty-five Emily Lanes, and what's it gonna say? *Hi Emily, it's me Zack, the guy you just met. Hey I just swapped phones with a professional assassin by mistake and he might come after you so please stop what you're doing, get up from your desk right now, leave your office, leave your job, and run for it.*

Yeah, right.

And the effort would eat up so much time, and she might not see it anyway. Or see it too late.

Jesus. He can't reach Emily to warn her. Not fast enough, anyway.

He starts to shiver. He feels his stomach tighten, start to cramp.

The guy only knows her first name and her face. Doesn't know her last name. Doesn't know where she lives. Zack's pretty sure it's not in any of the texts. His own apartment, yes—*15H, come on up*—but not hers.

There's not much time until he's due at Aldo's. The fifteen minutes are ticking away.

Maybe he *has* to go to Aldo's so the guy doesn't move on to Emily.

And if Zack's *not* going to Aldo's, then he has to protect Emily somehow. Get to her office or her apartment before Joey does. But *how* is he going to protect her? Make her run too? And what, run forever?

No. He needs something else. For Emily, and for himself. Something besides running. Some plan that turns and faces it somehow. And he needs it fast. Before he's absent from Aldo's, leaving Joey sitting there alone. Making things even worse than they already are.

Joey's not stupid.

Joey can hear it in Zack's voice.

Zack's not going to show up at Aldo's.

Joey can tell already that idle threat is not going to cut it with this kid Zack. He can tell already he needs to up the ante. Up the ante to even *get* this kid to come to the table.

Then maybe Zack *will* show up—scared, frightened, obedient. But the thing is, maybe he won't. And Joey will not leave himself in a position to just be sitting there, shuffling his feet, twiddling his fingers, diddling his dick.

He will not accept being dissed like that. He can imagine it—imagine it too well—and will not tolerate it.

He needs to avoid being a fuckup. For practical reasons. And for his own vision of himself. He needs to think ahead, anticipate. Take control. Be unpredictable.

He needs a way to *guarantee* that Zack will come to the table. Will show up with his phone.

He wanted to do it without upping the body count. Without increasing the risk to himself unnecessarily like that. He wanted to lure the kid, convince him, persuade him, terrify him into it, but fuck it, that doesn't look realistic anymore.

Zack is asking for the hard way. So it looks like it's going to be the hard way. The traditional way. Damn this kid.

He's been following Steve this whole time. Onto the subway platform. Sitting across from him in the subway car. Making the call to Zack while Steve gobbled a donut in a pocket park thirty feet away from him. Kid's oblivious. Looking down at his phone the whole time. Of course.

Emily was pretty cute looking.

But Steve—Steve is right here.

8.

ZACK IS AT a cluttered desk deep in the 11th Precinct, waiting for a detective named Lopez.

Precious minutes ticking by.

Waiting.

It's business as usual in here. Patrol cops flowing past, carrying their lunches. Couple of Hispanic guys being shepherded by in handcuffs. Fluorescent-bright, busy, almost like any other office. He's bringing them something that will interrupt their office day. That's not business as usual.

The diePhone is back in his pocket. He signed in with the desk sergeant. Nervously took the diePhone out of his pocket and put it in the little tray along with his keys and wallet, heart pounding as he watched it pass through the metal detector. Like any other cell phone. Like no other cell phone.

He made up a quick story about a burglary at his apartment, just enough to get in to see a detective, knowing his crazy phone story would raise eyebrows, was too crazy-sounding to justify even *seeing* a detective, and if he showed the photos to the desk sergeant, they might cuff him right there.

And now he's been assigned to a Detective Lopez, and he's waiting, *waiting* to see him—for how many more minutes? Ten? Fifteen? A half hour?—while Joey stews in fury at Aldo's and maybe figures out, somehow, what Emily's last name is, where she lives, where she works.

But Zack had to do something. This is what the police are here for. Citizens in trouble. Protection from imminent threats. Precincts all over the city that the average citizen can walk into and the desk sergeant will look up and ask, "Can I help you?"

For a burglary, maybe. Or a theft, or even an assault. But for this?

He's starting to worry that this is the second brilliantly dumb thing he's done today. First, noticing the guy's code and calling him. Now, thinking the police can act quickly and protect him.

Because when Lopez gets here, what's Zack going to say exactly? *Well, you see, I accidentally swapped phones with a guy in a GreenGirl but I also accidentally saw him entering his phone code earlier so I was able to call him but while I was waiting I looked at his phone, and the photos of all these dead bodies, taken from all angles, told me he was a professional killer, and now he's called me from my own phone, which I gave him the code for, and he's coming after me, and he's planning to kill me, I can just tell.*

Would a street-smart, street-weary detective believe it for a moment?

Two swapped identical phones? That *both* of them managed to get into? One of them belonging to an assassin? Hanging out at a GreenGirl Coffee before a hit? Leaving the phone inadvertently in a GreenGirl before a hit?

Really?

To Lopez, he would clearly be another crazy New Yorker. In the middle of some weird, crazy fantasy they couldn't hope to attach to reality. Classic bipolar paranoia. *Son, now calm down. You need to get back on your meds.*

But here, Detective, just take a look at these pictures! He could cut to the chase. They'd presumably find them as shocking and disturbing as he had.

But would they? Or would they be disturbed for different reasons? With the cynical eyes of cops dealing with some out-of-breath kid walking in off the street.

Maybe they'd think the photos could have been downloaded from the Internet. Could have come from anywhere. Could be a pervert's staging. Could be some weirdo student art project.

And here's this disturbed kid now trying to make his paranoid fantasy into reality. Make it line up somehow with photographic evidence so the cops would finally believe him.

Wouldn't they find it way more likely that these were *his* pictures, that *he* took, that it's *his* phone—and who knows how long they would hold him there until they could ascertain otherwise. Figure out what those photos really were.

Holding him there while Joey sits at Aldo's getting madder. And finally gets up and goes after Emily.

No, they wouldn't believe it. Not for a minute.

Hell, *he* wouldn't believe it. Not for a minute.

And speaking of minutes, the clock is ticking. The traditional clock on the precinct wall: second hand sweeping, minute hand clicking, both silently taunting and torturing him. Precious minutes that he's losing forever, sitting here waiting for this Lopez.

He should never have tried the code and called the business-man. It was an impulsive mistake that could cost him his life.

It's not too late to learn from that first impulsive mistake. And not make a second one.

"Hi, I'm Detective Lopez. So sorry about the wait." Over-weight, moving slow. Like a symbol of the whole department, thinks Zack. How fast can they really move?

The only rescue, Zack realizes, is going to come, somehow, from him.

"So what can I do for you?" says Lopez, settling slowly behind the cluttered desk.

"Nothing really," says Zack, standing up. Smiling his big, barista-winning smile—his artificial version of it. "No need to waste your time, Detective, I'll…I'll just file a report online." And he turns to go, just catching Lopez's confused expression.

A confused, befuddled expression that says it all. Captures instantly and perfectly for Zack, the whole bureaucratic, methodical, standard approach to a criminal complaint.

The criminal of the complaint now moving swiftly, focused, sharklike, toward his friends and toward him.

Zack hurries out of the precinct.

Turns the phone back on and nervously checks for messages as he exits.

Christ. There's Zack's phone number on the screen. A missed call from Joey.

What new threat? What new twist? *I'm at Aldo's, Zack. Where the fuck are you?*

The cops can't help him. They'll never believe him. Zack is on his own.

9.

JOEY HAD DONE a dime. Armed burglary with assault.

It was his third stretch. His longest by far. All told, he'd spent more of his life in prison than out. Not a surprising or uncommon stat in his crowd. In his world.

He's been out a year now. A busy year. A productive year.

He'd come out planning to go clean. Start fresh. Doing a full dime took it out of him. Just about killed him, literally and figuratively. So he really did want to fly right.

But he needed money. He talked himself into an apartment but he needed to pay the rent. And there was no job an unskilled guy like him could do to meet that rent. He filled out applications at the big box stores, which turned him down flat, even when he left off his convictions. Smaller places—dry cleaners, mom-and-pop grocers—couldn't give him enough hours.

So within weeks, he went back to the crew he'd worked for, been so loyal to, but they had nothing for him. Which pissed him off. Although he knew why they had nothing for him.

Because no one liked him. No one liked being around him. He didn't know what it was about him, or *why* it was, but it had always been this way, and he could see it and feel it from a mile away. No one liked spending time with him, and their work, if you wanted to call it that—hijacking, debt collection, illegal gambling, dock work, airport work, organized burglary—was always done in teams. And the team had to like you.

But there was one job he could do for them, he learned. And it paid really well. 'Cause the risks were way higher. And you worked alone, you had to, occupational necessity. And you had to be smart.

But nobody trusts him to do his job. Again, he doesn't really understand why. He's always been totally stand-up, never ratted anyone out, always kept his mouth shut in prison. It's just…well, it's just that he isn't like them. Tried to be, tried to fit in with the crew, but couldn't. And they don't trust anyone who's different.

So they've made it a condition of his new job that he has to show them that he's doing the job correctly.

You'll use a cell phone, they told him. You'll take pictures on the cell phone. You'll contact your clients on the cell phone, and tell them that *you* contact *them*, and they never contact you back. Don't keep anything on the phone but what you need. This camera on this phone is how you prove to us what you've done. Welcome to modern crime, Joey. You been in the Crowbar Hotel so long, welcome back to the world.

Cell phones. He had to learn them. In all his years in prison, he'd kind of missed out on cell phones. Hadn't grown up with them. He didn't really know everything they could do.

They were prized in prison culture. Guards would smuggle

them in, offering them to special prisoners in exchange for special favors. The prisoners traded in them. Old models, pretty limited in what they could do, but prized and prestigious on the inside nonetheless. Having one meant you were pretty high in prison hierarchy. Meaning Joey never even got close to one.

But for his new job, they got him a brand-new one. Explained to him just what he needed to know about it. *"Now look, Joey, you ain't the swiftest guy around."* (They all knew about his concussions from street fights as a kid, and maybe that's when he started getting kind of different, and he knew that by "different" they meant slow, stupid, even though he wasn't, was he?) *"So for your Apple ID password, we're just gonna pick something simple, Joey, something your scrambled brain won't ever forget. And for your code, look here, Joey, don't even think of it as a number. Just straight down the middle like this, 'cause this phone's pretty much staying in your pocket anyway, and this way if something happens to you and any of us need to get into it fast, we can."*

Like Joey couldn't even be trusted to choose a code for himself, like he couldn't even remember four numbers of his own birthday or his mom's or his dad's. Like they half expected something *would* happen, and they'd have to get into the phone someday. But that's what they wanted, that's how they saw him, so what could he do?

And his bosses disabled something on his new phone called the Cloud, some kind of backup system, so the pictures would only exist on the phone itself. They didn't want those pictures existing anywhere else. Only for Joey and them. For no one else, anywhere, ever.

"We find you your clients, Joey. We refer them. We take thirty

percent for that, up front. And you're takin' all the risk here, Joey, so you get the big share, seventy percent, cash straight from the client to you so it never gets connected to us. But you gotta do your job perfectly because it's a reflection on us, understand?

"You're gonna be good at this job, Joey. 'Cause you never really connect with people, you know? This is perfect for you, Joey."

They didn't trust him, because they didn't understand him. Everyone was a little uncomfortable with him around. From when he was a kid on the streets, to reform schools, to prison, to now. He didn't know if it was his IQ, if it was too high or too low, or his being a little different from everybody, or not one of the guys, or what. In prison he learned from the staff psychologist that besides the damage from the concussions, he might also have something called Asperger's, that he was "mildly autistic," that he was "on the spectrum," but he couldn't tell if that meant he was smarter, or dumber, or both at the same time. The psychologist wanted to give him some tests to find out more but the state said no to the cost.

But Joey figured that's what the pictures were really about. A way for them to verify the hit. And to keep an eye on him.

And well, he liked the work. Liked it a lot better than he thought he would. His own hours. His own decisions. He liked the careful planning. The sense of control. Not having to answer to other people. Spending half your time inside, with the prison population who and what it is, he had already mostly picked up how to do it. If he wanted to say no to a certain job, for any reason, he could. But you didn't want to be a guy who got a reputation for saying no, or for being picky, or they wouldn't recommend you for the next job.

And you had to do the job right every time because one

little fuckup and you'd be toast. You'd be caught. You'd be finished.

He was okay with all that.

And the money was really good. Even better than they said.

One thing about the job though. It reinforced his being alone. He had to work alone, had to cut himself off from pretty much everyone, and while a part of him liked that, actually preferred it, at the same time it made him feel isolated, and anxious, and well, a little crazy. Limited human interaction, only the most careful human contact, he was okay with it but he could tell it wasn't good for him, and that, whatever was already a little off about him, this was making it worse.

And the cell phone kind of reinforced that even more. Regular people got to use their phones to stay in touch, keep connections, have more people in their lives. But for him, the phone was a way of keeping people away. Avoiding human contact, doing it by phone. A device for business. For making arrangements. For documentation. And nothing more.

And then, after being so careful at his work, so good at it for so long, he was on his way to "finalize" a job, as he liked to say, and was double-checking his phone's camera like he always does but for some reason it wasn't working, his code wasn't getting him in. He tried his code twice, three times, and couldn't figure out what was wrong but *fuck*, now he had no way to document the hit. He was getting more and more frustrated, wanted to stomp the fuckin' phone under his feet, and suddenly a call comes, and he answers, confused, 'cause he sees his own number, and a kid says "Sir, were you just at the GreenGirl? We swapped phones. You've got mine, and I've got yours." *Fuck!*

He thought fast enough to get Zack's code—*hey, if I have some problem, what's your code so I can call you?*—but fuck, he can't document the hit on some kid's phone. He can't suddenly use some kid's phone for his business. Some phone that *does* connect to the Cloud and could send the photos fuck knows where.

And since he couldn't document the hit, he had to let it go.

And having to let the hit go means no money, of course. Not collecting on it yet, like he was counting on. And no money means no rent payment.

And not doing the hit means risking not being given more. Not being trustworthy.

One little fuckup and you're toast.

And that's why he's so mad. So truly smoking mad. 'Cause in a way this dumbass kid doesn't understand, everything is suddenly on the line for Joey.

And that's why just now he dialed the kid and hung right up. Just to rattle the kid. Just to confuse him. Just to add a little extra terror for missing Joey's call. Not knowing whether to call Joey back or wait obediently. It made Joey feel a little better, upping the terror. But not better enough. He's going to do a lot more, to really feel okay again.

10.

HEY, IT'S THE Internet. There's more than one way to reach someone. Zack opens the diePhone's browser.

No, he can't reach Steve through Facebook or Instagram, since he doesn't remember his own passwords, and he doesn't know Steve's email, but he realizes there *is* another way to reach Steve. His little one-man Internet design company—he's probably got a website of some sort, right? Probably with a contact email address. Zack hadn't thought of it—the context of their friendship has always been texts and photos and parties and friends but Zack has sat across from Steve while Steve obsessively and desperately checked for any new freelance assignments. So Zack now googles Steve Furman Design and clicks on the site, and sure enough there's an email contact. Yes!

Zack goes into his own Gmail and quickly keystrokes in the email address. His fingers dance on the diePhone key-board: Dude, it's me Zack. I accidentally swapped phones with a guy, too much to explain here, but that's why I missed you at GreenGirl, sorry. Text me at 2120739909. Do NOT text my old phone. He had wanted to keep their texts off the diePhone. But he can't worry about that anymore. It's more important now just to reach Steve, who must figure something has come up for Zack and is presumably trying Zack's cell phone and not getting an answer because Joey is probably ignoring the texts. Although if Steve is continually texting Zack's phone, Joey may eventually text him back to suggest a rendezvous. Jesus. Hopefully Zack will reach Steve first.

Joey is still following Steve. Deciding what to do to Steve. Where, when, and how badly to hurt him. What exactly to hurt him with. Enjoying the fantasies, the vivid possible scenarios, starting to piece them together into a convenient, expedient reality.

Deciding whether to take a picture of the resulting reality and send it to his own phone for Zack to see. Let Zack see what his pal Steve is up to.

Maybe taped and tied up in his apartment—to lure Zack there, to get the phone back that way—as the only way for Zack to save the life of his innocent, terrified friend.

Or maybe send a photo of Steve dead. Bullet to the head. Let Zack see how it's just one more to Joey—just one more photo on his phone. *And I'll keep going, Zack, don't you see? It's nothing to me. Emily is next on the list, until you get that phone back to me.*

But Joey recognizes the problem. As soon as he suggested

the meeting at Aldo's and as soon as he heard the hesitation in Zack's voice, he recognized it.

Zack is smart enough to realize by now that having Joey's phone makes him Joey's target but having Joey's phone is also keeping him alive. It's undoubtedly occurred to Zack that if he shows up at Aldo's, or at a kidnapped Steve's apartment, but hides the phone somewhere beforehand, then Joey *can't* kill him because he needs his phone back before he does. Because Joey can't risk it being in any other hands.

Joey sees Steve checking his phone, no doubt looking for a call or a text from Zack.

He sees Steve suddenly sit down on a bench, shake his head, smile—and still smiling, texting something.

Fuck. Maybe Zack, this smart-aleck kid, has figured out how to reach Steve from Joey's phone without having Steve's number. Maybe through Facebook or Instagram or one of those sites they all have.

Is Zack hatching some plan? Fuck. Maybe Joey should have taken Steve out already. But if he did, he'd never get to Zack.

Is Zack arranging a meeting? No, that would be pretty dumb of Zack. He wouldn't want to risk dragging his innocent friend Steve into this. Maybe he's just apologizing for not being at the coffee shop. Or maybe Zack is asking his friend for help without telling him why.

Watching Steve smiling and texting is making Joey nervous. He feels time ticking. He feels some unknown action coming from Zack. He needs—he's itchy for—some parallel action of his own.

But how's Joey going to get around the problem of Zack not

bringing the phone to any meeting he sets up—knowing Joey would probably just kill him right there, or shortly afterward, once Zack gives him back the phone.

Suddenly Joey has an idea.

Suddenly he knows what to do with Steve. Don't kill him right here and send a photo. That would scare Zack off forever. His friend would be dead. He would run to the police. Zack would have no choice.

No, Joey has a better idea, and it goes against everything he's done in his professional life for the past year. It will be a big departure. But this threat to his livelihood and his freedom is a good enough reason to do it.

A huge part of his profession, the biggest part arguably, is making dead sure—so to speak—that there are no witnesses.

The photos are the only witnesses. Silent, trustworthy, unquestionable.

But maybe now it's time for an actual witness.

One witness.

Zack.

Watching his friend Steve die. Right in front of his eyes.

That would be highly motivating, wouldn't it?

That would get Joey's phone back, pronto. Screaming, trembling, blithering, blathering, vomiting, crying, helpless, Zack would give it back right there. Or retrieve it real quick if he did actually hide it.

Even if Zack simply witnesses the live *threat* to Steve, without Joey even pulling the trigger, that might be enough. Zack would hand it over. Do anything to prevent his friend dying in front of him.

And Joey would take the phone and shoot them both.

Steve first so Zack could see it and feel crummy and responsible, for a few seconds anyway.

Yeah, Zack as a witness.

That's a lot of power Joey could bring to bear on the situation. Psychological firepower.

Because seeing a photo is one thing. Seeing it happen for real is quite another.

11.

DUDE—OBVIOUSLY I got your email. Phone swap? Only you, Z-man, only you! 🙂

All right, thinks Zack. A text from Steve! A communication from the previous world.

How much to tell him? How much to explain? How much help to ask for? And what help exactly could his pal Steve provide? Design a nice website for an assassin, in exchange for the assassin letting Zack go?

He is reluctant to tell Steve too much, to implicate him in any way. Steve's number is on his own phone, in Joey's hands. Lots of text exchanges. This guy Joey, if he's even half-way smart, will figure out this is a good friend of Zack's. Who knows what this guy Joey will do, how far he will go, to get the phone back from Zack.

Yeah, well, I'm trying to get this dude's phone back to him. But we're having some problems with the actual exchange, Zack texts to Steve.

Well, let me know if I can help.

Less than a minute later, he gets another text from Steve.

Hey, dude, why not swing by my place? We can have a brew while I help you figure out your phone thing.

Nice offer, thinks Zack.

Steve's apartment. Only ten minutes from here on mass transit. It's a dump, a fifth-floor walk-up, but it's a place to stop running, to stop and think. To organize a plan.

Maybe he is going to have to involve Steve, after all. That's what friends are for. There for you in a crisis.

Although a crisis like this? That's asking a lot.

Maybe he'll have an idea that Zack hasn't thought of. After all, Zack isn't necessarily thinking straight. Steve is a sweet guy. A longtime friend. No, he decides, he doesn't want to risk dragging Steve into this.

I'll figure out the phone thing myself, Stevie. Thanks.

Well come on over anyway, says Steve's next text.

Ok, I'll try to get over there sometime this afternoon.

No, you should come now.

That's a little forceful, thinks Zack. A little uncharacteristic. Zack's heart starts to pound.

Dude. You need to come now, says the next text.

Oh no…Oh no…

The diePhone rings. Zack answers.

"Dude, there's a guy holding a gun to my head. He says you need to come to my apartment right now." Steve's voice. Shaking. Mumbling. Zack can barely understand the words.

And then Joey's voice. "Guess we missed each other at Aldo's."

Zack is silent.

"Your pal's apartment. Ten minutes, asshole."

A wave of nausea washes through Zack's torso.

"Ten. Not eleven." Adding, in a shifted tone, eerily empty, devoid of emotion, "Eleven minutes is too late."

"Okay. Ten minutes," says Zack.

Now, with no choices. None he can see.

12.

ZACK RUSHES TOWARD the subway.

He's thinking a million miles an hour.

Would Joey really do it? Would he really kill someone—or *two* people—because of a smartphone?

A guy who kills for money. For a living. It wouldn't be very professional. It wouldn't pay very well. Nothing, in fact.

Maybe Joey, when he calms down, will decide it's not worth it. Maybe it's all a bluff to get his phone back.

Can Zack take that risk? Take that risk with his friend's life?

He scampers down the stairs to the subway platform, turning over the odds in his head.

He yanks his subway pass from his wallet, inserts it, and blasts through the turnstile.

And waits.

Waits.

Checks one of the electronic info boards dangling above the platform. NEXT TRAIN: 3 MINUTES.

He watches the board obsessively, leg jiggling, heart thrumming, waiting to see it change.

It does.

Next train: 5 minutes.

What? Oh no…

It changes again. Next train: 8 minutes.

Oh fuck. Delayed. Some kind of problem.

Maybe not even running.

Holy shit. He can't get there in ten minutes.

Wait here and hope it comes? Go upstairs to hail a cab? Call an Uber, hoping there's one close by? What's fastest?

The same question a million city dwellers wrestle with when they're late for a meeting. When they're about to get reamed out by a boss.

That's in the real world. The real world going on around him.

He's in an alternate world, a dark world right next to it, where if he's late for his next meeting, a friend could die.

Shit. He can't even dial or text from here to say the subway isn't running. No cell signal in this subway station.

He flies up out of the subway, three stairs at a time.

Brushing frantically past the clot of people flowing down the subway stairs, he bumps into one guy pretty hard. "Hey, asshole!" the guy says. Zack keeps going. But it's true—he's suddenly one of those arrogant assholes people can't stand, going against the flow.

He emerges at street level and throws his right arm high in the air, searching the traffic frantically to hail a cab.

He's picturing Steve's walk-up. Old run-down building. He's never seen anyone go in or out of it besides Steve. The apartment is at the back. It's easy to imagine that Joey has him there, at gunpoint, that no one even saw them go in. No doorman. No security. Unfortunately perfect for this guy Joey and his purposes.

Zack reaches into his pocket for the diePhone, to call his own phone and say he's on his way.

The diePhone isn't there.

Shit.

Holy shit.

His heart seizes. His legs feel wobbly.

It must have dropped out of his pocket when brushing past the crowd on the subway stairs. Bumping into some of them.

An empty cab pulls up to him where he was standing with his arm up. He stares at the cab.

"You gettin' in, buddy?"

All the other cabs are passing by full. He's lucky to get this one.

Shit. He can't show up at Steve's without the phone. No way. That won't save anyone.

He has no time. But he has no choice.

He turns and heads back down the subway stairs.

What if someone already grabbed it?

What if someone stepped on it?

He squints in the dimmer stairway light, bending forward, scanning desperately.

This is where he bumped that guy. Nothing.

This is where he brushed past those people. Nothing.

He looks farther down the stairs.

There.

Against the wall at the bottom of the landing.

Shit, no—did it tumble down the stairs? Will it still work?

He reaches the phone and scoops it up. Glass cover intact. He can't try dialing till he's out of the subway again. Another precious minute, lost.

Ten minutes, asshole.

He looks at the diePhone.

It's still working.

Showing him much of those ten minutes already gone.

Back on the street, Zack dials.

Feels only a moment of relief that the phone works. That the call goes through.

"What?" Gruff, impatient.

"I'm on my way. Subway trouble."

"You expect me to buy that? Just when you had to be here to save your friend, that's when there's subway trouble?"

"It's true. I'm on the street. Trying to get a cab."

"Try harder. Now you've got six minutes."

Dial tone.

Shit.

Zack waves frantically. Sees a cab pull in across the street. He dashes out across the street, narrowly dodging a delivery truck, in order to grab it.

Jumps in. Gives the address.

He aims the phone's camera at the cross street sign. Shoots a photo. Texts it to his phone.

Proof.

Proof he's on his way.

The guy respects photographic proof, thinks Zack.

The text comes back. You better go faster.

Okay, he got the photo. He knows Zack is on his way. *You better go faster.* Making Zack sweat. Giving him a little shit. Fooling with him a little. Someone who's fooling with him a little isn't going to kill his friend, is he?

Zack shoots another photo, a cross street ten blocks closer. Sends it.

The next text comes back. I don't think you're gonna make it. Are you?

Making it a game. Good sign.

He'll make it.

He'll be a few minutes late, sure.

But he'll make it.

Zack presses the icon to switch the camera around. Takes a selfie. Sends it. More proof. Clear proof. *On my way.*

Joey paces in the apartment. Gun in his belt. Steve gagged and tied on a kitchen chair in the middle of the floor.

There's nothing here. Kid's got nothing worth taking. This annoys Joey. He thought there'd be something here to pay himself back a little for the hit he lost. Make it worthwhile. The fact that the kid has nothing only makes him madder.

Subway not running? All of a sudden? Come on.

And now this kid's sending him travel photos. Like this is a game.

Sending him "proof" photos. What, mocking Joey's photos?

And now Joey's phone, his business phone, has Zack's cross-street photos on it.

And then the kid sends a selfie.

A selfie!

Joey is wondering, too, whether two people will be too much to handle in this little apartment. His victims have always been unsuspecting. Now he'll be facing them. Will he do it? Will he follow through once he has his phone back? Or will one of them try to jump him?

And he's thinking about that girlfriend, Emily. He has to admit, he's been thinking about her instead of this loser Steve. And what Emily might offer, what it might be like to tie her up, as opposed to this short, nerdy guy.

Joey looks at his watch, and Zack is now officially a few minutes late.

He doesn't take it seriously, this guy Zack, does he?

He pretends to sound scared. But he's not. Not scared enough.

Joey dials his phone.

"Hello?"

"Where the fuck *are* you?"

"Still in the cab. Almost there, Joey."

Joey!

How the fuck does he know his name? How did he figure out his name? It's nowhere on the phone. Fuck. Does he know his last name? Does he know everything, this smart-aleck kid? Fuck. Fuck!

Okay. That's it.

He puts the phone on speaker.

Zack can still be a witness.

"Zack, you're too late."

* * *

Zack hears the shots.

Followed by silence.

And then:

"Zack, you're too late. And this girl I see, Emily? She's next, Zack. And it won't stop until you give me that phone. On *my* terms. On *my* schedule, Zack. On *my* schedule."

The cab pulls suddenly to the curb.

The passenger door opens.

Zack struggles out of the cab.

Pukes on the sidewalk.

He's shaky. Dizzy. The city is spinning around him. The city he loves. Spinning out of control.

Steve.

Oh my God. Steve.

He pukes again.

Straightens slowly. Blinks. Breathes. Tries to focus.

Steve knew about Emily. Zack had told him about her—smiling, excited at this turn his life was taking, sharing it with his oldest friend. Did he ever mention her last name to Steve? Or where she lived? He doesn't think so but isn't sure. So he doesn't know what Joey could have gotten from Steve about Emily. Could have forced out of Steve.

Steve.

Emily.

Zack's world is being sliced apart. Piece by piece. Photo by photo. Smile by smile.

Because of his own phone in an assassin's hands.

Because of the diePhone in his pocket.

13.

EMILY'S AT WORK. Sitting at her desk. It's been busy. But when she stops and looks out the window for a moment, she notices she's still smiling.

She's a little surprised she hasn't heard from Zack yet this morning. He usually checks in with her. What did he say he was doing? Oh yeah. Meeting his friend Steve. He said he didn't have a lot to do. A light day. Like all his days.

She smiles. Maybe he's busier than she thought. Maybe there are things he hasn't told her yet. She really doesn't know all that much about him. It's really been about the two of them together. Not their individual lives. And that's part of what's made it special.

Usually, at this early stage of a relationship, she plays a little hard to get. She always waits for the guy to do the reaching out.

But it's so much easier with this guy. All those games are put aside. There's something more real and authentic and connected going on with Zack Yellin. For whatever reason. Through whatever mysterious chemistry.

So she's delighted to feel no hesitation, to feel totally comfortable, as she texts him.

What's up? How's your morning?

The text comes right back. Good! How bout yours?

Did you get together with your friend Steve?

Yup, I did.

Emily sees the ellipses. There's more coming.

Hey, so when can we get together?

Well, he usually has a more stylish way of asking, something wittier, slyer, more romantic. This is a little blunt of him but she forgives it because obviously he wants to see her as much as she wants to see him.

Well, I can probably grab lunch with you, she texts him.

Great! Where should we meet?

That park in front of my office?

There is a little pause in his response. She waits.

Great. Hey, what's the cross street again?

Oh, come on. How could he not remember?

You know where it is.

> Yeah, but I need the exact
> address cause I want to
> send you something
> at your office.

She smiles.

Ok. It's 109 Union Square South.

> Ok, see you in the park, 12:30.

Emily smiles in anticipation. She can't help herself.

Joey smiles in anticipation too.

14.

STILL DIZZY. STILL nauseous.

Zack vomits again.

And thinks again about those photos.

What kind of assassin has photos? It's completely counterintuitive. *Keeping* the evidence.

Zack tries to calm down. To think it through. And a couple of things occur to him. When he first called Joey, it was pretty clear that Joey was surprised to find he had the wrong cell phone. And Joey, for whatever reason, always took pictures.

So when he found he had the wrong cell phone, he might have called off the hit he was headed out on. Which helps explain why he is so crazy mad. 'Cause his system, his method that he relies on, is suddenly messed up.

And now Zack thinks again about the number he called from Joey's phone. The mysterious, surprising woman answering.

Everything go okay? It's all done?

When he'd hung up the phone suddenly like that, why hadn't she called him back?

Maybe this woman hadn't called him back because she was

told *not* to call back. Was told that's the rule. That she has to wait to be called.

Everything go okay? It's all done?

Meaning the hit.

And while Zack originally assumed it was some female associate or go-between on the phone, now he senses her as someone being careful, nonspecific, because she's scared.

Meaning, this might be a client.

A client who presumably comes from a safer, mainstream, everyday world—the world Zack left just hours ago—where killing someone is not something you know anything about so you hire someone, and the whole process is terrifying. Whether you feel justified or not—whether you want someone killed because they are abusing you, abusing your children, or have scammed you out of your savings and legal approaches have given you no other recourse, or whether you have less understandable motives—you are now dealing with a world that is dark and frightening and unknown. A *subworld* you've never experienced before so you tiptoe around in it. If you're a paying client, it probably means one thing: you're too scared, too lily-livered, too squeaky clean, to do this for yourself.

Leverage, thinks Zack.

Zack takes out the diePhone. Brings up the woman's phone number again in recent calls. Sends a text:

No, everything did not go ok. It's not all done.

Need to meet you to
discuss, as soon as possible.

He doesn't know whether she's close by or a continent away. Maybe close by, for a cash payment. They wouldn't risk bank deposits or transfers for something like this, Zack doesn't think. He hopes to figure out if she's close by, by how she responds to "as soon as possible."

She texts back immediately. Waiting by her phone, apparently.

> But you said we can never meet in person???

Yes, thinks Zack. A scared client, trying to stay within the rules.

> Now we need to. There's a diner called Mali's.

> Ok, Mali's. I can be there in fifteen.

Close by. Thank God.

He swapped phones with a professional hit man. His oldest friend is dead. But the universe is finally cutting him a break.

15.

EMILY WAITS FOR Zack in the park across from her office.

She's only got an hour. He's already a few minutes late. Where is he? He shouldn't have suggested lunch if he couldn't make it.

Where are you? she texts.

On my way. Sorry. Hey btw, my friend Joey works near you. I told him he could stop by and meet us in the park. Dark-haired guy in a trench coat. Dresses like a typical businessman but he's nice. Hope that's ok???

Jeez, it's a little early to be meeting your friends, thinks Emily.

A guy in a trench coat approaches Emily, waving at her, smiling broadly, big friendly grin.

Emily texts, Yeah I see him now. We'll wait for you.

She waves back to Joey and smiles as he approaches.

16.

ZACK LOOKS AT a woman through the window at Mali's. Sitting alone. Clearly terrified. *Clearly* the client.

Late forties. Petite. Pretty. And who knows—maybe she was trying to have an abusive husband killed? Or a sexually abusive boss? Maybe she felt as cornered as Zack does.

Zack is pretty certain she has no idea what Joey looks like. Nothing done in person. All arranged by phone call.

Zack slides smoothly, silently, into the booth across from her. She looks up, startled.

He stares at her silently, blankly. Channeling an assassin he's never met.

He watches her shift uncomfortably. Senses her struggling to breathe evenly.

"Joey?"

Zack waits before answering. Thinking it through. *This needs to be right.* "Joey couldn't make it," he says. "And here's your problem, Miss Whatever-Your-Name-Is, and don't even tell me. In my hands here, I've got Joey's phone, and on it is clear evidence that you ordered a professional hit from Joey, tried to have someone killed, and I can take this phone right to the police, and I will, unless you do exactly what I say."

He sees the expression on her face. Her eyes go wide. Absorbing it. Absorbing how she has fallen into this dark hole. Stunned. Terrified.

"Do what I say," Zack says, a little less harshly, sympathetically, "and you won't get hurt."

Stunned, terrified, she nods understanding.

"Lucky for you, your hit didn't happen so you can still go free. We can both pretend you never hired Joey."

She nods mutely. Obedient. Ready to get out of the trouble she's in. Ready to emerge from this world that she foolishly, mistakenly entered.

"I will explain what you need to do…but first, we have a phone call to make."

Zack dials the phone.

Joey picks up. Gruff. Insolent. "Guess you're finally—"

Zack cuts him off. "I'm sitting here with your client, Joey. Say hello, client. She's not too happy that you screwed up, Joey. Not too happy to be with me. Not too happy the evidence against both of you is on this phone. Pretty scared overall. Here's what's gonna happen, Joey. Your client and I are going to meet you back at the GreenGirl in full view of dozens of people so you don't put a bullet into anyone. And you're gonna take your phone back, and I'm gonna walk out with your client, and—"

Now Joey cuts Zack off, furious. "Your timing's pretty good, Zack," says Joey. "'Cause *I'm* here with Emily. Say hi, Emily."

Muffled, whimpering, terrified, "Zack, help!" before the phone is yanked away.

"So yeah, we're gonna meet back at that GreenGirl. And you're gonna give back my phone. And after that? We'll see…" Joey says threateningly.

Oh my God. Joey has Emily.

But Zack has the client.

He feels the nausea rising again.

"Fifteen minutes, Zack."

My terms. My schedule.

"Fifteen minutes," says Zack.

He looks across the table at the client. They mirror each other's terror.

The woman is shaking.

"I don't know what you did or what your victim did," says Zack, "but we're both in a world of trouble. And you're going to help get us out. I'm assuming you're paying him in cash, no bank deposits or transfers, and I'm guessing you brought the cash you owe him for the hit. Am I right?"

She nods.

"How'd you find him?"

"I was put in touch with him."

"Too bad we don't have his last name."

The client looks at him. "Joey Richter," she says.

Zack looks back at her.

She shifts uncomfortably. "Someone said it by mistake once."

Zack looks at her, puzzled. "Who would make a mistake like that?"

She looks at Zack. "He did."

Zack stares at her, waiting.

"'Joey Richter doesn't fuck up,' he said." She looks at Zack. "He wanted me to know."

Zack feels her bitterness rising for a moment above her fear. 'Cause Joey Richter *did* fuck up and put her in this mess. A foolish moment of pride, thinks Zack. Joey reassuring himself, as well as his client. *Joey Richter doesn't fuck up.* The assertion indicating to Zack that, indeed, Joey sometimes does.

Joey Richter.

Zack had made the mistake of saying Joey's first name aloud to him. He knew it was a terrible mistake the moment he'd said it. The moment before the earsplitting sound of gunshots came cracking back at him through the diePhone.

Before the spinning, the vomiting at the curb.

Now Joey had made the mistake of saying his own last name. Could that somehow save Zack and Emily?

But how? Giving the police the name to investigate? Staking out Joey Richter's apartment? That was hardly going to save himself or Emily in time.

He thinks back to the original moment at the GreenGirl. When Joey entered his code, dialed and turned away to talk.

"Wait. Did Joey call you this morning?" The hit man looking for one last confirmation of the contract? One last chance to change her mind?

She shakes her head no.

Zack has learned by now that there are virtually no personal calls on Joey's phone. Chances are, with Joey's profession, Joey erases any evidence of personal calls once he makes them. But that last call, of course, Joey didn't have a chance to erase because he left his phone in the GreenGirl. And it wasn't made to her.

Zack brings up the number. He dials it. Waits.

At this point, anything he can learn. Nothing left to lose.

"Federal Department of Corrections, New York East," says the voice that answers. "How may I direct your call?"

Zack hangs up.

Was Joey Richter calling someone who was directing the hit? Approving it? Or calling another prisoner? Someone worth calling in that noisy, crowded GreenGirl moment.

But either way, calling someone on the inside.

Yes, Joey was sitting in the GreenGirl. But he wasn't *really* in the GreenGirl, was he?

Sure, inhabiting the world around him, amid all those GreenGirl patrons hunched over their phones, chatting and texting with their friends. So joining in their world for a moment? Calling a friend? Trying to fit in?

What kind of person has nothing on their cell phone? No apps. No photos of friends. No events, no memories. Maybe not just a person who doesn't *want* anything on their phone. Maybe also a person who just *got* a phone. Who is new to cell phones.

Like someone who's done a long stretch in prison.

Whose life has perhaps been mostly prison.

Like a pale-looking "businessman" who hasn't seen the sun in years. Trench coat maybe hiding tattoos. Back of the hand and back of the neck tattoos that Zack thought were simply reckless youth. Maybe a whole torso of tats beneath the trench coat.

What kind of idiot uses 2580 for his code? Maybe just someone who doesn't know any better. Someone new to technology. Someone back in the world.

A prisoner. Who had experienced years, maybe a lifetime, of prison's dehumanization. Who has totally lost any other identity.

Something Zack would never understand.

But he might understand just enough of it.

Zack enters the code on Joey's phone. Opens the browser. Goes online.

"What are you doing?!" says the client, anxious. "We've got to get over to the GreenGirl! You don't know what we're dealing with!"

"Oh, I think I know exactly what we're dealing with," says Zack.

And we'll know soon enough if I do, thinks Zack.

The client watches Zack tapping away furiously on the phone's keyboard. Squinting at the screen. Squinting at the keyboard. Typing. Nodding. Typing.

The client is growing frantic. Rising from her seat. "We've got to get over there now!"

Zack finally looks up.

"Yes, we do. Let's get to that GreenGirl."

17.

BACK AT THE GreenGirl. A table in the back.

Two couples are having coffee together.

Zack and the client sit on one side.

Joey and Emily sit on the other.

Joey won't do anything here, Zack figures. The GreenGirl is full. Joey needs to stay anonymous; it's part of his job. But it's terrifying nonetheless.

The four coffees sit on the table untouched. Only there for show. To blend in. Things are a little too tense for enjoying a cup of coffee.

No pleasantries. No smiles. No discussion.

Zack takes Joey's phone out of his pocket.

He still knows that when he hands the phone back, he loses his leverage. But what choice does Zack have?

In full view of everyone at the table, Zack turns on Joey's phone, once more enters Joey's code—2580—where all the trouble began, and flashes the familiar home screen at Joey.

Proof. Proof to this guy who needs a record of proof, for some reason. Proof it's his phone. Proof it's still working.

He starts to pass it across to Joey.

And drops it into one of the large, hot coffees.

Joey, Emily, and the client are momentarily shocked.

Joey's eyes go wide in alarm. He reaches frantically for the coffee cup.

Zack pulls it away. Out of Joey's reach. Dangles it there.

Joey looks at Zack, furious. Opens his coat. Ready to reach for the Glock. Ready to kill Zack right here in the crowded GreenGirl. *Fuck it. Fuck it all.*

He looks at his phone. Immersed in the coffee cup Zack is holding.

Then, slowly, Joey nods and smiles, suddenly understanding that Zack has voluntarily and completely destroyed the evidence.

So that *no one* has the evidence.

And if no one has the evidence, then *there is no evidence.*

Now Zack hands Joey a sealed white envelope. Joey slides it open beneath the table but he already knows. The client's cash. As if he has actually done the hit.

As if Zack somehow knows how much Joey needs it to pay the rent.

Adding a little sweetener to the deal to make it go down better.

Joey gets it. And he realizes something else, something remarkable: this kid is trusting him. Nobody in his own whole goddamn world likes or trusts him—everybody requires proof—but this redheaded, smart-alecky kid he doesn't even know is trusting him. Trusting him to get it. Trusting him to understand. Huh. Well that sweetens the deal a little too, thinks Joey.

But Joey can have no loose ends. "You know I have to destroy yours because my number is on it. All our texts. All our back-and-forth."

Zack nods, understanding.

"I know your whole life is on there," says Joey.

"Hey, destroying it will *give* me a life, won't it?"

Joey nods. Slides Zack's phone gently into his own coffee. Holds it there. Looks up at Zack questioningly.

Zack answers the technical question so Joey doesn't have to ask. "After a minute, they're cooked. Unrecoverable. The heat. The milk. The sugar. A quick immersion in water, beer, or a toilet bowl, an iPhone can be recovered. In hot coffee, with sugar and milk, no way. It's dead forever."

Die, phone.

Die in an Americano Grande. Let the milk and sugar sweeten you into nonexistence.

"So now all evidence is gone. Now it's just a story no one would believe," says Joey.

The client nods. She accepts it.

"What story?" says Zack. Proving how thoroughly he is willing to forget. If Joey is. "And hey, your next phone? Maybe a different code," Zack suggests. Quietly. Politely. With a tight, sad smile. *So this never happens again. So some nosy smart aleck doesn't see it.*

Zack hands the hot coffee with Joey's phone in it to Joey.

Joey hands the hot coffee with Zack's phone to Zack.

There might even be a little toast. Coffee cup to coffee cup.

If a short, nerdy kid wasn't dead in a fifth-floor walk-up.

18.

ZACK WALKS OUT of the GreenGirl with Emily.

Free, he thinks.

Free, he's pretty sure.

Free. But thinking about prison.

Prison, where you lose your identity. Your humanity. So you can come out and shoot people for a living. Or maybe you had trouble with humanity to begin with, and prison only hardened you.

Where you cease to be a name, cease to be Joey Richter, and become only a number.

As he had sat with the client at Mali's Diner, suddenly learning Joey's last name, learning where Joey's last call went, Zack had gone quickly onto the federal prison registry. Where Joey's incarceration would be a matter of public record, he figured.

He had quickly typed in Joseph Richter.

Up came a federal eight-digit prisoner number: 54095ENY ENY for East New York region.

Even a mug shot of Joey with the number on his orange jumpsuit pocket.

Eight digits, numbers and letters.

Just about perfect for an Apple password.

His prisoner number. Who he had been. What he had been turned into. And Joey the ex-con, new to cell phones, choosing an Apple password he'd never forget.

Zack had seen Joey enter his four-digit code. That was just lucky. Or terribly unlucky.

But this, thought Zack. This was—well, luck too. A lucky stroke of intuition. And psychology, and social commentary, and sadness. A lifetime lost. The number overtaking the name. A glance not just at someone's cell phone code, but into the truth of their life.

Enter Apple ID and password. Zack had quickly entered the eight-digit code.

He was in.

He had checked Joey's Apple settings.

Sure enough, the Cloud was disabled.

Zack re-enabled it.

All the data, all the photos—all suddenly, instantly, sent to the Cloud. Without Zack touching another button.

"We've got to get to GreenGirl," the client had said then in a panic.

The Cloud that Joey probably never really understood anyway. The Cloud that somebody must have disabled for Joey so the evidence would exist only on Joey's phone.

Zack can now pull it down, with Joey's Apple password.

All those pictures. All that evidence.

The diePhone. Still very much alive. Awaiting Zack.

* * *

As he and Emily exit the GreenGirl, Zack is feeling pretty good about it. How Joey took the deal.

He's even thinking of explaining it to Emily. But not here, not now, not yet.

When should he pull the diePhone data down from the Cloud?

As soon as he and Emily are somewhere safe?

As soon as he tells the police about Steve?

Or as soon as he picks out a new phone at the Apple store. *'Cause silly me, I dropped my old one in my coffee.*

19.

JOEY RICHTER EXITS the GreenGirl coffee shop.

A little after Zack.

Not feeling free.

Not just yet.

He can tell the smart-alecky kid likes the neatness of it. The symmetry. Both phones dead in the coffee. Hell, even Joey appreciates the neatness of it. And the fact that the kid has trusted him with this deal—well, that still amazes him, makes him feel good.

But the kid doesn't understand how it's not really neat just yet.

He falls in behind Zack and Emily.

He sees Zack turn a couple of times to look for him. But Joey's a pro; he knows how to avoid being seen. Until he's ready to be seen.

He loves the deal Zack silently offered. He really appreciates it. Very clever. A good attempt. It seemed like it took care of all the problems for both of them. But unfortunately, it didn't.

It's loose ends. It's Hit Man 101. He can't have them walking around. Just can't risk it, plain and simple.

Zack thought he could solve it with his cleverness. But Zack doesn't understand that some things are bigger than cleverness. Have bigger consequences.

When they get close to Zack's apartment, on a narrow side street with almost no pedestrian traffic, Joey catches up with them. Draws alongside them without their noticing.

"Hey, Zack."

Zack and Emily turn.

Joey is pleased to see the happy, upbeat, smart-alecky expression finally leave Zack's eyes.

"One last thing," says Joey, drawing the Glock from under his trench coat, smiling.

One last thing. Get it, Zack?

See, Zack, I can be clever too.

Joey calmly levels the gun.

Emily screams.

Zack closes his eyes to fate.

A fate he managed to deter...

For a little while...

But no more.

A chaos of images, a compression of time...

Places, faces, moments, collapsing together, uncontrolled...

The mind's Cloud, storing all memories, unleashing them now...

"Drop it."

A voice from elsewhere, stern, commanding, some place outside but deep within, because all the imagery as instructed suddenly drops away, swept aside in some final accounting…some final moment of memory, turning liquid, melting, cascading…

"Drop it!" the voice booms at them. Comes from confusingly close by. "Drop it! Now!"

Detective Lopez is only a few feet behind Joey, his own gun out, with a much leaner partner approaching from the front, gun also drawn.

In seconds, Lopez is behind Joey, his gun against Joey's back.

A moment later, Joey is spread-eagled, hands cuffed.

A moment after that, he's in the back of a police cruiser, one of four that has screeched in at them from out of nowhere.

A chaos of images.

A compression of time.

Zack stands there.

Stunned.

Alive.

Lopez looks at Zack with the edges of a satisfied smile. Answering before Zack can even ask.

"You had something to tell me at the precinct but chickened out at the last second," Lopez says, brown eyes sparkling. "Which meant it was either nothing—or something you were too scared to say. I saw the look on your face, Zack."

Lopez's confused expression at the precinct when Zack

suddenly got up. Apparently not the only telltale expression between them.

"So I looked at the desk sergeant's check-in log. A burglary at your apartment, you said, but you gave an address that doesn't exist. Something was up.

"I checked the precinct's surveillance camera mounted in the corner. You're running out, obviously scared. You checked your phone as you got a call. I froze the frame with the phone number on it, zoomed in tight, traced the number. It belongs to a Zack Yellin. *Your own number*, calling you. Something was definitely up."

The street is already returning to its usual rhythm. The rush of pedestrians, the flow of traffic, the unremarkable sight of a single police cruiser still at the curb.

"I guess it won't surprise you that the GPS was disabled on the phone in your hands. But on your own phone, it was turned on. We headed toward its signal but it was moving around on us. At the same time, we pulled your phone's most recent calls, several to a Steve Furman, and we found his address, a fifth-floor walk-up, and made the discovery..."

Oh God...

Oh no...

Zack feels the vomit start to rise again.

"He's in the hospital," says Lopez. "We got there in time."

The relief that floods Zack is so overwhelming, so dizzying and disorienting that he struggles to follow the rest of what Lopez is saying.

"We were also checking Zack Yellin's most recent credit card purchases, and we tracked you down to a GreenGirl, and just missed you there apparently. Almost lost you in the crowd when I caught sight of you, but you've got that red hair." Lopez smiles.

Zack stands there, momentarily speechless, amazed.

He thought he'd been pretty smart about the eight-digit prisoner ID.

He was clearly just an amateur.

"Jesus. You move fast, Detective Lopez."

Lopez taps his palms against his considerable belly. "Only when I have to." Then he tilts his head inquisitively. "Something tells me you've got something for me, Zack?"

"It's in the Cloud."

Lopez grins. "I love a Cloudy day."

Three hours later, their statements completed, Zack and Emily exit the precinct.

Detective Lopez had offered a police cruiser to give them a lift to the hospital but Zack said he needed to walk a little first.

He just needs a couple of blocks. Of fresh air, decompression, a couple of minutes before they hail a cab to go over and see Steve.

A few precious minutes. Of not being chased. Or threatened. Or terrified.

A few precious minutes. On a day—Jesus, a single day—that came at him full force, unrelenting, frenzied, furious, no time to think, only to react.

Just a minute or two, to walk a few blocks with Emily.

Just the two of them. Taking each other's hands. Walking silently. Together.

Alive.

No cell phone in his pocket.

And boy that feels nice.

SIX MONTHS LATER

20.

JOEY RICHTER AWAKENS.

Lies staring at the bunk above him.

It's empty, thankfully.

An empty, quiet jail cell where, for most hours of the day and night, nothing intrudes. No guards. No prisoners. Nothing. The drone of the TV in the corridor—for Joey, it's familiar, soothing background noise.

Months now. Days that have stretched to weeks that have stretched to months while the wheels of justice…don't spin. Remain in place. Held by the brakes of lawyers jostling— venue discussions, admissibility of evidence, jury selection. All the legal maneuvering that he experiences as a lot of noise, a version of the blaring TV in the corridor.

Joey doesn't mind the jail time. He's comfortable back inside. The booking, that fat pig Lopez, the grinding gears of the system, it's all a blur. But he's back now where he's comfortable with the routines, with the predictability and rhythm of the days and nights and the familiar sounds and familiar pace, with the feel of time itself.

Almost no one to deal with. He could stay here forever.

He won't though. Because although it's stretched to months, this jail cell is, by the rules of the justice system, only a temporary home.

He'll end up in prison somewhere. A permanent one, no term or release date discussion, no parole hearings, consecutive sentences of hundreds of years, he is sure. A hired killer, after all. An unfeeling, mercenary "cold-blooded assassin," paid in cash.

On the other hand, his lawyers have been asking him about his "cognitive issues." He doesn't know how the justice system will view those. Is it a handicap? A mental defect? He can't tell. He inhabits his own brain, the only brain he knows, so he's in no position to judge.

The death penalty is no longer enforced in the state of New York. But it's still on the books. So could he still be executed? His lawyers shake their heads but he doesn't really know.

Deeply immersed in the routine of recurring light and recurring sounds, drifting in and out, barely conscious this morning, at first he merely notices the clank and hum of the metal bars and their electric motor control. He assumes it's a different cell on the corridor; it almost always is. In a moment, he realizes it's his own cell door and figures it's a meal being brought or a cell inspection.

But as he sits up, swings his feet to the floor and focuses, now there are several guards, and between them another prisoner.

A bunkmate. Fuck.

His peace is over.

"Meet your bunkie, Richter."

He'd figured he was so high profile that they were leaving him alone. They didn't want to risk any communication, any contamination.

Clearly he was wrong about that.

"Be cordial to one another. Respect each other's space. Respect each other's privacy wherever possible. Act civil." The guard—Griggs—practically reading from a script, expressionlessly, as if to inject the words with all their ironic content. Then going off script. "Joey Richter, Will Shale. You two get acquainted. It's a party."

21.

ZACK YELLIN AWAKENS.

Lies staring at the cracks in the plaster ceiling above him. A riot of morning light streams in. He shifts a little and feels a responsive shifting beside him as Emily's arm settles comfortably across his chest.

There are few pleasures more taken for granted, he is sure, than waking up next to someone. It's still a new pleasure for him. When he'd slept with girls before, he rarely stayed, and they didn't either. When he did stay, it was only to await a decent-seeming moment, anticipating escape, getting out of there, so it had no pleasure and comfort in it, only anxiety and careful plotting.

This simple pleasure. His parents spent a lifetime waking up next to each other and never said a word about it. Millions spend a lifetime the same way and seem to hardly notice it.

Emily shifts again beside him in bed.

"You awake?" he asks quietly.

"Mmmm, no," she mumbles.

A minute later, she groans and grumbles and rolls out of bed. Emily Lane is heading to work.

Zack is heading…nowhere. Again. Staying right here.

The crime drew them together, of course. Surviving it. They were drawn together anyway, and here, with the crime and all that followed, fate was only confirming it. On some level, he doesn't know if they'll ever be apart now. On some level, he knows Emily feels the same way.

All the "heroism" coverage afterward had been embarrassing. Foiling an assassin. Going toe to toe with a killer. He had pushed aside all the interview requests, and then— worn down, giving in—he accepted a couple, immediately regretted it and pushed aside the rest. Over the months, it had died down. As he hoped it would, it became yesterday's story.

They moved in together a month ago. It was as natural, as inevitable as the turn of seasons. Zack couldn't even remember any discussion about it. Certainly no brooding about it, no listing the pros and cons, no weighing it or thinking what friends or parents would say. They were in their own little world, had been from the moment they set eyes on each other, and it made perfect sense to formalize that world, to establish its beautiful but exclusive boundaries and borders, to respect and formalize their feelings for one another, to seize all the joy, all the hours with one another that life was offering them. Given what they'd been through together, everyone around them—parents, close friends, Emily's coworkers—were willing to grant them their privacy and space.

And now, lying here in the morning light, he squints against the brightness. They need to get curtains or shutters, although this way, it's always a light-flooded reminder of how lucky they are to be alive each day. Alive and with each other, and for now, there isn't anything more to ask of life than that.

As Emily does a few wake-up stretches, fingertips to toes, and starts to dress for work, the little note of darkness in their lives tolls lightly in the background once more.

"How's the job search going?" she says into the mirror, putting on makeup in quick, expert dabs and touches. Smiling—with affection, yes, but with sarcasm and annoyance too. Because she knows—they both know—it's not going anywhere.

He has no answer. He's paralyzed. His arms and legs stiffen up as he lies there. His pleasurable morning hard-on deflates.

It's the little wedge between them. Their first hurdle. Such an absurd hurdle, of course, such a small, nagging thing, compared to outwitting and surviving a professional assassin. But it's there in the room with them, in the bed with them, at the back of both their brains, acting in different but complementary ways inside each of them. For her, frustration. For him, embarrassment.

A small thing, but not a small thing, they both know. Drive, ambition, direction in life. Responsibility. Willingness to go forward, leave childhood behind. Their discussions are oblique. Dancing around it. But the issue is ever-present. Lying in bed with them like an infant, quiet now but ready at any moment to wail and scream.

This morning she digs in a little more. It may be easier for her when she's heading out the door, he surmises. "Got your interviews lined up? Got your spreadsheets going?" She is smiling now because she knows, they both know, he doesn't. "You'll probably have a job by the time I get home," she says.

Jamming the eyeliner into its holder with a little too much force, Zack notices.

She turns to him and looks at him, awaiting some kind of answer. Any kind of answer.

He shifts. "Em, I still don't know what I want. Besides you."

She frowns. A well-turned phrase, a romantic notion, is not going to cut it with her this morning.

"Do anything. Take a job at GreenGirl. Anything. We could use the money." She pulls on her boots and begins to lace them up. "Heroism doesn't seem to come with a paycheck, unfortunately."

My job is to be here with you. He doesn't say it. He knows it will only annoy her.

Disaster, drama, life and death drew them together. Gave them a rare, special bond. Will ordinariness, the everyday, the mundane every couple faces, pull them apart?

Reality…intruding.

"GreenGirl," she says—half kidding, half serious, checking her boots one last time in the open doorway, the building's dingy hallway framed behind her. "While you try to figure it out, Zack. Anything, Zack. You think I love my job? You think anyone does?" Yet, before she closes the apartment door, giving him the bottom line, she says to reassure him, "See you later."

22.

HE'S A KID, this Will Shale. And you'd say right off, based on his age and his smooth baby face, that this is probably his first time inside. But his ease in here, his familiarity, his swagger, indicate it's not.

He's wiry. Tatted up like a long-term con but several of the tats, Joey sees, are letters and numbers—formulas, weird equations, when Joey dares to take a closer look. Mean-eyed like a con but alert-looking, intelligent, and he seems, well, kind of amused. A little bit of college kid to him. College kid gone bad. Very bad.

At first, they tolerate each other silently, moving around each other warily. And when both sense there's no physical danger from one another, they start to talk.

And soon, jail time turns a lot more interesting for Joey Richter.

It takes a while—shared irritation with the guards, complaints about the food, teasing about snoring, descriptions of the neighborhoods where each of them grew up—for Joey to get to the stage where it's okay, enough time has passed, to pose that most basic jailhouse question: *What do they got you for?*

"Oh, they don't got me," Will replies confidently, bouncy, with a little smile. "They just *think* they got me..." He stretches a little. "It's temporary."

"For what?"

Shoulder shrug. "Bunch of stuff." Looking at Joey with a bemused, suspended expression that says, *I can explain it but I don't know if I can trust you yet, like you don't know if you can trust me.*

Bunch of stuff? What could that mean? "Try me," says Joey.

Another shrug. "Cybercrimes."

Joey repeats the word blankly. "Cybercrimes." Saying it in a way that reveals he doesn't really understand what Will means.

Online banking shit you couldn't even follow at first. But soon enough, Joey did. Joey got the gist of it anyway. Installing malware that rides invisibly on a bank's overdraft protection program; the code takes pennies out of accounts "and re-inputs them a nanosecond later," Will explains, "redirecting them as banking fees, fees that don't really exist and so are easily electronically collected from account statements and transferred to other accounts. Accounts that are held by me and my bosses," says Will with a smile.

"How'd you figure all that out?"

"Well, I didn't really figure it out, did I?" says Will. "I wouldn't be here if I really figured it out." Glum, bitter, fierce, jokey, all at the same time.

There was another reason they'd initially stayed away from each other. Both were experienced enough to know that a prosecutor could ask for information learned in conversations in the cell, and a prosecutor might offer reduced sentences or other considerations in exchange for such testimony, but they soon came to understand that neither of them would give any information about the other to anyone, and that's when they began to talk. They assumed one or the other of them would be shifted out of this particular cell soon enough. Both their cases were now in motion apparently, so their time together seemed limited.

Will explained more. Told Joey about his previous scam. Setting up an online bank that looked, to even trained eyes, like a legitimate division of a major institution—Citibank or JPMorgan Chase—whose CD and "safe" short-term bond investments were just attractive enough to win over wealthy older investors.

Told him about winning an ATM servicing contract with phony paperwork. And eventually, making phony uniforms for a phony service company. "These little mom-and-pop service companies, they can incorporate quick, and they can dissolve quick. It's tough for law enforcement to check them out, they come and go so fast."

He'd been caught and served time on the ATM scam, he said.

The online bank division, he'd gotten away with for a while. Salted away plenty of scratch.

Joey listened, fascinated. Mind expanding. Drinking in every drop.

This kid Will. Super-tough, super-hard, but super-smart, and getting to know him a little, listening to him, Joey starts to see him as a criminal from the future, while Joey is embarrassed to be a criminal from the past—as far in the past as you could get. *Thou shalt not kill.* A gun. A murder. It was still a blunt instrument and blunt use of force, something still awfully close to medieval or biblical, where this kid's crimes were much better designed to get you where you want to go, to make you rich. Rich enough to be left alone.

Of course, they're both caught. But this kid at some point will be getting out, will serve some time and then be free to stroll out, disappear, erase his identity online, and start over, correcting past mistakes, modifying the past's little slipups so they don't happen again. While Joey's crimes—taking lives—mean no do-overs, no learning from your mistakes, no learning curve.

Will is lean. Taut skin and bone. Looks like he'd curl right up in a fight. But Joey recognizes this kind of kid immediately. He's seen this kind of kid before. Able to ignore pain, seems literally not to feel it. Can somehow take any infliction the world brings him. Seems—in that impish, smug expression—almost amused by it. Seems to require no food or drink, seems to have no physical needs. Day and night don't seem to matter. Body merely a vessel, pretty much ignorable. It's scary. A superior kind of criminal, from a more advanced civilization or something.

"What about you?" Will asks him suddenly.

The neatness of it occurs to Joey. "You're a cybercriminal?" says Joey. "I'm a cybervictim." Thinking about his phone—the phone submerged in coffee—Joey only learned later how that kid Zack had gotten all its texts and photos into the Cloud before that.

"Hired assassin, they told me." Will gestures to the guard

station. "That's all they said. Told me to rattle me, I guess. Putting me in here with a real criminal." Will gives a thin smile.

And when Joey begins to describe what happened—telling about his "business" over the past year, telling about the photos—Will listens silently, intently, and at a certain point shakes his head.

"Joey, Joey, Joey...that's all the evidence they got you on?" Will seems genuinely upset. Genuinely mournful. "You could have avoided this. You could have junked the evidence on your phone, made the evidence destroy itself, even in the Cloud. Joey, Joey"—still shaking his head—"there's so much more you can do with an iPhone."

And the look Will gives Joey—pity, plain and simple. But in that look, too, maybe a little sympathy, a little friendship.

Maybe the start of something, thinks Joey. The fact that they're only temporary cellmates, maybe it's even better for both of them. Maybe a reason for both of them to open up.

Tell me.

Show me.

23.

"RED!" SAYS THE cute Latina GreenGirl barista with a big smile. "I remember you!" She's clearly delighted to see him.

Zack smiles shyly.

"Last time I saw you, you were dunking your iPhone in coffee. On purpose, apparently."

"You saw that?"

She smiles. "I was keeping an eye on you." She continues making an order. "I've seen you since then, of course."

Zack knows where this is going.

"On TV! On the news. A hero." She smiles broadly again.

"Yeah, well..."

"The guy with you that day...that was the killer?" She is suddenly serious. Quieter. The terror of it, the proximity, apparently coming back to her. She seems to push it forcefully away. Becomes brighter again. The cheerful, welcoming barista. "So what brings you back here, Red? What can I get you? On the house." She looks at him.

He is quiet, earnest looking, attentive. And suddenly she

breaks into a huge, knowing grin. "A job! You want a job. That's what I can get you, huh?"

He smiles shyly again and nods.

"A TV hero like you? And you need a job?"

"Being a hero doesn't come with a paycheck." It's not the first time it's been said today.

She tosses a rag on the counter. Her expression darkens suddenly. "So what, you come in here, figure we'll hire the local hero, the hero from the back table, so you can work here and make a few bucks while you figure out what you really want to do with your life? Is that it?"

Zack is blindsided by this sudden hostility.

She looks at him testily, irritably, challenging him to answer.

He looks back at her silently. Doesn't deny it. How can he?

"You still with that girl you used to come in here with?"

He nods.

"So she's tired of you hanging around the apartment, doing nothing, and she's telling you to get a job, find something, anything, and this is the only thing you could think of."

Zack looks at her with quiet astonishment. With admiration. An indication of how right she is.

She regards him appraisingly. Picks up the rag, slaps it over a shoulder, and says neutrally, "I'll go talk to the manager, see what they'll do."

24.

JOEY AWAKENS IN the middle of the night to see a glow of light emanating from the bunk above.

Fuck. A cell phone. As if out of nowhere, Will's got a fucking cell phone.

Joey shifts enough to see for sure. The cell phone's glow illuminates Will's face.

Will is texting speedily. Fingers flying. Second nature. Joey glares at him. In response, Will just gives him a little smile.

Joey sits up, is about to say something, ask Will where he got it, who he knows, but Will simply adds to his little smile a finger across his lips—*shhshhshhshhshh…*

Will's been here before. Knows his way around. And not only are cell phones a big commodity inside prison—above cigarettes, amphetamines, barbiturates, and even opioids in desirability—but new prisoners are also a special commodity of their own. They're still so connected on the outside that they can get outside "favors" taken care of. If a guard gets an inmate a phone (and Joey assumes that's how Will got this one), it's usually by providing the guard a favor that the new inmate's outside friends can handle for him. Will doesn't offer up what kind of favor or favors these guards wanted, and Joey doesn't ask. All he knows is Will's got himself a phone.

Joey understands the way it works in prison. You cultivate relationships over time, you barter and trade and develop trust, you pass some tests, but this is *jail*, temporary holding, shuffling people in and out. Who does Will know, how did Will work it, to get a phone?

"Aren't you worried they're gonna catch you with that?"

Will shrugs. "So what, they'll put me in jail?"

Most of the prized prison cell phones are older models. Flip phones, earlier generations. Fewer records of them, recovered from lost and founds, liberated from electronics stores, no paper trail. But this phone is brand-new—looks like it just came out of the box.

"Can't they tell you've got it, you know, from the signal?"

"Nah. Geolocation's only accurate to within a few yards. They'll just assume a guard has it."

Joey watches Will.

"You stay in touch with people," says Will. "You check your email and Twitter and your social media. You can almost forget you're in jail. Your life goes on. Hell, people don't even need to know you're in jail."

You've got some juice here, thinks Joey. He knows enough about the inside to know this didn't just happen because Will's got a charming smile and a winning style.

"It's good to have," says Will blithely, flipping the phone between his hands playfully. "And now that I've got it, maybe I'll teach you a few things. There's so much it can do."

What is this sudden friendship about? Joey is confused by it. Maybe it's respect for Joey? Maybe underneath the hard shell, the kid has, well, some admiration for an older, career criminal?

"Yeah, well, you don't need to teach me," says Joey. "'Cause we both know I'm not gettin' out of here."

Will smiles. Makes a point of not looking at Joey as he says, offhand, casually, "Oh, I don't know about that, Joey. I think you need to learn. 'Cause I think you're gonna need a cell phone again."

25.

ZACK WALKS DOWN the street.

Everyone on their cell phones. No one looking at one another.

Normally that shared isolation—people marooned from each other—bugs the hell out of him. But today it doesn't. Today his walk is a stroll with a little extra lift to it.

They're going to start training him in a couple of days.

The cute barista—Roseanne—returned from the back room with a smile on her face. Followed by the manager, Chris.

They asked for his cell phone number. He admitted he didn't have a cell phone.

"We don't require a lot to work here," said Chris with a tight smile. "But you do need to have a phone so we can reach you."

Zack resists rejoining the world. Caving in to its demands and conventions.

GreenGirl is temporary. They know it. He knows it. Maybe they're intrigued by having a local celebrity on staff.

He's been on hold. Hanging on to his previous life. Paradoxically but powerfully, the crazy events of the phone swap, of the twenty-four-hour nightmare that followed, the murder attempt he survived—all of it has kept him in his previous existence, kept it suspended over and around him, trapping him in that identity. Trapping his image in the newspapers, on social media, trapping him as if in a looping video.

This is a step. Maybe more symbolic than actual. On the way to something. Putting not just an episode behind him but a stage of life too.

He heads purposefully down the street. Not sure where he's going exactly but sure now it's somewhere. He feels a sense of momentum. He feels himself shrugging off, finally shedding, his previous life.

Soon, soon, to leave it behind.

He will remember this walk. This feeling. This little moment when everything seems to be shifting. This sense of lightness and liberation.

But he will remember it for entirely different reasons than he thinks.

He will remember it wistfully, longingly, and grimly. As a vivid, tangible, tactile memory—of what never truly was.

26.

"**STATE OF NEW** York versus Joey Richter. Borough of Manhattan, Courtroom 104B. Judge Burton Sherman presiding. All rise."

An obedient shuffle of two hundred boots and shoes—court stenographers, attorneys, jurors, print and television journalists from a wide range of news organizations, well-known and obscure, victims' families, and a smattering of court rats clever and quick enough to secure a seat.

Joey is sitting at the middle of the defense table. By this time, there are three lawyers on his team, the original one assigned to him by the state, Simms—hunched over, hollowed out, a scarecrow in an undertaker's suit—and two more flanking him, who have materialized, as if out of nowhere, in the past few weeks.

One of them is a slickly dressed attorney named Darwin Cope, who Joey soon realized had been hired by his old boss, Karloff. (Karloff isn't his real name; no one knows his real name. Apparently, he's from Russia or some country around there so he's known only as Karloff.) Joey has no clear idea why Karloff has gotten involved or is footing the bill for this high-priced mouthpiece. He knows enough to know he doesn't really rate in the organization. He's always been just a foot soldier at best so this special counsel, this sudden special treatment, is a mystery to him.

The third lawyer, Len Carter, a straight-laced, well-spoken black dude, is some kind of technology whiz who Cope or somebody else is paying for. That's not clear to Joey either.

And while all three technically represent him, none of them really talk to him. It's almost like they've all forgotten about him. His defense seems to be something that goes on around him, that doesn't involve him much at all. Cope and Carter slap his shoulder, and Cope even occasionally ruffles Joey's hair, which makes Joey pretty uncomfortable.

The lawyers consult with each other in hushed murmurs. For weeks now, they've rarely even asked Joey a question. Cope and Carter interviewed him in his cell when they were first assigned to the case, and during those interviews, he noticed that Cope never looked at him directly. As if Joey was merely an annoyance, a distasteful but necessary hindrance in the process of ascertaining the facts, of doing his job.

The first attorney, Simms, the lean but jowly sad sack who was assigned by the state, has definitely retreated—or been pushed—into the background, overshadowed by Cope and Carter.

There is excitement and energy between Cope and Carter, and Joey hears them refer to something they call "strategy."

The state has been presenting its case clearly, method-ically. Joey and the jury have looked at all the photographs that were on his phone—gruesome shot after gruesome shot, never intended to be blown up to the size of a big screen in a courtroom. The photos brought gasps from the gallery.

Joey looked at the jury. Several of them turned away. Two of the women looked like they might retch. Joey thought the prosecuting team would relent—*you get the idea*—and not make them suffer through every photo, every angle. But no. They made the jury sit through every photo and angle.

Photographic evidence pulled down from the Cloud. On a phone originally registered to one Joseph Richter. They even showed the bill of sale for the phone. Other cases undoubtedly hinged on witnesses, DNA, taped conversations. Here were photos. Photo after photo after photo.

It seemed pretty open and shut to Joey.

It wasn't.

"Let's talk about the Cloud," says Darwin Cope to the courtroom. Squinting his eyes and shaking his head at the prospect of trying to explain, to even understand, this concept of the Cloud. "Anyone on the jury want to try to explain it to us?" A rhetorical question of course but he pauses. "Anyone at the prosecution table care to take a stab at it?" Another pause, while looking at each of the assistant DAs, as if inviting them. "Want to call your own technology expert to explain it to us? You're welcome to, of course. But I'm going to save us all the trouble. I'm going to try explaining the Cloud in the simplest, clearest terms I can."

Setting down his expensive fountain pen. Taking off and

setting down his eyeglasses, as if preparing for a school-yard fight.

"The Cloud, as we all know, is where information is stored. What is it exactly? No one in this courtroom knows. But that's okay, because we know it works, right? Okay, so *where* is it exactly? In a field in Kansas? Under a mountain in Colorado? Satellites in space?" A few nervous laughs. "Different places? All one place? Most people think of it as just…everywhere. Which it sort of is, since we can all download from it and access it from anywhere. But can it *really* be everywhere? And, if it's everywhere, is it anywhere?" A few more laughs.

He looks around. "I'm guessing no one in this courtroom is all that clear on any of that. And again, that's okay with us, be-cause we know it works. That's the important thing, right?"

He pauses, frowns a little. "Or at least, it works as far as we know." He pauses again. Taps two fingers to his chin, a pose of inquiry, of philosophical exploration. "In fact, sometimes it doesn't work. That's no surprise, right? Technology. It works mostly, works amazingly, but sometimes it suddenly and un-expectedly stops working. We've all experienced that plenty of times, right? But we tend to forgive and forget because it *generally* works for us, because we, or someone, eventually gets it working for us again."

Darwin Cope shrugs. Smiles a little. It sounds, for a moment, like his little discourse on technology has come to an end. Like his problem is solved. It's not.

"But here's the thing. Someone's on trial for murder. His life is on the line. And if the technology suddenly and un-expectedly doesn't work—well, for you, sitting in judgment of him, it's suddenly a matter of life and death for you, too, not just for the defendant. Technology's little blips and burps are suddenly a lot more serious. And your judgment of this defendant all hinges on this thing called the Cloud that no one really understands. So now we *do* have to understand it. Now we *do* have to be able to explain it. But unfortunately, we can't."

And then Darwin Cope does something that mystifies Joey at first but that he eventually finds brilliant.

Darwin turns over the oral argument to his co-counsel, Len Carter, the straight-laced tech specialist, who carefully, methodically, patiently, attempts to explain the Cloud more thoroughly. To explain the technology and the breakthroughs and advances that have allowed it. He starts to explain bits and bytes, and how data is stored, and how data is transferred, diving into the complex, highly technical matters…

Judge Sherman doesn't stop or interrupt him because the technology of the Cloud—how and whether it works—is directly relevant to the case.

And as Darwin Cope must have known very well, no one can really follow the explanation.

Zack Yellin's testimony comes right in the middle of the trial. Dressed the same as always, T-shirt and jeans and an open flannel shirt and shoelaces undone, no concessions to the seriousness of the proceedings.

"State your full name for the record, please."

"Zachary Yellin."

"You promise to tell the truth, the whole truth, and nothing but the truth?"

Zack nods affirmatively throughout the question. "Yes. Absolutely."

He is alert. Prompt in his answers as the prosecution probably instructed him to be, thinks Joey. Crisp yeses and nos. He has no long soliloquy or explanations, and yet, out of his yeses and nos come a coherent story of bravery, of action, of quick thinking and quick intelligence that you have to admire. Hell, Joey admires it. Smart kid.

But Cope brings a different shading, a different flavor, to all that bravery and action.

"Just a moment, Mr. Yellin. I just want to remind the jury— and everyone in this courtroom—that you got Joey Richter's phone code by looking over at him while he entered it. Sneaking a look. Intruding on his privacy. You don't find that pretty intrusive?" Cope asks.

Zack shrugs uncomfortably. "I wasn't trying to, sir. I just happened to see it, and I wasn't even sure of what I saw. I only knew I got the code right when all the icons suddenly appeared. That part was just lucky. Or, well, unlucky."

Scattered laughter in the courtroom. A shrug, an embarrassed smile, from Zack.

Just right, thinks Joey. The kid is working the crowd perfectly.

Joey should jump across the defense table and get his hands around the kid's neck. Do what he should have a long time ago. He'd be pulled off Zack before any damage could be done but the point would be made. And what harm would come of it? He's going away for life, or worse, and one last stranglehold isn't going to make any difference.

"So you just *happen* to see his phone code. And next, you *happen* to guess the password for his phone ID? His NY State prisoner number? You came up with it, right at the moment you needed it? You expect anyone here to believe that?"

Another shrug. "It's all I had. Hey, he's the one who chose those numbers for his ID code. Not me."

Cope ignores the kid's response. "Wouldn't you agree, Mr. Yellin, that such a lucky string of circumstance and guesswork strains credulity?"

Zack shrugs.

Cope asks again, "Wouldn't you agree? Wouldn't *anyone* agree?"

Zack shrugs. "I guess."

"Mr. Yellin, have you ever been to Vegas?"

Zack looks puzzled. "No."

"With your luck, you should definitely go," says Cope, to sudden, broad laughter, before the judge warns him about relevance. "Mr. Cope…"

"Withdrawn…" But the point was made.

The kid is on the stand for a couple hours. Questioned, cross-examined, re-crossed. It makes Joey think of a speed bag, opposing attorneys on opposite sides, punching, backhanding, slapping, demonstrating their prowess to one another, showing off for one another, working the bag with skill and relish and delight.

In his two hours on the stand, Zack never looks at Joey.

Joey, on the other hand, stares at Zack the entire time—never takes his eyes off the kid—but Zack pretends Joey isn't even there. As if the trial is taking place without Joey present. Like Joey himself is somehow just another of Joey's lawyers.

When Zack steps down two hours later, he looks the same. Not wrung out. Not beaten down. Like he just got there. Curly red hair springing as he steps. Like it was a walk in the park.

Which is where he's probably headed now, Joey thinks. He caught a glimpse of Emily in the back of the courtroom. There for support.

Headed to the park with Emily while Joey is certainly headed back to prison, and maybe worse.

The jury room on the fourteenth floor is flooded with light from a line of windows along one wall but the windows all have frosted glass to prevent jurors from gazing out onto the city, probably intended to encourage a jury's focus.

Schoolteachers, store clerks, city employees, midlevel marketing people, all doing their civic duty or secretly happy for a change of pace from the tedium of their routine. Truly a jury of Joey's peers, they didn't seem to understand the Cloud any better than Joey. Couldn't agree on the Cloud. When they tried to explain it to one another, as Cope suggested they do in the jury room—"Go ahead, explain it to one another. That will be helpful, won't it?"—it confused them even more.

The Cloud. Too cloudy for them. But the concept of habeas corpus. That the accused is required to appear in court only if there is a clear charge. That *the evidence must be there*, as the judge had instructed them. *That* they understood. That was clear to them. And because it was something they could understand, they seized on it and didn't let go. Like a log, a life raft—a familiar, recognizable object to cling to—in the swirling sea of Cope's technological explanations. So they seized on it—*habeas corpus, the evidence must be there*—and held it hard. Too hard.

How could you really trust the Cloud? How could you be sure that what was in the Cloud came directly from Joey Richter's phone and hadn't made stops at some server farm under a mountain in Colorado or some satellite above New Zealand because of the requirements of technology, where signals could have gotten rerouted or misrouted or messed up? How could you really be sure—to a judicial certainty—of something you couldn't see and hear and touch? How could they really be sure that the photos came directly from Joey's phone? A phone, after all, completely destroyed by a cup of coffee. *That* part they could picture clearly. *That* was evidence. Evidence has to be based on something tangible. Not just the say-so of young, eager, politically ambitious prosecutors or the state. You needed to be absolutely sure because, in a capital case like this, someone's life is on the line.

The other judicial concept they discussed in the jury room: *reasonable doubt.* Using your ability to reason, to ask questions, to doubt. Wasn't that what the term meant? And given that, weren't there reasons to doubt? If you couldn't understand something like the Cloud, wasn't it reasonable to have doubts about it? To have doubts about its structure, its accuracy, its reliability? If it wasn't clear, well that was the very definition of doubt, wasn't it? Cope's closing argument echoed in their minds, reverberating with the sound of both American values and common sense. "Look, I'm not saying Joey Richter *didn't* do it. I'm his lawyer, and I'm admitting, maybe he did. But I *am* saying that we haven't heard the proof, the pretty much doubtless proof, that our law and our system requires and that this courtroom must deliver."

Yes, there is doubt. And if there is doubt, there is *reason* to doubt. Is the doubt truly reasonable? That is a distinction lost on many juries. Including this one.

Joey stares at the pocket squares of his attorneys, Cope and Carter. At their alligator shoes, shiny beneath the defense table. The pocket squares and shoes tell him a lot. He isn't asked to contribute a dime. If Karloff is footing the bill, as he assumed (and no one would confirm it to him, which told him it was true), then there will be, he knows, an expectation. He doesn't know what it is. But he knows Karloff isn't coming to his spirited defense out of the goodness of his heart. As far as Joey knows, Karloff has no heart.

Joey can feel the grim seriousness, the tight silence, close around his legal team, as arguments conclude and the jury files into the jury room.

And the longer the jury takes, as the minutes and then hours tick away, he can feel the energy, the excitement, the anticipation, starting to fill his team. The looks they begin to exchange. Slight smiles, amused, even cheerful. Their thinking is obvious: the longer the jury is out, the more evident it is that there is substantial disagreement. And while disagreement might mean the jury is deadlocked, unable to reach a verdict, it can also mean the jury will vote to acquit.

Seeing the growing anticipation and the bounce in his team's steps as they go for more and more coffee, Joey begins to feel a little dizzy. Disoriented. He has done everything the prosecution is accusing him of. Every little thing. They had been careful, methodical, and he doesn't think they'd gotten a single detail wrong. They have the photo evidence, of course, to make sure they got everything right. They have timelines to make sure everything connects. Their methodical care is impressive.

But his dizziness, his loss of balance, is related to the fact that none of that matters. That the truth might not matter at all. Joey finds it disorienting, more than anything. Not exciting, like his attorneys did. Not ironic. Not depressing. Mostly, just…disorienting.

"Has the jury reached a verdict?"

"We have, Your Honor."

A moment later, there is pandemonium at the defense table. Chaos in the courtroom behind him. Shouting, a babel, the judge's gavel. The big irrepressible grins of his attorneys, the fist pumps of victory and vindication and pure joy, the chest heaves of relief.

Amid it all, the world seems to spin faster around Joey Richter. To become even more dizzying and disorienting. Not sure what will happen now. Sure that something will though. Sure that this result will bring other results—some chain of events he can't yet foresee.

And Darwin Cope, exultant, exuberant, says with a wink to his fellow attorneys: "I love a cloudy day."

Joey is so dizzy, he actually feels like vomiting. But he doesn't.

He stares down, expressionless. He waits.

Cope turns to him. Puts a hand on his shoulder. It's almost an afterthought, it seems to Joey—remembering to clue him in, to mention it to him as if in passing. "You're free."

Free to starve.

Free to sleep in the street. No money. No place to go. No one to turn to, no one to count on, no one to trust.

Free to do whatever it is that Karloff has in mind for him. For whatever reason he has harnessed all this legal firepower.

Joey is dragged through the courthouse corridor on the flowing contrail of judicial victory, carried along by the scrum of attorneys and reporters and guards. As if he is a quarterback being protected. But he's not, he knows. He's a lineman. Less than that—a water boy.

The scrum moves out through the exit doors into the blinding morning light.

He can see nothing momentarily. But then at the periphery, in the crowd of reporters and onlookers and bystanders, one stands out.

There is Will Shale.

Will, who'd been transferred out of Joey's jail cell only days after he'd come in, gone as quickly as he had appeared.

Will, whose case had been dismissed or pleaded out. The guards who informed Joey hadn't been clear on that.

Lean. Grinning. At the victory? Or at what is to come?

Joey steps toward his old cellmate. In the chaos and human crush at the courthouse doors, not knowing where else to step.

"Follow me," says Will.

Joey follows wordlessly. Obediently, unquestioningly. Nowhere else to go.

They slip quickly past reporters who are milling around the courthouse entrance, none of whom were expecting the defendant to ever exit the courthouse through the front doors to freedom. They're just now organizing their cameras and their mics, harnessing and hefting and aligning their equipment as they get word from inside the courthouse and start looking around for the defendant.

Joey briskly follows Will across the street, ducks into Will's nondescript Japanese sedan, and they're gone.

27.

ZACK AND EMILY are nowhere near the courthouse when they learn the verdict. They are at Emily's apartment.

In fact, as it happens, they've just had sex. In fact, they are naked.

Now, naked and exposed.

The call comes on her cell. New York Police Department, says the caller ID. Even naked, you pick up.

"Emily Lane?"

"Yes."

"Are you sitting down, Ms. Lane?"

She doesn't answer specifically. She puts it on speaker so they both can hear.

The next few sentences will remain a blur in her head. Where meaning and feeling will collapse together in her, becoming tangled and confused. *Prosecution presenting first- and second-degree murder charges only...Jury misconstruing the judge's instructions...Evidentiary confusion...Acquittal and release pending separate charges...*

"We don't believe you're in any immediate danger. We'll be keeping a close watch on him every moment that he's out. You should live your life, put this news aside if you can," says the officer gently. "I would have called Zack Yellin but he doesn't have a cell phone, as you probably know. Will you tell him?"

"Of course, Officer."

She hangs up.

In the silence of the apartment, Zack can hear the officer perfectly clearly.

Emily and Zack look at one another. Stunned. Wordless.

Something changes in the room. Something subtler, deeper, than just the news of the verdict. Some shift has taken place.

They suddenly feel their nakedness. They cover up. Turn away from each other. Dress quickly.

Emily is shaking her head, unthinking, without processing, side to side. She feels a sudden vertigo. A sickening feeling overwhelms her. She's close to retching but she holds it in.

Joey is free. So she is not. Cause and effect. Like a switch flipped. Like an hourglass turned.

The fact feels so instantly stark. So transformative. So upside down.

She wants to get out of the apartment. She knows that's irrational; she knows the police will be keeping an eye on him; she knows her apartment is hardly the place he would head to straight from his release from jail but still, she doesn't want to be there. She doesn't want to be anywhere.

She wants to keep Zack here, next to her, holding her, forever.

At the same time, she suddenly wants nothing to do with Zack. Zack who has brought this to her. Zack whose fault this is. Inadvertent, unintended though it was. An accidental by-product of his charm, his curiosity, his incredible smarts, his natural affinity for people—that he earned the enmity of an assassin.

Where will she go? Will she need to leave the apartment? Really leave it? Start over in a new place? She doesn't know yet. She's not thinking clearly yet. It's too new. Too strange, too incomprehensible right now.

And then her heart plunges again. She turns to Zack and finally speaks.

"Steve," she says. "Oh God. Poor Steve."

Who had been shot, barely survived, lucky to be alive at all. Physically recovered by now but still traumatized by the events.

Zack pulls on his shoes and throws on his jacket. "We have to get over to Steve before he hears on his own," he says.

"So we're going to tell him?" Emily asks.

Zack shrugs. "Someone will. Better if it's us."

And it's something for them to do. Some purpose, some distraction, some activity, while they try to adjust. Emily pulls on her boots, grabs her coat, and they're out the door.

28.

WILL SHALE DRIVES through the streets of lower Manhattan and crosses the Brooklyn Bridge. He weaves circuitously through Brooklyn, then Queens, as Joey looks out silently from the passenger seat.

Joey watches Will check the rearview and side mirrors carefully. The police may be following already, afraid of what crazy Joey Richter might do the first moment he is released. But Joey also knows it's just as likely that they'd made no official plan for this outcome, had no surveillance in place, were caught pretty much off-guard by the verdict. That they saw the prosecution's case as a slam dunk. Certainly, Joey did.

Somewhere in the factory district where Brooklyn becomes Queens, they pull into a garage next to another nondescript sedan. Will gestures to Joey to quickly switch into it with him. Will grabs a small blinking electronic device off the first car's dashboard and puts it on the dash in the new car.

Will sees Joey looking at it and smiles. "Watch it. You'll see how it marks the movement of all vehicles around us, and it'll signal if the same vehicle is continually near us, in which case it beeps. Actually pretty simple technology."

They are back on the street in a moment.

"You're taking me to Karloff."

"I am," says Will.

"You've always worked for him, haven't you?"

"Almost as long as you."

"So you were, what, put there in my jail cell to baby-sit me, keep an eye on me? Make sure I didn't squeal or get turned?"

"Something like that."

"For what?" says Joey "For some reason that I'm about to find out, I guess."

"I guess."

"How did you get in there?" Joey asks, dumbfounded. "How did you get put in my cell like that?"

Will snickers. Like it's child's play. Nothing to it.

"And you can get out just as easily?" Joey still remembers how he had awakened one morning and Will was gone. Transferred out before the trial, Joey presumed, at the request and agreement of lawyers on both sides as well as the judge— standard security procedure before a trial begins, to eliminate the temptation to discuss trial proceedings and details, but now Joey starts to realize there was another power at work.

"It's pretty easy to hack the state of New York's jail and prison databases," says Will, watching the device carefully as he talks and drives. "They're pretty old tech, as you can imagine. Wasn't the smartest IT team, just a bunch of state employees in Albany, who put the original programs together. Still waiting for funding to update them. If you've already been *in* the prison system, it's easy to work yourself back into it. After all, no one's *tryin'* to do that."

Will looks around him before turning down a narrow one-way street. "There's literally thousands upon thousands of prisoners cycling into, out of, and around the state's prison system all the time. I'm just another name in their fucked-up databases."

Will suddenly possessing that fancy phone is no longer so impressive. Clearly there are guards and administrators on the take from Karloff, facilitating what Will just described. Crooked guards—what a surprise.

"Well, you're not so smart," says Joey. "'Cause with all this"—he gestures to the device on the dashboard, the nondescript sedan—"you're still just another soldier like me. A soldier from the future, with cooler toys and scams, but just a soldier working for Karloff."

Will is silent.

"It's almost like you replaced me, isn't it? You replaced me when I went inside."

"There are lots of us," says Will, emotionless.

"What does Karloff want with me?"

Will shrugs. "Guess we'll both find out."

They are headed, Joey knows, to Karloff's headquarters. But he doesn't know where it is. Because no one does.

Because it moves every day, he's heard. Sometimes twice a day, he's heard. Sometimes hourly.

He's never met Karloff, of course. Almost no one has.

The assignments always come through intermediaries. The organization has always been run that way. For everyone's protection.

You don't want to meet with Karloff. Ever.

You want to go through life without ever meeting with Karloff. If you're meeting him, there's some problem. Something not going smoothly.

The legend has always been that the first time you see Karloff can be the last time you'll see him.

Or your last time seeing anyone, for that matter.

Joey figures—assumes—that's an exaggeration.

But a meeting with Karloff is not a good meeting to have.

29.

STEVE'S RECOVERY HAS been steady, but slow.

Rehab. Physical therapy.

The two bullets had entered high on his abdomen but missed his heart. They'd done as much damage as possible without actually killing him.

For months, Zack and Emily have felt burdened by guilt. Zack remembers standing by his hospital bed with Emily in those first weeks. "Hey, man."

"Hey, guys." A whisper. A struggle to speak. Steve grunting as he turns toward them to see them. To greet them.

Zack thinking: Joey's victims, who are all dead, me and Emily, who are alive, and Steve, who is somewhere in between.

"How you feeling?"

Steve struggling to even shrug. To smile.

Zack had jumped in to speak for him. "You're making progress. You seem better than you were last week, for sure."

Their visits continued, and slowly, slowly, he's come back.

Physically, anyway.

Shepherding him home in a cab. Helping him up the stairs. Cooking meals for him.

The three of them drawn inevitably closer to each other. Survivors of a catastrophe.

It hasn't been lost on Zack or Emily that the delay caused by Joey stopping to deal with Steve gave Zack the extra time he needed to put his plan into motion.

It hasn't been lost on Zack that it was Detective Lopez who actually saved Steve, who figured it out, who got the EMTs there in time. Zack had left the police station but Lopez had followed up. If Zack had said something, if he'd gotten Lopez to believe him right then and there in the police station, then Steve would never have been shot. And Lopez's subsequent behavior, his curiosity, his following through, showed Zack that Lopez probably *would* have believed him. And if Lopez hadn't followed up, of course, Steve would certainly be dead. Because of Zack.

Luckily, as a freelance designer, Steve can work from home so he is soon back to earning a living and paying his rent.

He still gets bleary, confused, a little dazed sometimes, which the doctors say they expect to pass. His brain and his body are still recovering, and full recovery probably takes a year or more. But he's headed in the right direction, and they all know it.

"I'm still here," says Steve one day, shaking his head in astonishment. The tears suddenly run down his cheeks. Sheer gratitude at being alive.

A statement like that, out of the blue, reverberates with Zack and Emily, who are there with him, who can't help themselves, who are glad to shed tears along with him.

Still here.

*　　*　　*

And now they are at Steve's apartment. He's buzzed them up.

There are multiple locks on the door now. Cameras. A little fortress that Steve has made.

Steve has a handgun now. He's shown it to them, and taken lessons with it. He keeps it by his side. He walks around with it. It's a different Steve.

"Hey, guys. What brings over the happy couple? Want to get a GreenGirl?"

Zack and Emily look at each other. *Which one of us will say it?*

"We have bad news," says Zack.

Steve's brow furrows.

"He's out."

Steve doesn't seem to process it at first. He stands perfectly still, paralyzed for a moment.

Suddenly his legs give way under him. He bumps roughly against his bed as he collapses to the floor.

"Oh God!" Emily cries out.

Zack and Emily leap toward him, lift him up together and sit him on the bed.

Steve takes a moment to recover there. Zack hears him breathing heavily and only then realizes it's because his breathing had momentarily stopped.

A few seconds later, Steve looks up at them. "When did this happen?"

"Today."

He looks confused. "He's an assassin, Zack. A professional killer, who was caught."

Steve suddenly unbuttons his shirt and looks down at the

scars of his two bullet wounds, as if to remind them all, to confirm once more, the reality of what had occurred. Six months later, the scars are still very prominent, a part of his flesh's topography. He shakes his head slowly with incomprehension. "How can he be out?"

Neither Zack nor Emily answers. They don't really have an answer. An overconfident prosecution team, a confused jury, confusing evidence, a narrowly focused set of charges that were misunderstood anyway—they don't have it within them to even begin muttering their way through it, to try to explain a system that clearly doesn't work, that clearly has failed...

There is more silence. Steve looks quietly at his scars again. All of them looking. Emily is forcing herself not to turn away. To share the reality. Those scars are like the ineradicable memories of what happened that day.

"We'll stay with you," says Zack. "We'll camp out here, order food in, trade off lookout shifts, and be with you until he's back inside." All of them know this is impractical. Just emotional. Just a show of solidarity and support.

"Let's double-check with the police," says Emily. "Make sure they're following him."

"Maybe they can set up extra security in this area, Steve."

"Extra security for a pro like him to skirt around," says Steve glumly, flatly, absently. As if not even aware that he is speaking aloud.

"I'm sure they're watching. Maybe they can make him wear a monitor," says Zack.

Emily shakes her head. "I don't think they're allowed to," she says. "You can't monitor someone who's found innocent under the law. That's harassment. He could sue."

"Let him sue," says Zack.

He and Emily are drifting off into unknown territory. Talking nervously into Steve's silence.

Steve gets up and goes unsteadily to his window, looking out nervously for a moment. Then suddenly, he violently pulls the shades. In fear. In anger. In frustration.

Sits back on his bed. Curls his knees up. Looks silently up at them again.

You can't let him win, Zack wants to say. *You have to live your life. He's never going to touch you.* But he stays quiet.

And is there something in Joey, crazy Joey, that will want to attend to unfinished business? Prove himself once more to his bosses? Follow some code? When they submerged each other's cell phones in coffee, Joey tried to accept the deal but apparently he couldn't. Didn't have it in him. Couldn't accept unfinished business.

And now? Zack doesn't really know, of course. The mind of a career criminal. He is out of his depth here.

And then Steve reaches over to the bedside table, opens the drawer, and takes out his handgun. A big, heavy, ugly thing.

Zack recoils a little. The last one Zack saw looked pretty much like this one, and it was being held against his temple. The memory comes roaring back like a red light flashing, an alarm sounding, somewhere deep in his head.

Steve turns the gun silently in his hands, inspecting it closely like he did his scars just a minute ago.

This gun is not a good idea, Zack knows. This is only trouble.

"I've been going to a firing range once a week," Steve says, looking up at them. "You guys should each get guns too." Knowing that they won't. Knowing they don't approve.

So you're going to defend yourself from a professional assassin by having a gun? But again, Zack doesn't say anything.

"I feel better having it," says Steve.

"We'll be here," says Emily, not knowing what else to say. "Whatever you want. Whatever you need." Zack can tell she's trying to avoid looking at the gun, act as if she hasn't seen it, as if none of them have. "We're here for you."

"Thanks," says Steve. Leaving the gun out, right next to him.

30.

TO ANY OBSERVER, it's completely informal-looking, casual-seeming, although Joey's heart is pounding through his chest.

In greeting him, Karloff gives merely a curt nod.

No handshake. No Mafia don hug. No ceremony. Nothing.

Short, steel-wool white hair exploding out from his head in all directions, Karloff looks exactly as Joey has heard. As Joey imagined. A short, tough dockworker who has built a business, a cult, a world of illegality around him.

They're in some sort of back office of a factory space, with no factory there anymore. Karloff motions Joey to the chair in front of his. Joey sits facing him. Will backs away silently and leaves them.

Karloff looks at Joey. Starts right in. His accent is thick but his voice is low and rich, and Joey can understand every word he's saying. "One of two things will happen to you, Joey. Either the state will retry you on other criminal charges or some of the families will bring a wrongful death suit, which is civil court, not criminal. Whichever can be put together faster. Whichever means a better chance of conviction."

Joey is surprised by Karloff's keen interest, his clear, instructive summation of Joey's situation. He'd expected Karloff to talk in gruff, grudging single syllables. It's a reminder to Joey that, despite the dockworker appearance, the man does, after all, run an extensive criminal enterprise. It makes sense that he's as smart as he is brutal.

"Either way, your case is getting fast-tracked. The dumbass prosecutors got caught with their hands up their asses by your brilliant attorney's argument about the Cloud. Cope's jury research showed the argument would work. But next time, the prosecution will be ready. They can still try you on a lot of lesser charges—attempted homicide, weapons possession, assault, grievous bodily harm—which all come with a lot of sentencing discretion. You're going away forever, Joey. So I figure you've got a couple weeks at most. A couple weeks of freedom in this life. Just so you know."

He says it flatly. Factually. Information only. Like a white-coated cancer doctor, telling Joey he has just months to live before checking his watch and moving on to the next patient.

A couple weeks of freedom.

Freedom? That's not how Joey would describe it.

"But that's plenty of time for your next assignment, Joey," Karloff says with a little smile and an affirmative nod of his chin. "The assignment that will let you pay us back for our considerable investment in your defense." He looks at him. "The assignment that is the whole reason for our investment in your defense."

As Karloff continues to speak, certain phrases echo in

Joey's head: *A big assignment, Joey. The last thing we'll ask you to do.* It's being explained to him in the context of making things right with the organization. Of doing his duty. Of what Joey owes them. He is only hearing the broad strokes: a detonation of some sort to not only get the target but also destroy the surrounding evidence beyond recognition or forensic usefulness. No more specifics are mentioned, which is typical at this stage, keeping details about when and where purposefully unclear.

But Joey starts to sense the edges of something darker. Darker than a hit. To understand more fully the investment in his defense. And the reason for this special meeting. And the babysitting presence of this kid Will. It all starts to come together for him in a very uncomfortable way.

He starts to sense it's not a standard assassination assignment.

Then why would they turn to Joey? Because no one else would agree to do it?

Is it because he's an outsider? Someone who has no social network? Someone who's only going back inside to ultimately rot to death, as they see it, someone who will be of no use to them afterward? With his little two-week window before going to prison for the rest of his life, does that make Joey the perfect candidate? And Joey's Asperger's oddness (*a lack of connection*, the prison psychologist had tried to explain), they were never comfortable with that anyway. So is that somehow making him an ideal candidate too?

Yeah, something is different here. A big assignment, okay, but big how exactly? Do they figure that with Joey's lack of connection, he won't even realize something's different? That he'll just go along dumbly? He *would* have gone along dumb and unquestioning before. But all the interaction with that kid Zack has smartened him up a little. To things not being what they seem—like a phone dunked in coffee not being a dead phone, as it turned out. To there being another layer underneath. He credits the kid. Making him now pay a little more attention. Maybe just enough. Or maybe too much, he thinks gloomily.

Because Joey realizes he *has* to go along dumbly. He has to play dumb, for now. If he doesn't, if he protests or complains or tries to dodge or escape it, they'll just kill him. Right here. In this empty factory space. Maybe the real reason for being here, he realizes, is so they have that option, depending on Joey's reaction.

Maybe Joey's misreading it. Maybe being suddenly in Karloff's presence is clouding his judgment, making him unduly fearful and anxious.

Even if, as Karloff says, he's headed to prison for the rest of his life, prison is still a place where they feed and clothe you. Where you look forward to new episodes of the latest Netflix and HBO series. Where you hear the latest songs. Where there is a kind of life. A kind of life that Joey has come to know.

A place where, importantly, you are actually alive.

Karloff doesn't get Joey. No one gets Joey. But Joey is finally starting to understand Joey.

And Joey is starting to understand that he's in a corner. In a life of dark corners, maybe the darkest corner of his life.

"Welcome back, Joey," Karloff says cheerfully, but only as an afterthought, it seems. Only because he knows he should say something like that. Joey can see that Karloff has already moved on to something else. Scribbling some new notes on his pad. Joey thinks of the cancer doctor again.

"What does it pay?" Joey asks. Still being a good, dumb, dutiful, ambitious soldier. Still trying to believe it's just another assignment, that it's his big chance to prove himself to the boss.

Karloff looks at him, pausing a moment. Looking for a suitable answer, he almost shrugs.

It's suddenly clear to Joey: Karloff has never even thought about the pay because he doesn't expect Joey to be around to collect.

Will successful completion of the assignment mean never knowing he successfully completed it?

They got him out of prison. But because he's out, is he now—ironically—being sentenced to die?

Karloff smiles generously, magnanimously. "Name your price, Joey."

Confirming to Joey that he is not expected to survive.

31.

ZACK IS ASSIGNED the last shift at GreenGirl—six in the evening to one in the morning. He knows, he accepts, that this shift is the least desirable. The mornings are what you want. You're busy, productive, and employed people leave generous tips in the register jar, people who identify with and admire the baristas' hustle.

The last shift is customers hanging around with nothing to do, no better place to go, at loose ends, marking time. The last shift is when the drunk and high come in for a sober-up cup or two or three. The last shift is statistically when there is trouble in the store.

The hot Hispanic barista, Roseanne, works the more desirable morning and afternoon shifts so he can't train with her. He trains with Shaquille, fairly new himself, who's stuck on the evening shift for now. They initially give Zack just two shifts a week. The money per week is paltry, a joke really, but it's a start.

"Dude, you got to get yourself a phone. What if we got

to reach you? Change your shift around? Need you in an emergency on one of the other shifts? How can you not have a phone?" Shaquille asks.

Zack shrugs. He doesn't want to explain what happened with his last one, in a GreenGirl no less. He likes that Shaq doesn't know anything about that, and he wants to keep it that way. "You can call my girlfriend and leave a message. She'll let me know," he tells Shaq.

"What if you two break up? You got to get yo'self a phone, okay, man? They ain't expensive no mo'." Assuming that Zack has never been able to afford one. Simply doesn't have the money. "You got to join the world, my man. No choice."

Zack nods noncommittally.

"Yo, let's go over the register one more time."

32.

THE MEETING IS short. Just a few minutes spent sealing his fate before Will is summoned and hustles Joey away from Karloff, out of Karloff's sight, into yet another dull-colored, blend-in sedan.

At the end of the meeting, at Karloff's nod, Will hands Joey a new cell phone. A stripped down, cheap disposable, untraceable Joey assumes, many functions disabled, presumably hot. "This is how we'll reach you." Karloff looks wordlessly at him after that. *Another cell phone, Joey. You're back in the club, Joey. But don't fuck it up.*

Joey is dropped off on a street corner in Brooklyn. The warehouse section. Two streets Joey's never even heard of. Will presses a fifty-dollar bill into Joey's palm and takes off, without a word.

Joey Richter has nowhere to go. Has nowhere to spend the night.

He'd already spent all his earnings on rent and basic living expenses before he went inside. And he's not about to make his way to jail to retrieve his wallet and personal items that were being held for him during his imprisonment.

There was two hundred bucks in his wallet but he's sure that's been lifted by now. A couple of credit cards, canceled he's sure, since the bills haven't been paid in six months. He didn't even think about trying to make the minimum payments on them. He never expected to be out.

And the client's cash that the kid Zack had passed him at the GreenGirl to forget everything, to call things even…boy he could use that now. But the state isn't about to hand that money back to him, and who knows where it is anyway?

He's sure his crummy apartment is gone. He's behind six months on the rent now, and the fat, lazy landlord, big TV blasting in his ground-floor apartment all the time, probably saw the news and has learned all about Joey Richter.

If he shows up there now, he can't pay him any of the back rent, and the guy will be terrified to have a guy like Joey living there anyway. Of course, the apartment is so crummy that maybe nobody else wants it, and if it's empty, he can hand the landlord a fifty for the night. Muscle his way in, frighten the guy, just for the short-term.

Karloff didn't offer him an advance, and he didn't dare ask for one. Maybe Karloff assumed Joey has something saved from all his previous work for them. Or maybe he knows how fast Joey's cash disappeared in high-roller hotel suites, on high-priced dope and expensive call girls to pay for a temporary connection to a world that otherwise passes him by, and how it is always pretty much gone by morning. Most likely Karloff doesn't care either way.

Basically penniless, homeless, newly employed in a job that will pay nothing, Joey Richter heads down the street. A free man. Who is anything but free.

Just fifty bucks and a cell phone to his name.

33.

"DUDE," SAYS CHRIS at GreenGirl—this time visibly annoyed, no longer laid-back and friendly—"you've *got* to get yourself a phone."

They needed to contact him to change shifts and tried Emily, who didn't answer, and Chris didn't bother leaving a voice mail, not knowing if Zack would get the message in time.

But Zack can't convince himself to get a new phone. Even holding Emily's in his hands for a moment brings everything back.

Everyone forgave him at first for not having one, knowing what had happened. Knowing the trouble, the pain, the terror his last one had caused. Everyone cut him some slack, although Emily and his friends and family have found it increasingly ridiculous.

But over the months, it has become something else too. Zack has gotten *used* to being without a phone. Without texts, without a connection to Instagram and Snapchat and social media. It was a tether, that phone. Being without one was weird and eccentric but it was gradually more liberating too.

That's not how Emily saw it. Or, she saw more to it. She was patient with him at first but in the time they'd been living together, she was starting to pick up on something else, something subtler, that his lack of a phone was really about.

"So you start working at least but you still won't get a phone. It's like at some level you want to keep away from adult responsibility *somehow*. Okay, I'll get a job but I won't have a phone. As long as it's something, right, Zack? Not having a phone is your latest way to avoid growing up."

And finally, simple exasperation. "Zack, I'm tired of being your secretary, a messenger between you and the real world. Get yourself a new phone or get yourself a new girlfriend."

Not meaning it, Zack senses, but sure as hell thinking it at least. The sentiment is clear.

He's plenty smart, plenty educated, capable of doing anything really, but he doesn't do anything. Doesn't know what he wants. Doesn't even have a sense of where to generally focus. He *resists* doing anything. He can feel it in himself.

Is he lazy? No, he's full of energy; he's ready to give all his considerable energy to *something*. But he doesn't know what. Someone suggests something—grad school, a training program, an in at a corporation through a friend's dad, a spot at a tech start-up through a friend's brother—and it just feels so far away somehow. He doesn't feel any connection to it. It doesn't feel like *him*.

Emily has started calling him Pete—as in Peter Pan. Asking him if there's anywhere he'll be flying today. Gonna see any of the Lost Boys from GreenGirl on his days off?

*   *   *

"Need a new phone."

Zack holds out the old one.

"What happened to it?" says the Apple store clerk, turning it over in her hand, seeing no external damage. She is looking every bit the Apple Genius Bar rep—her glasses are thick and black and sexless. Hasn't combed her hair in a week.

"Dunked in hot coffee."

She is looking closely at it, thinking it might be salvageable.

"Sat in the coffee for several minutes," says Zack. "Don't even ask."

She shrugs, reaching into the display case for a new one. "What color?" Zack points. She takes it from the case. "All your data is backed up to the Cloud?"

"Yup," he says. His photos. His contacts. His email. His digital history. His online life. All in a suspended state in the digital ether, waiting to be reignited, summoned back down, reunited with him. With the touch of a button and the swipe of a credit card. Like he's a computer—his plug pulled while he sat quietly and contemplatively in the dark and then he's plugged back in, lighting up, connected, as if he'd never been gone…

"Amex, Visa, or Mastercard?"

Zack looks at the row of fancy phones. At the prices. Remembers all the heartache. Thinks about Steve.

Walking over here to the Apple store, everyone on their iPhones. Everyone living their lives on their little screens. Zack is sick of it.

She sees him hesitating. "So you want it?" asks the clerk.

Zack shakes his head. "Nah."

*   *   *

Zack heads out of the Apple store, feeling the fresh air fill his lungs like he'd been holding his breath.

He strolls down the street and stops into a nameless electronics store run by immigrants.

"You sell disposable phones?"

"Yes, of course," says the Middle Eastern salesclerk in a shiny suit, leaping up off his stool. "I bring you. You choose which you like."

"Give me the most basic one. Just a phone and texting. That's it."

"No internet? No apps? No geolocation?" The salesman looks disappointed.

"Nothing. An old model. The simplest, oldest model you've got. I don't want it to do anything. I want it to barely make a phone call."

He needs it for GreenGirl to reach him. To reach Emily, since Joey Richter is free. For his parents to reach him. It's not fair for Emily to be his secretary forever.

The salesclerk shrugs and reaches for a disposable on a bottom rack with an evident touch of disgust.

It's an off-brand. Some Indian company. Zack can't even find the brand name anywhere on the case. "It's really disposable?"

"You throw in trash when battery is done. It works maybe few months. Then you come back here for new one, yes? For good customer discount."

He shrugs. "Sure."

"When you want upgrade, you come here, yes?"

The phone feels as familiar in his pocket as his apartment key or jangling change. It's no object of love. Its case is basic and void of design and he's sure the speaker is lousy but the reception is the reception, the network is the network, whatever phone you have, so Zack feels fine about his purchase.

He can reach and be reached. He's rejoined the world.

34.

JOEY STANDS ON his old front stoop, talking to his old landlord, Gerardi. Fatter and slower than ever, Joey notices.

"Hey, Mr. Gerardi."

"Joey," says Gerardi nervously.

The way he barely opens the door—when he used to throw it wide and chatter on about the New York Jets, whose hat he wore constantly—tells Joey that Gerardi knows exactly where Joey's been for six months.

"Listen, I was wondering—"

"It's rented," says Gerardi. "You were behind six months, and it's rented."

"Yeah, well, I couldn't get you the rent. See, I—"

"I know," says Gerardi gruffly. "I watch the news."

There is a pause while Joey debates asking for a room for the night. "Look, if I gave you a fifty, could I—"

"Fifty! Hah! You jokin', right?" The landlord shakes his head. "I don't want you here. Or anywhere near here, okay?"

Pretty bold way to talk to an assassin, thinks Joey. An increasingly pissed-off assassin.

But then Gerardi suddenly throws his apartment door wide open, sweeps out into the hall, and waves for Joey to follow him.

Joey follows Gerardi down the hallway to the storage area at the back of the building. Gerardi inserts a key from his thick keyring into the lock and throws open the storage door.

"Your stuff," says Gerardi. "All of it. We tossed it all into these boxes for you. No charge, if you get out of here."

Four cartons. Clothes, linens, toiletries, shoes, a few plates, a couple of pots. All his worldly goods, in four cartons.

"I'll go through them, just take what I need, whatever'll fit into a cab, okay?"

Gerardi shrugs, a little annoyed but obviously glad to be putting this episode behind him.

He walks away as Joey yanks open the cartons.

Looks like they just threw all his stuff into them as fast as they could. It was a complete mess. But it looks like everything is here.

He sifts through to find what he's hoping for. Fingers crossed.

He'd always been super careful about it. Stripped and disassembled, he's always been able to hide its pieces in shoeboxes, in a locked cutlery box, and in a couple of hollowed-out hardcover books.

There in the storage area, he quickly reassembles it. His Ruger.

Beautiful gun. Gleaming black in the slanted light of the storage room. Transforming it.

The rounds are there too. Stuffed into various socks and shoes.

He throws the gun into one of the cartons, covers it with some clothes, grabs a couple pairs of running shoes, T-shirts, and some underwear and socks.

Closes the single carton. Lifts it and heads to the front door to hail a cab.

"Toss the rest," he calls to Gerardi over the landlord's blaring TV as he heads out the building's front door.

35.

JOEY STANDS ON a curb at Aqueduct Avenue in the Bronx. Looking across the street at a small house he thought he'd never see again. He'd thought he was done with forever.

But he has nowhere else to go. Nowhere else to sleep, to find a meal, nothing. This is where people turn when they have nowhere else.

Are they still here? Are they both still alive?

He left home so long ago that he doesn't even remember the exact circumstances of his leaving. Has he somehow blocked it out? He doesn't think so. He knows there was no blowup or drama. It was just a drifting away. There was no particular love there, none he could feel or remember in either direction, him toward them or them toward him.

He'd been an only child, as if they'd quickly decided that children were not really for them or that they were not really meant for children.

He knew now that his strangeness—his diagnosis "on the spectrum"—made it harder on them both. On them all. He wondered now in passing, for the first time, standing there, whether one or both of them were on the spectrum too. But he couldn't even remember their behavior clearly enough to say. He'd left at fifteen; home life in his last few years there was a blur—not an unpleasant blur, not a pleasant blur, just a blur.

He picks up the carton where the taxi dropped him. He tucks it under his arm, crosses the street, sets it down on the lowest stair of the stoop before ascending to ring the bell.

Twenty years. That's the math.

A stooped older man he doesn't know opens the door. Balding. Dangerously thin. Wispy white hair. Thick, black-framed glasses.

Damn. Joey was wrong. They no longer live here. He should have figured.

He is already starting to figure out some other plan—a men's shelter, an SRO, somewhere he can skip out on the payment in the morning—while the man blinks at him.

"Saw you on the news," says the man in a thin voice, and Joey realizes now the stooped old man is pretty sick, cancer or something.

And he realizes it's not just a stooped old man.

It's his father, Sam.

No hugs, of course. No handshake. They are strangers. A man who rang a doorbell. A man who answered it.

"What are you doing here?" asks Sam, and then sees the carton under Joey's arm and looks up in a kind of sudden, frozen fear and shakes his head slowly. "Oh, I don't know, Joey…"

"I got nowhere else to go…"

"I don't know. We seen you on the news…"

"They let me go," says Joey.

"Don't mean you're innocent," says Sam.

Not knowing how to respond, Joey just repeats, "I got nowhere else to go."

Sam Richter looks again at the carton, again at Joey. Holds the door open wider and gestures with a nod to come on in.

Sam and Joey in the dark hallway.

Sam calling out, "Irma, I got a surprise here for you."

"What kinda surprise?" The voice from the back of the house, even darker than the hallway, is strong in contrast to Sam's reedy voice. And it does not sound at all receptive to any kind of surprise.

A wheelchair rolls up out of the darkness.

"Guess who?" says Sam to Irma, with no joy, no surprise in his voice.

"I know who," says Irma, looking up at him from the wheelchair. "Well, well, you're back." A statement of fact. Nothing more. She looks at the carton. "You can stow it in the front closet for now. Just keep it out of the way of my chair."

*　　*　　*

They explain quickly enough. Diabetes for her that's put her into the wheelchair. Prostate cancer for him. Debilitating for both of them but only slowly, the doctors say. So this existence in this dark apartment is open-ended, interminable, unpredictable.

So fucking dark in here. No wonder he can't remember anything from childhood. He couldn't see anything the whole time.

The piece of cake they serve him is stale—but it's cake. Obviously she doesn't care much about her diabetes.

They don't know what to say to him but they don't much care, it seems.

"I got nowhere else to go," he repeats, not knowing what else to say either. It's a mantra. He kind of likes saying it; he likes the simple truth of it.

Until finally Sam responds to it.

"Well, what does that tell you about your life, Joey, if you got nowhere else to go? Except to your old, sick parents who you don't even remember and who barely remember you."

To which Joey says, "Can I stay here?"

His dad shrugs. "You can stay here tonight. You can stay here tomorrow. Then we'll see."

His old room. Which he barely recognizes. All personal effects cleared out long ago, and he can't even tell you what they were to begin with. Some toys, he assumes, clothes he can't picture, something on the walls he remembers vaguely, but nothing he can recall exactly. Only the single bed remains.

The room was green, he remembers that, remembers curling up and looking at the green wall as he waited for sleep. Which sometimes came and sometimes didn't—he remembers that too—but now the wall is white. As if to erase, to bleach, any memory at all.

He retrieves the carton from the hall closet, closes the bedroom door, opens the carton, and riffles through it until he pulls out the Ruger again, holding it up in the dim light and tossing it hand to hand.

It was never his favorite. He preferred the Glock—its weight, firing action, grip, balance, everything. The Glock that was with him his whole adult life until it had its star turn in the courtroom, in the spotlight as Exhibit A, and was now in secure storage somewhere, awaiting his new trial or maybe it was already melted down, scrap metal.

This Ruger was second-class all around. You wouldn't know it unless you held and shot the Glock. The Ruger was a VW to the Glock's Mercedes. It was like a second kid—ordinary, unnoticed in the glow of the superstar, but in the absence of the first, you could get to know this one, get to love it, feel affection for the underdog...He smiles.

A polite knock.

"Yeah?" Not bothering to hide the gun or open the door.

"Come get something to eat."

"Yeah, okay, on my way."

Like the boy he was twenty years ago, he puts away his toy and heads to dinner.

* * *

It is silent. He sees his parents moving cautiously around him. He sees his father making sure to avoid eye contact. He sees his father's hands shaking. His mother swallowing for her dry throat.

"What the hell, you afraid I'm gonna kill you?"

"We're afraid you won't," says his mother bitterly. "We're afraid people will discover who Joey Richter's parents are, and we'll be hounded forever, and I'll be accused of giving birth to a monster."

It shuts everyone up again. He doesn't remember if that bitterness was always in her personality. He doesn't remember anything.

"We know who you are," says Sam.

"What you are," says Irma.

It's soup. Not bad. Nice and hot with nice warm bread.

"Yeah? Go ahead. Who am I?" Daring them to say whatever they have to say. Figuring they will go silent and meek with the challenge.

"You're someone we don't know, Joey," says Sam quietly. "Someone we've never met."

"You're a killer, Joey! A hired killer!" Irma is direct. Franker. Louder. As if freshly stunned by the idea of who he is, as if waiting for years to confront her son. "I can't imagine anyone less human. No human feeling at all, if you do that job. If it's even an actual job. And I can see how successful you are at it...since you're back here begging for a place to spend the night."

"I have been successful," he says, and suddenly he wants to tell them about his successes, his triumphs, his patient craft, the loneliness, the discipline. But he is disciplined enough, lonely enough, to keep it to himself.

"How can you be out?" Sam says. "I don't get it."

"I don't get it either," says Joey.

"You think the police will just let you go free? They're probably following you, and now you've come here and dragged us into it."

He shrugs. "They're not following me. And even if they are, you don't have to talk to anyone. They're not gonna bother sick people. You can just keep to your bitter, sick selves."

"Well, if they're not following you...please don't tell anyone you're here. Don't tell anyone about us."

"I got nowhere else to go."

Irma twists the words around and sends them back bitterly to Joey: "Go anywhere else but here, Joey."

Nothing about the past comes back to him, yet it all comes back to him. No specifics, but all the feeling, the frustration, the bitterness. He can't remember anything but in an instant, he sees again how it was, how it always was here.

And what...should he bring it full circle, go load the Ruger...come back and put them both out of their misery, and him too? Put all three of them back where they started...dead to each other? A woman in a wheelchair, a cancer victim, and a killer who is about to be killed himself on his final assignment? It would be a favor to all of them, and a favor to the world.

He considers it. He considers it for several bites. Putting down his spoon, heading to his room to retrieve the gun, loading the clip, coming back to dinner, shooting all three of them right here in the kitchen. Why not? It's one way out of Karloff's suicide mission. Karloff might then realize Joey had figured it out. That he was smarter than Karloff thought. Of course, Karloff might just think he was crazy.

But Joey won't do it. He doesn't want to do the world any favors.

He eats in silence. Watches CNN with them silently.

Goes to bed with the gun tucked under the covers with him. In case Sam or Irma decide to try something heroic. Something dumb and heroic. In case they have the same homicidal thoughts he does.

But as he curls into sleep in his old bed—quiet, anciently familiar—his thoughts soften, and some deeper thing begins to reverberate, to come up from the old bedsprings, wiggling up from the past. Maybe over the course of a couple days, they'll all warm up. Learn a little about each other. Maybe there'll be some thin string of connection.

He opens his eyes in the middle of the night.

A figure is standing over him in the dark...

Its right arm coming toward him...

Fuck! How the fuck...?

Joey's left hand forcefully slaps away the arm as his right hand grabs the Ruger from between his legs and brings it up out of the sheets, pointing it before he sees the figure's two hands go up high in surrender and he sees that it is his father.

In Sam's right hand is a roll of bills.

He holds it out to Joey.

"We can't sleep with you here, Joey," Sam says. "We've been lying in our bed, terrified, arguing about what to do about you." He is shaking. "Here, take this. Three thousand, cash. Three thousand cash to get out of here now, right now, and not come back. I know you can use it, or why would you be here? And it's worth it to us."

Sam Richter watches as Joey gathers his few things back into the carton, pulls on his pants and shirt and shoes and leather jacket, lifts the carton, and heads for the door.

When they emerge from Joey's old bedroom, Irma is sitting in her wheelchair in his parents' bedroom doorway. She watches silently, hands in her lap.

Sam hands Joey the money roll.

Three thousand dollars. Probably enough to live on until Karloff gives him the call, and then he doesn't need anything to live on anymore.

Three thousand dollars. The cost of getting him out of their house. He knows it's a lot for them. A stash of cash kept hidden for an emergency. For them, this is that emergency. Three thousand. That's how much his presence troubles them. Is that three-thousand-dollar sum a point of pride or a point of shame? Or both at once, in his twisted life?

Three thousand. Clients would typically pay him ten. Ten to kill another human being. To take a life.

Three to get out of a couple of lives that he'd never been in anyway. Three to just walk down a hallway and out a door.

Very different, of course. But something in it feels the same to Joey. A payoff. A transaction. With nothing more attached to it.

Carton under his arm, he heads out the door. For the last time. For forever, he assumes. They all assume.

36.

THE PROBLEM WITH GreenGirl—a busy GreenGirl—is that, well, people drink coffee.

People you know. People you never expect to see. People from your old life.

And it is Marcie from junior high school in suburban Cleveland who happens to stop in and happens to see him.

"I didn't know if it was you. I couldn't be sure. You look so much older and bigger but of course your red hair…it's one thing that's the same. It's the giveaway," Marcie gushes with a smile. They exchange pleasantries and catch up. He's the staff, he's a barista, he needs to be nice, and why not be nice anyway?

Yes, she has a job in the city, in ad sales for Google, and besides Google headquarters in California, this is really the only place to be.

And the next week it is Marcie and Meghan, clearly not an accidental appearance this time, clearly planned so Meghan can see him too. Meghan who works in publishing and is Marcie's roommate on the Upper East Side.

And obviously word went out because he soon gets a call from his parents, who he has dutifully resumed talking to every week, now that he has his own cell phone again. "Hey, we heard! And you never said a word about it. You're working at a GreenGirl? Is that right?"

Oh Jesus.

"Just a couple of shifts, Mom. Just to get me out of the apartment and out of Emily's hair." They have heard about Emily. Haven't met her, are eager to, but don't want to intrude.

"A GreenGirl," says his mom.

"Good coffee," says his dad.

They so obviously are trying not to pass judgment, so obviously trying to let him live his life and not be critical, but it has the reverse effect, making him feel worse about where he is in life.

His dad is a successful contractor with thriving businesses in the suburbs of both Cleveland and Austin. High-end homes. A peerless reputation for construction quality. Moves equally comfortably on the golf courses of exclusive clubs and out on the job with Ukrainian sheet rockers and Irish framers and Nicaraguan painters. A man's man—who nevertheless reads the latest fiction at night and the latest thinking on Buddhism. An impossible role model.

It's a prosperous business. One Zack could easily slot into. His dad would never ask or insist but would welcome him completely if he decides that's what he wants. Which he doesn't.

His mom is in her third term as mayor of their little town

of Moreland Hills. Successful, well loved. Opponents have stopped running against her for the time being. An impossible role model as well.

Only two failings, Zack would argue, and he would also argue that they aren't really failings at all.

One: they never had any other kids. He's never asked why and they've never offered. They could easily have handled four or five, from what he can see. He's never gotten any whiff of fertility issues or any sense the marriage was ever in a fragile state. He senses—and fears—that the reason for just a single kid is they were so happy and fulfilled with little Zacky that they felt no further need or longing.

Two: which is an offshoot of one, he supposes—they always let him do whatever he wanted. No discipline. No expectation. Well, that wasn't quite accurate. A high expectation of decency. A high expectation of fairness. Of respect for others. But as far as achievement or accomplishment? They had it covered themselves. Don't worry about it, son. Live your life. That's why we work as hard as we do. For you. To find meaning in your life that you want. To see you happy.

Leaving him to cast around blindly for meaning and happiness, apparently.

And he knows he has only himself to blame. And it's such a subtle thing. Because of course, they only want what's best for him. They are rooting for him in all things. At every moment. Boosters. Come on, Zack! You can do it! Whatever it is, you've got the goods!

He's more than a little ashamed to have such conflicted thoughts about his own good fortune. He keeps them to himself, even with Emily.

Lately, he's been thinking about the opposite end of the good-fortune scale. Thinking about someone who, he assumes, has had as much bad fortune as Zack has had good.

With Joey out, he's been wondering about him. Anxiously, of course, but curious too.

Where Joey sleeps. Where he eats. Where he is. Is he close? As close as he can get, getting closer? Or far away, as far as he can get, trying to get even farther?

And wondering, therefore, about Joey's past. Joey's parents. Who are they? What were they like? Anything like his own? Some kind of subtle burden like his own? Or some kind of inversion of them?

Leaving one child a highly focused, emotionless killer. And the other a directionless lover, in touch with his emotions, with his softer, gentler side, arguably to his own eternal detriment.

Zack knew he would regret getting a phone again. Starting the dutiful calls home again. "You're not going to come surprise me here, are you?" asks Zack.

"Well, if we did show up, it sounds like it wouldn't be much of a surprise," says his mother coyly.

"I can't talk to you when I'm working," says Zack.

"I know. And relax. Nobody's told us which GreenGirl, and we didn't ask. Your dad and I will have to drink a lot of coffee to stumble across you at random."

Letting him live his life. To a fault.

And then the conversation turns suddenly more serious. Deadly serious. The shift in his mom's tone is pronounced. "We heard the news, Zack. Even out here in the hinterland. I presume you weren't going to tell us because you didn't want us worrying."

Which is exactly right. "It feels weird to always have you inside my head, Mom."

She laughs affectionately. Her entertaining, brilliant boy. He can do anything. Someday, maybe he'll actually do something.

"We're not going to make you come home or ship you off to California or Australia to start a new life. We'd love to, of course. We'd be able to sleep at night but we're not going to do that."

Of course not. They won't insist on anything.

"All we can say is be alert, be safe, be careful. All the usual parent stuff."

Zack is almost certain that his mom—a mayor—has used her position to reach out directly to the city's police department, explained the situation, and is making sure the police are monitoring the situation closely. She may have done it charmingly or she may have read them the riot act. She is equally capable and accomplished in both styles.

"You know, if you insisted that I come home or that I leave for California or Australia, I might actually do it, Mom. If you insisted, I might."

"Oh, Zack, I would insist, absolutely, except for one thing. Emily. I know you well enough to know you won't leave her. Because you want to be with her, of course. And because you don't want to leave her unprotected. So I know it's stupid for me to even ask."

"Mom, it's time to leave my head now, okay?"

She laughs again. "I don't know if I know how to."

He laughs now too.

"Be alert. Be safe. Be careful," she repeats.

"Got it. See you soon. Don't come searching GreenGirls. I'll fly back home in a couple of months, okay?" And then he says what he knows will delight her. "And I'll bring Emily."

"Now who's in whose head?"

"Bye, Mom."

37.

IN HIS NEAT new three-bedroom on eastern Long Island, sitting on his little porch with a cigar in the morning, Detective Lopez, NYPD, 11th Precinct, Ret., puts down the newspaper. He's read the two paragraphs closely three times now, and they reveal nothing more than he already knew.

He's so used to the failure of the justice system over his thirty years on the force that it no longer bothers him. Usually.

This one bothers him a lot. Because in this one, he had intervened. He had personally been there to keep the kid and his girlfriend alive. It had been a matter of seconds between life and death. Two nice young kids are walking around today because of Lopez's instincts and quick judgment. It isn't usually so personal and close as that.

And this is a bright kid. Unusual kid. Bravery with brains. With modesty. With curiosity. Straightforward, honest. And this is a kid who'd come in looking for police help, who sensed he could trust and count on the police—even if he got spooked and didn't stay.

On the job, Detective Lopez's weight issues had finally gotten the better of him. He joked about it—*I only move fast if I have to*—and they joked right back at him in the station house until it was no longer seen as a joke. He was a hero, a highly decorated cop, but he suffered from morbid obesity, and he and the department had differed on the issue of treatment. They wanted him to have a procedure. They'd pay for it and his recovery but he explained and believed that this is simply who he is, how he is, and they should accept it. And rather than everyone being dragged into court or arbitration over the issue, the department had offered him a package.

His service had been meritorious from day one, and he took the package and sits now, looking out on the sun rising over a potato field—but reading about an assassin going free. An assassin whose eyes he had looked directly into, at the moment the guy was about to pull the trigger, and Detective Lopez, from amid his deep reservoir of experience and intuition, did not like what he had seen. He wouldn't mind seeing whatever it was—whatever was in those eyes—through prison bars, but he sure as hell minded the idea of those eyes and what's behind them, what he sensed, being out on the street.

He called his friends on the force immediately. To make sure this guy Richter is being monitored. To make sure the correct mechanisms are in place. He even went so far as to ask who is on the detail and how smart they are, how alert, how streetwise.

"We've got a couple of good kids on it, Sanders and Singh."

Lopez frowns. A couple of "good kids" is not at all adequate.

"No worries, Detective. The guy is pretty predictable. We

staked out his old apartment and his parents' house, and sure enough he shows up at both places less than an hour later."

"Wait. An hour later? Where was he before that?"

"Well, everything's fine now. But truth is…"

Uh-oh.

"We did lose him briefly when he left the courthouse…"

What?

"Confusion, cameras, a lot of traffic…and a pretty unexpected outcome, you've got to admit. We weren't totally prepared for it, I guess…"

Detective Lopez does not like this.

He brings his bulk up out of the porch chair. Looks across the field.

Looks down at his protruding stomach. Which he has a lousy feeling in the pit of. A reliable barometer, he's found.

Another reason he'd resisted the procedure.

38.

JOEY RICHTER, WALKING around, thinks Zack.

Wherever he is, whatever he's doing, he's *somewhere*, he's doing *something*.

It puts a sudden new stress on Zack, on Emily—to say nothing of Steve. And extra stress on Zack and Emily as a couple.

"He's just walking around out here," says Emily. "He could be waiting downstairs, on the sidewalk outside, across the street, watching."

"Look, we have to just try to go on with our lives."

"But we can't, Zack. That's the point! We can't just go on with our lives if he's out there, lurking around a corner."

It's taking its toll. They're on edge. Snapping at each other. Which shocks them both since they haven't snapped at each other before.

"Where is he this morning, do you think?" says Emily sarcastically, irritably. "What's he up to today?" Speaking of Joey as if he's a friend. As if he's a casual but inevitable part of their lives.

Joey walking around. It occupies them. It consumes them. They can't think about themselves because they're thinking about Joey. Emily talks about it incessantly but it's working silently inside Zack constantly as well.

"Look, Em, think about what the cops told us. They're watching him all the time. The state's putting together its case as fast as possible. And the cops heard there's a wrongful death case by a victim's family, as well as the criminal case on lesser charges. Two approaches. The state's embarrassed by what happened; they got caught flat-footed. They're not going to let it happen again."

"Yeah, well, if we know the state's putting together its case again as quickly as they can, Joey knows it too, right?" says Emily. "He's got to figure this time he'll be convicted. So Joey has to assume that this couple of weeks might be the last freedom of his lifetime."

His last chance to do whatever he wants, whatever he needs.

His last chance to tie up loose ends.

"And if he does something horrible, what are they going to do to him, put him in jail?" says Emily. "Lock him up forever? That's happening either way."

Would someone in that position choose to go out in a blaze of glory?

These are the questions and worries that occupy Zack and Emily. Every time they leave the apartment in the morning, every time they turn a corner or board a subway, it is anxious, fraught, nerve-racking.

Emily has inquired about separate police protection but the police reiterated that they are watching Joey already so a separate protection detail is redundant.

Emily can't sleep.

Zack awakens to find her staring at the ceiling.

"It'll just be a couple weeks. And we know they're watching him."

But Emily cannot be soothed. Rationality can't always calm you when you've had a gun held to your head.

39.

JOEY, WALKING AROUND. But in fact planning nothing.

No master plan. No standing across the street from Zack and Emily's or Steve's apartment. Not thinking about Emily or Zack or Steve, or any of that.

Thinking about Karloff.

Thinking about himself.

Trying to figure things out. For instance, what had Will really been doing in jail? In Joey's cell?

Joey had first assumed—when Will admitted to Joey in the sedan that he worked for Karloff and explained how he'd gotten in to share Joey's jail cell—that it was to keep an eye on Joey, to make sure Joey didn't flip or squeal or consider a plea deal in exchange for leniency. Maybe, too, Will was even there to protect him, to make sure Joey stayed alive because Karloff wanted him out to do one last job for Karloff, one last job Karloff seems to feel Joey owes him.

But now he's rethinking it all. Did Will really get in there the way he said? Is it really that easy to manipulate prison system records and computer programs? Or was that a bluff on Will's part? A lot of smooth bullshit? Meaning, did he come into the cell some other way, with official assistance, which seems much more likely?

Joey's suddenly seeing some deeper, subtler, trickier possibilities.

For instance, the prosecution must have been asked at some point if it was okay to put a cellmate in with Joey. Their eyes may have lit up at the prospect, and they probably said yes, figuring that the cellmate might relay something to them—especially in exchange for consideration or release—never realizing that putting Will in there achieved the exact opposite. Having him there guaranteed they'd learn nothing from Joey. They'd cut off the information flow with exactly the move they thought might open it up.

Maybe the prosecution wanted to plant an informant in there with Joey, and when his defense team or Karloff learned that, they managed to insert Will. That would make more sense, wouldn't it? That would be how he'd gotten a cellmate. One agreed on by both the prosecution *and* the defense. Maybe his slick defense team had cleverly engineered it to be Will.

What a great position for Will. He could make a deal with the prosecution using any information he got from Joey as a bargaining chip. Or he could supply them nothing but misinformation to mess up their upcoming case. Will could pass on anything he chose to either side, the prosecution or the defense, or only to Karloff.

Will's presence, Joey realizes, was just the latest version of not trusting Joey. Just the latest version of making him take photos of his hits. Just the latest version of *We don't really get you, Joey. You're too odd, too different, so we have to keep an eye on you, and it's a hassle and a burden keeping an eye on you.* Joey had never squealed, had been stand-up his whole life, and still this was how they saw him.

Was that what Will was doing there? Joey isn't sure. He realizes he'll never know. A new gloom descends on him like a blanket he can't throw off. There's so much he doesn't understand. So much going on around him, above him, beside him—teasing him, dangling just out of his mental reach. Connections he doesn't follow. That he'll never follow.

Is this part of being on the spectrum? Or due to those childhood concussions? Or some of both? Shit, if you can't think straight, if you can't sort things out, then what's the point? And if you're nothing but a problem and have to be treated like a child, then what's the point? If you have no connection to anyone, then what's the point? And he realizes grimly: that question—*what's the point?*—is the clearest thought he's had.

40.

IT HAUNTS JOEY. He can't stop replaying it in his head. If only he had listened to that kid Zack. If only he had taken Zack's deal.

That moment when they'd both destroyed their phones in the matching Grandes. If only he had accepted that ending, the fairness, the mutual evenness of that arrangement, instead of coming after Zack and Emily, he wouldn't be in this fix today.

He wouldn't have been in jail. He wouldn't be awaiting his permanent return to prison. He wouldn't have been released for Karloff's next project and be waiting for the suicide mission Karloff is about to send him on.

If only he'd accepted Zack's deal, he would have gotten away with having been a paid assassin.

Even though it turned out Zack had transferred Joey's data to the Cloud, Zack might have just left it there. Like an insurance policy, to make sure Joey didn't come after him. That's probably why Zack put it there in the first place.

It got pulled down from the Cloud, Joey is sure, only because

Detective Lopez asked Zack for what he knew. If Joey hadn't come after Zack, had not followed him out of the GreenGirl, Detective Lopez wouldn't have been involved at all.

Things might have been wildly different. Joey would just continue to be out and around. Zack would have never risked pulling the data down. Would never have taken the chance. Would never have risked Joey's wrath and fury. Would never have risked Joey's revenge.

They would each have left the other alone. Live and let live.

But no, Joey couldn't leave well enough alone. He had to tie up loose ends. Tying up loose ends is what has put Joey into this position.

His fateful, dumb decision to follow Zack out of the GreenGirl. More evidence of Joey's idiocy. Of his inability to read the situation.

That's why he always gets pissed off thinking about Zack. Zack is a reminder to Joey of how dumb Joey is. Of his mistakes.

Zack is a reminder of how close Joey was to getting away with it. And didn't.

Three thousand.

Probably just enough to get him to the end of his life, thinks Joey grimly. Just enough to feed him until he gets the details of the "assignment." His final assignment.

He finds a cheap room. Stows his carton one last time.

And then, as always, he has to just kill time. Killing time before killing time—one more time. One last time.

He pops the television on but can't focus on the news or on a movie. He tries some porn, usually a pretty reliable distraction, but can't even sit still for that. Can't sit in the room. He doesn't know what to do with himself.

So he hits the streets again. To walk. To wander.

It's like prison, he thinks. Worse, actually. Because in prison you know what your days are. There is predictability, relative safety, routine, clarity. You can shut down, go into yourself, whenever you want.

But this has none of that. The call from Karloff could come at any time. So it is all you can think about. It eats up your energy. You can't go inside yourself.

This is a prison of walking around. A prison that looks to all the world like freedom but is in fact the opposite. It's a prison of buildings and earth and blue sky and activity and all the bustle of city life. Joey trudges up and down the streets as if they are prison corridors. Keeping his head down, shuffling along. Marking time. Dead Man Walking. Counting down to his doom.

He knows he's being followed by the cops. He knows they're keeping an eye on him. He saw them when he was leaving his parents' house. And he's seen them outside his new room. Young guys. Inexperienced. He figures he can shake them when the time comes but he figures he might have only one chance to do it so he'll have to save it and live with the tail until then.

He'll have to shake them to do the job for Karloff. On the

other hand, he could purposely *not* shake them so that he can't pull off Karloff's job.

Who's he kidding? Karloff knows Joey's being followed by the cops with such a high-profile re-prosecution pending, and Will or someone else who works for Karloff will help him shake the tail when the time comes. For all Joey knows, Karloff himself has the power to temporarily get rid of the tail. To put in a call to corrupt cops on the inside who will find some way to divert the tail, leaving Joey clear for the few hours he needs to pull it off.

If the cops are following him, he also figures they're probably protecting Zack and Emily and Steve. So he can't take his last weeks before the Karloff job to terrorize Zack and Emily and Steve—terrorize or worse—although he finds himself thinking about it more and more in these days of wandering. A chance to prove himself to Karloff—and to himself. Define himself. Take care of unfinished business.

But he's been warned about that.

"You're gonna lie low, right, Joey?" Karloff had said. Joey had nodded yes obediently.

"You're not gonna try something foolish?" Karloff had asked. Warning him. "Foolish is what got you in trouble last time. And put all of us in trouble. And we're not going to tolerate stupid and foolish again from you, capisce?"

Joey nodded.

So now he wanders around the city.

A death sentence stroll.

41.

JOEY IS SPENDING down the three grand, coffee by sandwich by subway ride. He could probably shake the tail on the subway but that's just the ones he's spotted. There might be others.

He wanders the city, waiting.

The city, it seems, ignores him.

His wandering takes him—unconsciously? magnetically? inevitably?—back to a certain GreenGirl. He knows this might alarm the tail, although he bets they probably don't know the whole history of his case. To them it's just another GreenGirl, and there's nothing wrong with him going back there; it's not the scene of the crime. Just a couple of drowned cell phones, by mutual agreement. A mutual agreement he just couldn't leave alone, he thinks again regretfully.

Hey, maybe he'll have a coffee. For old times' sake.

He looks in the GreenGirl windows from across the street and heads impulsively toward it. As he passes the window to go in, he glimpses the familiar curly red hair.

What?

Impossible.

Did he imagine it?

The past has reared up suddenly, more vivid, red…He's so confused.

Meaty hands are quickly on his shoulders, pulling him out of the GreenGirl doorway onto the street.

He's down on the pavement seconds later.

"Not a good idea, Joey," says a male voice from behind him.

"Pick another GreenGirl," says a second voice. "Pick *any* other GreenGirl."

The click of handcuffs.

And when Joey is finally pulled up off the pavement, he glimpses the people staring out from behind the plate-glass window at the scene with him at its center. Some customers. A couple of baristas.

And Zack—staring at him—wearing a GreenGirl apron.

The bile, the anger, the irritation—irrational, uncontrollable—rises up off the sidewalk with Joey. Just seeing the kid triggers it in him.

I show up here, I don't even get in the door, and it happens again. It's that kid again. I see that curly red hair, and suddenly I'm facedown on the pavement, and there's handcuffs on me. Fuck!

The fury races through him. Itches him like a rash. He doesn't know why but he can't deny it.

He tries to calm himself down.

Kid finally got a job, thinks Joey.

Well, Joey's got one too.

Or maybe two.

Do Karloff's job. And get rid of this kid just before.

Or at the same time, he thinks vaguely.

And then, while the undercover cops, three of them, Joey notices, are getting things organized on the sidewalk, shooing onlookers along, Zack comes out of the GreenGirl.

Everyone else stays inside the coffee shop, terrified.

But Zack comes out. Steps toward Joey slowly, carefully, keeping a safe distance. He looks at the handcuffs. Looks at Joey.

Nods to him. "Hey, Joey," says Zack.

Like he wants to talk or something? Like he misses him? Wants to catch up on old times?

Joey tugs furiously, uselessly, at the handcuffs behind him.

Shit, this kid is really something.

42.

CHRIS, THE MANAGER, takes Zack aside.

"Look, Roseanne told me you're a hero. That you helped catch an assassin. But nobody knew the assassin was gonna get released and come back here, back to the same GreenGirl, obviously looking for you…"

"But he was stopped before he got in here…"

"Yeah…by cops. By the police!" Chris says, his usually calm voice rising, constricting with tension. "What if they weren't keeping an eye on him? An assassin, Zack. Look, man, we can't have a guy like that coming in here. Who knows what he's gonna do?"

"But he *didn't* get in here…"

"He got awful close. And he did it because you're here…"

"He didn't know I was here, I swear! He couldn't have."

"Oh, you think he was just coming here for a cup of coffee?"

Zack knows how it seems. How it looks.

"Zack, everyone on the team says you're a good worker. Everyone likes you. But you're gonna have to find a different GreenGirl, or another coffee shop, or another job altogether. I'll give you a good recommendation. But I can't risk keeping you here. Sorry."

43.

IN A COUPLE of hours, Joey is uncuffed and released from the 14th Precinct.

Did not enter the establishment, the police report says. *Remained in public space.* Since he never entered the GreenGirl, Joey did nothing bookable, nothing wrong. He was stopped before anything happened. Maybe the cops regretted that. Under the law, he was literally just a man crossing the street.

Now he knows how closely he is being watched.

Karloff and Will must know too.

So how do Karloff and Will expect him to pull off whatever they have in mind? Unless it has to do with *being* so closely watched. Unless that's part of it somehow. Being close to the cops. Being dragged back into court again soon.

Maybe the cops who were tailing him will be rotated off now since he's seen them, and new ones will be assigned. Or maybe it doesn't matter. Maybe they're happy to have him know who's watching him.

And he knows that if he has to shake them at some point, he'll probably have just one chance at most—and he begins to think about how.

44.

ZACK DECIDED NOT to tell Emily or Steve about what happened outside the GreenGirl. Who had shown up. Who he might have served coffee to.

Emily would be paralyzed by fear, unable to concentrate at work, afraid to leave the apartment.

Steve would reach for his gun, not able to stay in his apartment like a target, like a sitting duck. Might even go looking for Joey.

"Wait. So it's not working out? They're letting you go?" says Emily, back at the apartment that night when Zack explains how there's no longer a place for him at the GreenGirl.

"Well, Chris told me I'm doing a really good job and that people like working with me…" Zack pauses, searching the apartment for the right words. "I think it's just a staffing thing. He said he'd help me find some shifts at another GreenGirl."

Emily frowns. She's clearly surprised. Zack said days ago how well everything was going. He can tell she's not completely satisfied with his explanation.

He senses she's starting to worry he's one of those people who can't hold down a job. Any job. Not even a GreenGirl job, for Christ's sake.

"I'll attack it in the morning," Zack tells her. "I'll have something new very soon, I promise. Don't worry."

She pauses, looks closely at him before admitting, quietly, "I *am* a little worried, Zack."

He probably should tell her about Joey. Then she'd understand the firing.

But she'd be completely terrified that Joey will come looking for her next.

He doesn't like keeping this little bit of news from her and Steve. He wonders if it's a mistake. A mistake that will come back to haunt him—in severed trust, in a moment of doubt about him by his girlfriend and his closest childhood pal. They've shared the whole brutal experience, the three of them, and now he's letting something interrupt that sharing.

He doesn't know how they'll take that. Yes, he does. Badly, is how.

45.

JOEY ALWAYS WATCHES to see if anyone knows who he is. Looks out from under his baseball cap to see if there's a glimmer of recognition or not.

Mostly there's not. He's just another unremarkable New Yorker. Part street person maybe, part recluse, he knows he gives off those vibes but in New York there's nothing remarkable or noteworthy about those roles either.

When he is recognized, it's a quick glimmer, a quick little panic in the person's eyes. Almost always, Joey notices, the person steps back a little. Protective instinct. Or gets out of range somehow, a primitive instinct to keep out of his grasp, like he's an ancient beast or something.

The day clerk and night clerk at the Rooms4Rent don't recognize him. He comes and goes so they hardly even notice. His knack for invisibility has always helped him in his profession, and it's helping him now.

He lies on the bed in his little rented room, staring at the ceiling.

The cops have proven they know where he is. They've proven that they're watching closely. Will they come search his room? Do they have the right? He has a feeling they don't have the right but he doesn't know the law.

He hides the gun in a place they'll never find it in the rented room. Meaning, not in the room. In a custodial closet down the hall.

He'd lifted a key from the custodian's tool cart and had a copy made. The cops didn't follow him into the little hardware store. He would have seen them. He came out with a broom and some lightbulbs so presumably they didn't think about keys being made. And if they actually went in afterward and quizzed the store clerks, they'd all assume it was an extra room key he was making, not a custodial closet key.

The custodial closet was a complete mess. Good for storing a gun in there, which the custodians themselves will never find.

He can grab it at a moment's notice.

He doesn't know when, or if, that moment will come.

46.

JOEY COMES BACK to his little rented room a few days later and sees they've been in it. The stakeout cops, presumably. Checking. Inspecting.

Nothing is out of place. But it's easy for him to see what happened.

Items moved in the drawers. Shifted a little. Other items shifted in his carton.

He supposes they don't care if he knows they've been there. They probably want him to know they're watching, that he can't keep any secrets from them.

But nothing has been moved or touched so much that he can complain to anyone because they'll just say it's his imagination, they've never been in there, and it's just his paranoia, and who's he going to risk complaining to anyway?

Joey lies on the bed.

Staring up at the ceiling.

And waiting.

47.

"JOEY'S GOING TO be arrested again any day now. The prosecution is putting together its case. They won't make the same mistakes." Zack knows he's just repeating himself, not providing anything new, but that's all he can offer his fretful friend.

"Maybe they'll make different mistakes," says Steve, sounding anxious. "He had high-priced lawyers last time. Maybe he will again."

"I'm sure he's really close to being rearrested. So let's just watch out for one another. Stay in touch. Don't overreact."

The last sentence was intended more pointedly for Steve, whose gun was out again, in his lap again, there in Steve's little apartment.

In her job creating and channeling "content," Emily monitors various news sources, which lead her inevitably to other news sources, and she has been keeping the two of them informed on any developments, forwarding items to both of them as soon as she comes across them.

They've managed to learn quite a bit. The prosecution, of course, had originally presented what it thought was its strongest case—"Victim #4"—among Joey's ten or so hits. The problem with now gathering a "next strongest case" was that the primary source of evidence—the phone photos in the Cloud—was still the same, with the same risks of a confusing technology and a confused jury. Risks the prosecution might not want to take again.

The state was weighing the relative merits of the other possible charges, from attempted murder to manslaughter to criminal possession of a weapon, but while a conviction on any of them would get Joey Richter off the streets, anything short of a murder conviction would be seen as the prosecution's failure. How could a hired assassin not get convicted for first-degree murder? Was that a prosecutor or a DA anyone would ever elect again?

There was also some coverage about the relatives of one victim who were preparing a wrongful death civil suit. The standard of proof in civil court wasn't as high, a "preponderance of the evidence" as opposed to "beyond a reasonable doubt." But the punishment in a civil case could never match what the prosecution and the state and the public felt was called for. O. J. Simpson's civil conviction was the most famous example.

All the coverage that Emily shares with them, all the legal discussion, is only a source of growing frustration for Steve.

"You don't understand, Zack. He tortured me. I almost died." Irritable. Pissed off. The peaceful Steve has been fundamentally changed. "I don't think I can last much more with him out there. Out there somewhere."

"The cops are watching him. They told us. They *assured* us."

"Watching him only as long as he's perfectly willing to be watched. Believe me, first time he needs to dodge them, he's gone."

"Try. Try to hang in there, okay, Steve?"

Once again, Steve tosses the gun from one hand to the other, a playfulness that's not at all playful, from what Zack can see.

48.

"HEY, EMILY," ZACK says when she picks up his call.

"Zack, aren't you in the middle of your shift?"

Zack's previous manager, Chris, had followed through on his promise, getting Zack a few shifts at another GreenGirl ten blocks away. Nobody knows him there. Nobody knows the first thing about him. No unannounced visitors from his hometown. He's completely anonymous.

"Yeah I'm working but I'm worried," says Zack. "I've been calling and texting Steve and not getting any answer."

Silence on the other end.

"It's not like him at all, Emily. He's usually Mr. Responsive, Mr. Connected. You saw him playing with that gun, Em."

"You afraid he's gonna hurt himself?"

"Not just himself."

"What are you saying?"

"I'm afraid he's going after Joey."

"How would he ever find him? Unless you're wrong about

Joey staying away from us and Steve saw him 'cause he was looking for Steve…"

Zack doesn't answer. Doesn't go there. Doesn't want to tell her about the GreenGirl incident.

"Steve's a techie, Em. Maybe he figured out from police communications or some other way where Joey is staying. If he really set his mind to it, he could probably figure it out…"

Zack keeps picturing that gun in Steve's lap. Maybe Steve didn't want to just leave it in his lap.

He hangs up with Emily and takes off his apron.

"You're leavin' in the middle of your shift?" says his new manager, flabbergasted. Zack's been here less than a week.

"I'm so sorry, man. I've got an emergency."

The manager shakes his head.

Zack's GreenGirl career isn't off to a very good start.

Zack pounds on the door to Steve's crummy walk-up apartment.

No doorman, no neighbors around that Zack can see.

Since Joey's break-in, Steve's got so many new locks and so much hi-tech security on the place that Zack knows there's no way he can get inside.

There's no getting in from the fire escape either, he's sure, but he can at least go up and, if the shade's not down all the way, look in.

He's never been on a fire escape. He steps tentatively onto it, a rickety, skeletal structure, and tests the sturdiness of its metal side rails, watching each step as he goes, but the anxiety and urgency he feels about his missing friend propel him upward quickly. He's as nervous about being seen by some terrified or outraged neighbor as he is about the safety of the structure.

In a minute, he's at Steve's window. The shade is only partly down. He kneels carefully on the metal step and cups his face against the window glass. He can see the apartment's empty. Bed unmade. Dishes in the sink. He knows where Steve keeps the handgun, by the bed, but he can't tell from this angle if it's there or not.

Steve's not dead in there, at least. Thank God.

Suddenly, a text…

Dude, my camera's showing that you're trying to check on me. I'm FINE…

Zack texts back to Steve immediately. Worried, man. You're not about to do something stupid???

He waits for a response. There is none.

Where are you, Steve??

Nothing. A pointed, purposeful nothing. And then: I've got to do this, Zack. Don't look for me.

Oh Christ.

Where? Where in the city would he be looking for Joey? Zack's dumb off-the-rack disposable phone doesn't have a friend-finder program loaded onto it. He should have insisted on getting one with Steve, who maybe would have consented to it earlier.

To find Steve and stop him from doing something to Joey, he'll have to find Joey. In a city of millions, how is he ever going to find Joey? Find him fast?

One way.

He still has the business card that had been pushed into his palm. *If you ever need anything, don't hesitate to call.* He quickly dials the number. "Detective Lopez? It's Zack Yellin."

"Zack Yellin," the voice says warmly, "I've actually been thinking about you and your girlfriend since that crazy verdict, but I didn't want to bother you."

"Thanks," says Zack.

"I did check to make sure the police are keeping an eye on you. How are you?"

"Not so good, Detective. You remember my friend Steve?"

"Of course I do. Poor kid. How's he doing?"

"Detective, I think he's going after Joey. He bought a gun to defend himself, and now…" Zack doesn't bother explaining more. "Detective, the police assured us Joey's being watched. Can you find out where the stakeout is? Where Joey is? 'Cause I think that's where Steve is gonna be."

"Sure…but obviously you should let the stakeout cops handle it."

"I don't know if there's time. Steve could be there already."

"My friends at the precinct can tell me where Joey is. But they'll ask why…" Lopez pauses. "I'll have to tell them, Zack. I know you don't want Steve getting in trouble or hurt again. But it sounds like Steve is armed. I have to tell them that."

Oh, Jesus. Zack imagines multiple scenarios playing out on the street—Joey, Steve, weapons, stakeout cops. "Sure. I understand."

Lopez puts Zack on hold but he's back in a minute with an address.

"Joey's staying in a rented room at 301 West 122nd. The cops will watch for your friend."

"Thanks, Detective Lopez."

"I'm sorry this isn't over, Zack."

"Me too, Detective. Me too."

Zack hangs up. Tries one more text. They're staking him out, Steve. You're not in any danger from Joey. You'd be crazy to try anything.

Again, no response. As Zack figured. Steve has gone silent.

Please, please…not silent forever.

49.

ON WEST 122ND, Zack begins to look around. He quickly sees what must be the stakeout vehicle. Unmarked sedan. A white guy and a Hispanic guy in the front seat. If Zack sees it so easily, so has Joey.

And probably so will Steve.

The unmarked sedan. The Rooms4Rent front door. Being back on the street.

He experiences the same panic, the same anxiety that he felt with Joey chasing him. But this time it's exactly reversed, of course. Joey is the one being hunted. Hunted by Steve, who is somewhere. Anywhere.

Zack is beginning to think about where to wait and what to look for when Joey Richter comes bursting through the front door of the Rooms4Rent and heads down the street.

Joey Richter on the street. Zack on the street. A sick feeling goes coursing through him.

Does Joey have a gun on him? Zack can't tell.

Zack sees the unmarked sedan begin to slowly pull out, starting to follow Joey from a distance.

It's all happening in some different measure of time. Outside of him. All too fast. All too slow. All frozen. All too fluid.

And then Steve materializes. Out of nowhere. A narrow alley next to the building.

Falling in behind Joey. Heading down the block behind Joey.

Five seconds later, Steve pulls the gun from under his shirt.

Oh Jesus.

"Hey, Joey."

Joey hears his name and turns.

It's that kid. The nerdy friend. Steve. That kid Joey thought he killed, that he left for dead. Standing pointing a gun at Joey.

So this is how it is. Justice, shorthand version.

Joey raises his hands. Would this kid really shoot him? In cold blood like this?

Joey Richter will never know. Will never have to know.

Because Zack Yellin appears suddenly behind Steve, grabs for Steve's gun with both hands, and forcefully points its muzzle down and away.

He wrestles it out of Steve's hand a moment later, both hands wrapped around it, body-checking Steve to definitively separate him from the gun.

Steve falls back, stunned, off-balance.

Suddenly, Zack is holding the gun. Looking at Joey.

Joey looking at him.

A screech of tires. The unmarked sedan from down the street pulls to the curb. Its doors fly open. Both the white and the Hispanic cop are there on foot in a matter of seconds.

Joey's arms are still up. He watches Zack hand the gun to the cops.

Zack. Materializing out of nowhere. Like a superhero. Right place, right time.

As the undercovers steady Steve on his feet, check the chamber, and remove the rounds, they exchange a look that says how close this was, what could have occurred.

Steve, still shaking, shows them his permit. "You don't know what he did to me!" Steve wails. "You don't know!"

"Take it easy, pal. Take it easy now..."

Watching it all happen, Joey finally drops his arms but stands obedient, passive, observing.

Joey and Zack continue to regard each other silently.

I saved his life, Zack realizes, the idea startling, confusing somehow.

He saved my life, Joey realizes, and the fact makes him dizzy.

The moment is dense with irony, floating around them on West 122nd.

And while the white and Hispanic cop are occupied with Steve, calming him, waiting for backup, Joey knows this is his chance to escape them.

Just the right moment of confusion, of distraction. To disappear around a corner or down a building alley. They'd never catch up to him, they'd never fire at him, because he hasn't done anything and he is unarmed.

But escape them for how long? And to do what? Plead with Karloff for a different assignment? What difference does shaking the tail make? None.

You'd think it would have been his tail that would stop anything from happening to him. That his tail would, paradoxically, at least keep him alive.

Instead, it was the redheaded kid he tried to kill.

Joey stands there wordlessly. Waits for a cruiser or two to come and take Steve away for booking. Joey knows Steve will be released. He knows there are two justice systems. At least two.

Once the police cruisers arrive, the stakeout cops look at Joey, and Joey looks expressionlessly back at them before turning and continuing up the street, where he was heading—to get a goddamn sandwich for lunch.

50.

STEVE IS PROCESSED and released under a simple arrangement. Give up your gun, and we let you go.

Steve actually debates it. Isn't sure he agrees to it. Isn't sure he wants to be without his gun with Joey Richter loose.

Zack and Emily are there at the station to support Steve through processing. Making sure he doesn't try anything crazy again. Making sure he doesn't fall apart even further. Come further unglued.

Steve doesn't know how good he's getting it, for what he just tried. Zack had called Lopez once more as Steve was being processed, and Lopez had intervened, and this is what the police had proposed.

Zack looks at Steve. "Steve, this is a good arrangement. You're lucky. Don't risk this. Don't mess this up."

Steve still seems disoriented. Still not himself, outside himself, confused by his own thoughts and actions of the last few hours. "Okay, okay," he says to the two young detectives and to Zack. He nods acceptance and watches his handgun get carried away by one of the detectives, disappearing into the bowels of the station.

"You're going home, Steve," says Rodriguez, the Hispanic one—fit, handsome, oddly perfect features. "We're letting your friends take you home, and you're going to stay there and relax and not try anything, and not think about Joey Richter. We're watching him, okay? We've got plenty of eyes on him. We just proved it to you, right? We were right there."

Well, I was right there, thinks Zack, but he stays quiet.

Rodriguez nods imperially to Zack and Emily. "Take him home. Keep him there. He's lucky."

"Now he's walking around, and I'm unarmed, and he knows I tried to kill him," says Steve morosely, back in his apartment.

Zack and Emily stay quiet. Emily puts on water for tea. She bought some cookies for all of them. She opens them now.

"This is a guy who's eye for an eye. Who holds grudges. Who gets even. Who doesn't forget."

A guy who doesn't forget? Who won't let it go? Who's that, Steve?

"Look what he did after you made a deal, Zack. He came after you."

"Like they said, like they proved, they're watching him."

"You think he can't slip a tail? A guy like that? He's probably just waiting for the moment when he wants to. Or needs to."

"Steve, don't forget, he'll assume you've still got your gun, right? He doesn't know the cops took it away. His last view of you was leveling it at him…"

"Before you grabbed it and the two undercovers tackled me," says Steve.

Zack doesn't respond. It's not worth arguing.

"He's not gonna come messing with you, Steve. You heard the detectives. The state is putting the new trial together. They'll be picking him up shortly and the last thing he's thinking about is hurting you."

Steve doesn't seem to hear him. Is drifting off to another place. "He almost killed me, and he's walking around free. Strolling to the corner to get lunch or something. A guy who almost killed me."

"You almost killed him," Zack points out.

"Until you stopped me," says Steve, turning toward Zack, focusing on him.

"Would you have killed him if I wasn't there? Would you have actually done it, Steve?"

Steve looks out the dirty window of his crummy apartment. "I don't know." He shrugs.

"Now you don't have to know," says Emily.

Steve curls up onto his bed, the physical, psychological, emotional toll catching up to him. He is out within moments. Zack tucks him in. Like they're back in camp, and he's in the bunk above.

Zack and Emily drink their tea in silence, not letting it go to waste, and slip out, being doubly sure the door locks behind them.

51.

JOEY AWAKENS IN his rented room in the dark to the sound of his cell phone ringing.

He's confused at first. He realizes in a moment why. He's never even heard it ring before.

He could just not answer it.

He can't just not answer it.

He presses the green button.

"Joey."

Joey shudders a little at hearing Karloff's voice. "Yes, sir." He almost says Mr. Karloff but remembers, as he slowly awakens, that's not his name.

"Here's the assignment, Joey. It's simple."

"I don't know, sir. I can't see how I can shake the tail on me to do it."

"That's the beauty of it, Joey. You don't have to shake the tail. We *want* the tail. 'Cause soon your tail is going to be escorting you right where we need you. They're gonna knock on your door, pick you up, and take you for a retrial. Our sources say probably in the next couple days."

"But I don't get it…"

"It's inside the courtroom, Joey. *Inside* the courtroom. You'll do the job for us after they take you in there."

"But I can't bring a gun. You know, metal detectors, and—"

"We'll have everything set up for you. We'll have what you need for the job waiting for you. We've got all that handled. Once you're in there, we'll text you and give you the details of the hit, what you need to do. It's simple, Joey. I know you like things nice and simple, right? No photos needed this time. All you'll need to do is answer my text, Joey, and follow the instructions. We're doing the rest."

The courthouse? Inside the courthouse? He doesn't understand.

"So you keep that cell phone with you the whole time, you got that, Joey?"

"Yeah…"

"So you always have it when we need to reach you, right?"

"Yessir…"

"Good. And you'll have a way to call us if you need to. Good talking to you, Joey. I don't know what'll happen with the new trial, Joey, don't know how it's gonna go down, nobody does, but this'll put you even with us."

Click.

Joey sits in the dark, stunned, confused, processing it, imagining it.

It was a pretty clever way to do a last hit.

Do it right where he was gonna be anyway.

He gets it, from their point of view. He's going to prison anyway. This is the last work they can get out of him. A job he's uniquely qualified for and will be uniquely positioned to pull off.

He doesn't get it yet about not having his gun. Could they somehow hide a weapon for him inside the courtroom? But it's clear they don't want him to know anything about that yet, to risk his blabbing about it to the cops who'll be all around him. But he'll bet they have everything worked out pretty neatly, particularly with Will involved.

A courtroom. Armed court officers. Dozens of cops waiting to testify. Plenty of law enforcement hanging around. The belly of the beast…

He still has that initial feeling, overriding everything else. Even though he doesn't have the details of the plan yet. The same feeling he had when he first was taken to Karloff:

The unmistakable sense he's going to die in that courtroom. That this *is* the plan.

Maybe that's just the feeling everybody gets being near Karloff. Joey has no one else to ask about that.

See, he doesn't necessarily mind jail again…

And if he got the death penalty, well, it would probably never be carried out in New York State, and if it was, it would be years from now, when appeals had all run out, when he was an old man.

See, everyone's going to die eventually. He can accept that.

But he doesn't want to die next week. Violently. Needlessly. Thoughtlessly.

He had felt in his profession a certain freedom. Choice.

Independence. This is the opposite. This is trapped. This is no choice.

If he refuses, he assumes Karloff will take him out right now. Not even think about it. If he refuses, he has outlived his usefulness—and Karloff won't have that.

Lying there in the dark, finally given his assignment, Joey's feeling more trapped than ever. Desperate. And maybe it's out of that desperation, a new thought descends on him. A new thought that, it occurs to Joey, may even be part of Karloff's plan.

The new thought there in the darkness: that maybe Joey Richter is done here.

Done. Done with it. Done with all of it.

Maybe he's had enough.

Maybe Karloff knows it. The streetwise Karloff. Who knows Joey has no home, no money, no friends, no relationships, and is heading to prison for the rest of his life.

Maybe he reads Joey's psychological state and knows that even if Joey half figures that he's going to die, in the end, he just might be willing to do this.

More than willing to.

"This puts us even," Karloff had said. Joey had been mystified by that. Confused. But maybe dying *does* put him even. Puts him finally even with the world.

Death, nonexistence, sure evens everything out.

Maybe there is no way out. So maybe that *is* the way out.

He has no one to help him. It's obvious now that Will is no friend. He looked like a friend, gaining Joey's trust there in jail, picking Joey up in the confusion after the trial, but it was never to help Joey. It was all for Karloff.

Joey is desperate. But he's pissed off too. Pissed off and furious at being trapped and cornered into this situation. If he's reading it right, being set up to die.

Joey is alone. Alone as always.

But more alone than ever.

There's not a single person who has shared in his life, he realizes. No one who knows who he really is. No one to turn to...

No. Wait. There *is* one person.

Someone who might be able to figure this out for him. Understand what's really going on here. Someone really good at figuring shit out. Someone no one would expect.

Someone who might even come up with a plan. Something unexpected. Some way out of this that no one has thought about. Who has a proven record of having that ability.

Someone who—beyond all that—may have just saved his life. Maybe could do it again.

And if Joey is going to die anyway, wouldn't it be a good time to settle old scores?

This puts us even. Karloff's words echo once more.

Maybe this is what comes of being desperate *and* pissed off, Joey thinks vaguely.

Joey still knows the phone number by heart. The phone number that was kind of *his* number temporarily. He's sure the kid has a spiffy new iPhone, that he has pulled his old data down from the Cloud, and everything is the same for the kid, like nothing ever happened.

The rented room may be bugged. The cops have been in here riffling through it. So Joey slips into the hall and tiptoes to the end of it.

He dials.

*　　*　　*

Zack's cheesy-looking, cheap new disposable phone rings.

He figures it's Emily but when he looks at the number of the incoming call, he doesn't recognize it.

But he has a feeling.

The encounter in front of the GreenGirl.

The wordless exchange of looks when he stopped Steve from doing something stupid.

He has a feeling.

When his old data got pulled down from the Cloud, Zack's phone number stayed the same.

His heart sinks. His knees go weak. He starts to shake a little but takes a deep breath to control himself.

He doesn't know why but he feels compelled to answer. Feels it's important to. Maybe there's some closure, some understanding possible, that will, for instance, help calm Steve and take away his torment. Maybe Zack can engineer that.

He answers.

"Zack?"

Zack knows the voice immediately. "Joey," Zack says. Flatly. Evenly. *I thought it might be you. I knew it was you. And still, I answered.*

There is a pause on the other end, and then the voice—small, thin, desperate, nearly unrecognizable—"I need your help."

211

52.

"HE WANTS MY help," Zack says to Emily.

She looks at him, uncomprehending.

Zack shows the text to Emily. I need your help.

The text Joey sent following their brief phone call. Reinforcing it. Memorializing it. A silent plea that followed his spoken one.

Emily stares at it. Zack watches as the understanding crosses her face that it's a text from Joey Richter. He sees how she pins her arms and hands to her side, as if she's afraid to touch the phone, or come anywhere near it.

"You should have changed your number."

"We thought he'd be in jail," he says defensively. "We both knew there was no way we'd be hearing from him again."

"Still," she says. Hugging her own shoulders anxiously. Visibly upset.

Zack can tell that Emily assumes he won't respond to the text. That it isn't even in the realm of possibility. She turns away, goes back to the dishes in the sink and rinses out the yogurt containers for recycling.

"You should delete that text," she says.

Zack smiles. "What difference would that make?"

"Just…psychological." Adding, "For me. Do it for me, Zack."

Zack stands there, staring at the short text again. As if it could reveal some clue.

She turns to him from the sink. "Delete the text, Zack."

He looks at her and smiles a little awkwardly.

"You're not thinking of *responding*, are you?"

He looks at her silently. And then says, shrugging, "I guess not."

"You *guess* not?" She looks at him, stunned.

"It's just…he'd never send a text like that unless he was in pretty serious trouble, right?" says Zack. Trouble somehow more serious than his upcoming trial, thinks Zack. Somehow more serious than possible life in prison. Trouble even an assassin can't handle.

She looks at him evenly and starts to shake—in rekindled fear? In anger? "He tried to *kill* us, Zack. He aimed a gun at your head. What are you talking about?"

"Imagine what it would take for him to reach out to me, Emily."

"You mean, as in balls? As in, insanity?" And she reminds Zack, talking slowly, like a parent to a child, "He sent me a text to lure me to the park. You don't think that's just a text to lure *you* into meeting him? So he can finish what he started?"

"I highly doubt that," says Zack, shaking his head.

"How do you know? 'Cause you trust him?" Showing Zack the absurdity of his interpretation. "You suddenly trust a hired killer? A killer whose time is running out?"

Of course she's right. Of course he's being ridiculous.

She turns back to the sink. "You better not respond to that text. And you better delete it." And she slams the yogurt container into the trash.

Zack thinks about everything he's learned about Joey. Everything he saw sitting across from him at the GreenGirl. Dealing with him, playing cat and mouse with him that terrifying day. Joey's psychological disturbance. Joey's intellectual limitations. But now, also, Joey's pain. And Joey's crazy willingness, in his pain and need, to turn to Zack. Obviously, because he has nowhere else to turn.

The events had connected Zack to Emily. Maybe forever. The truth was, in a similarly powerful way, the events had connected Zack to Joey.

I need your help.

Zack stares at the text.

Ok, he types back. Impulsively. Surprising himself. And from some deep place in him that he doesn't even pretend to fathom.

Once it's sent, he deletes Joey's text and his answer, and he immediately shows the phone to Emily before Joey responds.

She sees that Joey's text is deleted.

He wants her to be able to sleep at night.

53.

ZACK AND JOEY sit across from each other in a GreenGirl. One that neither has ever been in.

Joey slipped the surveillance to be here. Down into the basement of the Rooms4Rent, along a narrow service hallway, through a sub-basement, and up into the next building. A route he observed a seventy-year-old plumber take one day, a private route that clearly very few knew about but the plumber did, maybe uniquely, no doubt from servicing the building for fifty years. Joey knew he might have only one chance to use it. Maybe more, if he could slip back before the cops in the unmarked knew he'd been gone. But they'd figure it out soon enough. So he had to use it only at the right time. The right time was this.

They are silent at first. Staring at one another. Coffees between them.

GreenGirl on 1st and 15th. Grab a coffee, come to the back. 9am?

215

Joey's question mark, Zack noticed, the first note of civility, of consideration, in their torrid, troubled history.

Ok.

Joey smiles thinly now. Clearly, Zack thinks, Joey is struggling a little to figure out where, how, to begin.

"Only one of us knows why we're here," says Zack finally.

Joey smiles a little more, seeming to relax a little since at least something has been said. "Always with the funny, huh."

Zack shrugs.

Joey, morosely, "I didn't have anywhere else to turn."

"Obviously," says Zack.

Joey looks up sheepishly. "I can't imagine your girlfriend feels too good about this."

"She has no idea," says Zack. Honest. Honest with Joey. Lying to Emily. What is he doing?

"I'm amazed you came," says Joey.

"Me too." Zack shifts back a little and waits.

"I think they got me out. My employer—"

"Who's that?"

Joey shakes his head. *Better if you don't know*, is how Zack reads it.

"I think they got me out for a last job. A big one. A job I think I'm gonna die doing." He looks up. "That they're counting on me to die doing."

"Are you sure?"

Joey shrugs. "I'm the right guy to do it. The only guy. 'Cause I do the job when I go back to trial."

Zack frowns, uncomprehending.

"It's in the courthouse."

"The courthouse?" Jesus. Surrounded by cops. At least half of them armed and hair-trigger.

"You see why I think they figure I'll die? Maybe they figure I'll be dying in prison anyway. What's the difference, right?"

"Do you know what they want you to do?"

"Not yet. And I don't think they'll tell me till the last second."

Zack furrows his brow. "I don't get this, Joey. You're gonna have to go through a metal detector. It's not like you can carry a gun or a knife in with you."

Joey shrugs. "I thought of that. They said don't worry. They're setting it all up. All they told me so far is I won't need to take any pictures no more. All I gotta do is call them."

"How you gonna do that if you're surrounded by cops?" *Or if you're dead?*

Something isn't making sense to Zack. Likely something Joey has missed, or misunderstood, or isn't explaining right. Zack can understand how they are purposely keeping him in the dark. But Joey does seem clear on one thing—that this is his doom. Zack senses this is one thing Joey is right about.

"What does it pay?" asks Zack.

Joey smiles bitterly. "They said I owe them. For getting me out. They said I owe them for fucking up in the first place and almost bringing them down. So I ain't seein' no payday."

Zack nods slowly. Just confirmation of Joey's instincts. No need to pay a dead man.

And now the big question. "What do you want me to do?" *What on earth can I do for you, Joey?*

"Help me."

"Help you?"

"Like you did last time. Figure it out."

So this is what's left of the most terrifying episode of his life, thinks Zack. This is what's left of surviving a murder attempt. Being misperceived as some sort of wizard.

Zack has no idea what to do. Where to begin. And most immediately, what to say.

A text comes in. He takes out his phone. Emily.

I didn't know you had a shift. When you gonna be home?

Soon as I'm done talking to Joey Richter. I decided to see him, Emily. To hear him out. Maybe help him out. I didn't delete his text.

Hah. Right. Zack feels awful.

Home soon, he texts her back.

If he just gets up and walks away from Joey, the lies can stop before going any further.

He's actually about to. About to stand up and step slowly back toward sanity.

He looks up at Joey. Joey is smiling broadly.

"What?" What could he possibly be smiling at suddenly like that?

Joey can't stop smiling. "Your phone."

Zack looks down at it. "Yeah, well, after what happened, I just got myself a disposable."

Joey reaches into his pocket. Zack sits up a little, nervously.

Joey pulls out his phone and slaps it onto the table.

"Zack, that's what they got me too! A disposable. Just so they could reach me. And, Zack, look." He's practically giddy. "It's the exact same phone! The exact same disposable!"

My God. They have the same phone. Again.

As if their fates are forever tied. As if it is some trick, some stunt of the universe. Some loop in the time-space continuum.

And Zack realizes immediately. They both have these simpler, dumber, off-the-discount-rack, do-nothing phones for the same reason. Because of what had happened with their previous ones. Stripped-down phones to stay out of trouble. To not get into any phone trouble again.

To stay out of trouble? Look what's happening. Look who he is sitting with.

Zack looks at the phones.

The same exact phones.

Only, they're not.

He picks up the two phones and turns them over, slowly.

"They look the same," Zack says cautiously. "They're the same model, for sure." He looks up at Joey. "But, Joey, they're not the same."

Joey squints at the phones.

"Look closer at yours. See how it's slightly thicker? And look along the back cover of yours. See how it's blackened along the seam?"

Joey leans in and looks silently.

"Joey, your phone has been opened."

Joey sits up, anxious, alarmed, roused into a different state.

"It's been opened," says Zack again, barely believing it himself, "and you'd never know except by comparing yours to mine."

"That's impossible," says Joey indignantly. "You're wrong. They bought this off the shelf for me."

"Joey, this is no longer an off-the-shelf disposable." He says it with exaggerated slowness, letting the logic sink in, for both of them. "Either someone's worked on it without your knowing or they switched it on you without your knowing." Zack sits up, pulling himself away from the phone instinctively. "Someone's been in it, Joey."

Will, Joey thinks. *Will.*

Altering the phone, thinks Zack.

Opened. Altered. Slightly thicker. To put something in there?

Zack and Joey stare at the phones on the table.

Zack slowly slides his own phone away from Joey's and puts it back in his own pocket. Leaving only Joey's between them.

Joey looks afraid to touch it.

"What is it? What did they do?" Joey asks, petulant, childish.

"Oh, it's still a phone," says Zack. "You texted me, then called me, right?"

Joey nods.

Zack looks at it. "But we've got to figure it's also…well, more than just a phone."

Joey looks questioningly. "Like what?"

Zack takes a long, slow breath before he says it. Something that would have never come to mind, he realizes, if he weren't sitting across from an assassin.

"Like a remote trigger of some sort."

"A trigger?"

"That sends a signal to detonate some device that's within range. Or…"

Joey looks alarmed. "Or what?"

Zack swallows hard. "Or it detonates itself."

A diePhone, thinks Zack.

More of a diePhone than Joey's previous one.

More of a diePhone than ever.

54.

WHO? WHERE? WHEN?

The primal questions about the target dance in Zack's head immediately, loudly, bouncing into one another, unanswerable.

A remote trigger makes the most sense to Zack. So is Joey just a convenient soldier who can get close enough to blow something—or someone—up? But can't you generate the signal from far away? Why do you need to get close? Maybe only to make sure Joey is part of the explosion? Part of the collateral damage?

Or is the phone itself the incendiary device? Can they do that nowadays? Probably they can do anything. And they'd trust that Joey can use it as a phone until the moment they explode it, with the phone still in Joey's pocket or in his hand.

The dumbest, simplest, disposable off-brand phone available. Is that the easiest phone to get into, to modify? Zack had wanted a phone for just one thing—basic communication. Maybe they wanted it for one thing too—detonation.

It was only by seeing the phones side by side that you'd realize one had been altered. Zack still can't process his luck in discovering that.

Although luck isn't quite the right word.

Joey had explained to Zack that he wouldn't be able to slip his tail more than this once. They'd have to communicate via phone.

That phone, thinks Zack, still staring at it. Because if Joey starts using a different phone, they'll realize Joey knows.

Zack wants to look inside it. He knows that could be suicide, of course. Anyone clever enough to rig this phone is probably clever enough to booby-trap it. Although it's likely they wouldn't have bothered, figuring Joey was never going to know. Maybe Zack and Joey should take the risk. To understand it? To disarm it? To turn its ultimate use around?

And Zack knows exactly who to take the phone to. Who will know whether to even risk opening it or not. Who will likely know what they're dealing with, technologically, at least.

If only he can get him to look at it...

If only he can get him and Joey to look at each other...

If only he can get him to be in the same room with Joey...

Because Zack really wants to take it to Steve.

55.

ZACK IS BACK in the apartment with Emily.

"I couldn't reach you today. I guess they had you working an extra shift?"

"Yeah..." *Lie.*

"You couldn't text me to let me know?"

"They make us keep our phones off while we're working. GreenGirl rules."

No such rule. But it sounds good. Sounds reasonable.

"Extra shift? Why?"

"They were shorthanded. People didn't show up." *Lie.*

"But you show up." She smiles warmly at him. "You're reliable. They can trust you."

His chest clenches. The lies actually hurt.

For once, a relationship had begun with no lies. Both of them completely themselves, their raw, truest selves, because of the threat they'd both faced. No time for posturing. No chance to pretend being anyone else.

And look what he was doing. Since he began with no lies,

no posturing, it somehow made the lies bigger, worse, now that they were occurring.

"Well, it's more income, isn't it? It'll help us with the rent."

And when the rent bill comes, what's he going to do? Open his pockets and show her they're empty?

"I know you hate the work, Zack. I know it's temporary. I really admire the way you're stepping up and doing something while you—while we—try to figure it out."

It was a relationship launched on trust. On immediate, necessary trust of the other person. Trust of the other person's instincts for survival. Trust of the other's good intentions. Of the other's selflessness. Of the other's mutual concern and personal good.

And look what he's doing. Look what he's destroying.

He has to tell her about meeting with Joey. She won't believe it. She won't accept it. But going behind her back is only making it worse.

Emily comes up to him suddenly and wraps her hands around the back of his neck, pulling him to her affectionately, sexually, totally. A moment of complete commitment and trust.

As if she knows and is making it harder. Making it as hard as she can.

Responding to Joey has put Zack suddenly, unpredictably, into a nightmare corner. He hoped that he could step in, hear Joey out, help solve whatever Joey's problem was and be done with it. But suddenly Zack is looking at some kind of detonation. And all Joey knows about the job keeps coming back to Zack: *It's in the courthouse.* Meaning inside a courtroom? Meaning innocent people could die. Dozens of them. Maybe more. Collateral damage from the actual target, whoever it is. All in the line of fire. All their fates held in the balance by a disposable phone in Joey Richter's hands.

Zack suddenly realizes he has a huge responsibility here. The huge, weird responsibility, at least for now, of staying connected to Joey. Keeping this "friendship" with Joey temporarily alive. Until he can see his way to some kind of plan. *Figure it out.* Joey's words coming back to haunt him.

But Zack needs to keep *this* alive too. Not risk what he has with Emily.

Will it be possible to do both? Or will he have to choose?

56.

JOEY WAS NEVER clear on why he was taken to see Karloff in person. In the flesh. Wasn't that unnecessary? Unnecessarily risky?

But now he starts to understand. The understanding seeping in slowly. It wasn't really about seeing Karloff. It was so they could give him his phone.

That phone now in his hand. The last thing he'll see? The last thing he'll feel? The metal against his ear? Like it's just another phone call?

They still haven't told him what the target is. Normally you're told in plenty of time for you to plan. But this time they're doing the planning. Joey is just doing the execution.

Meeting with Zack and discovering the altered phone, he realizes how much more trapped he is than he even thought.

Maybe so trapped Zack can't get him out.

Although the kid seems willing to try.

57.

THEY ALL CALL him Karloff, he'd learned.

Like the scary Russian actor who played monsters in old movies.

Scary. A monster. He is fine with that.

He had grown up in Bulgaria.

In Bulgaria, he was trained to murder as a child. Children are effective assassins because no one sees it coming and prosecution is so difficult. It was a terrifying time in Bulgaria, though comparatively brief, because it got so much attention that the police and other authorities acted swiftly. These were not boy soldiers in a lawless African proto-republic. These were killers for hire in urban centers run by crime syndicates.

In fact, when he was caught, after personally committing five murders, he was held while legal maneuvering took place around him. Extenuating circumstances. A child. How could he be responsible for his actions? Did he even understand the consequences? In a bureaucratic kerfuffle and a switch of ruling parties in Sofia, the capital, he was released pending a hearing (the adult perpetrators, the trainers, were not; they were eventually executed), and he boarded a steamer for Sardinia, and then one to Morocco, and eventually he made his way to the United States.

These are things only a few people know. And no one around him.

When Joey was released thanks to the mysteries of the Cloud, Karloff had of course seen such judicial results before. It reverberated with his childhood, with another lifetime.

He knows personally the limits of the justice system. He is here, alive, thriving, rich, because of those limits, those U-turns and side roads. And being ready and willing to take them.

The bureaucracy, the changing political parties, or the legal system had expunged his name completely from the public record. Only a child, after all. Let him start over. Like he never existed. Like he never killed. He saw how legal systems worked. He learned the considerable advantages of nonexistence. And he saw that the vaunted and prideful American justice system could be as flawed and as fragile and as manipulated as Bulgaria's.

He had learned more than murder in those days, working for that gang. He was wealthy now but pathologically quiet and always in motion. No monuments to himself, no showy testament to the good life, nothing to draw attention. His showiness is all in his reputation, whose mystery and whispers of ruthlessness are themselves useful.

He isn't nostalgic. He doesn't see something of himself in Joey Richter. Joey is an unimaginative idiot. Autistic, compromised. A tethered animal.

The stories of the five murders Karloff committed as a child were terrifying, jaw-dropping, but he prided himself on having had the discipline never to have told of a single one, not to anyone. They would have created more fear of him, perhaps amplified his reputation, his myth. But they could have been used to understand him, to analyze him, to predict him, and he didn't want that. The stories, though startling, were more useful to him untold.

Yes, Karloff has seen the weaknesses, fragility, and surprising malleability of the criminal justice system, which is supposed to be pure and transparent, based on case law, precedent, regulations and rulings available for all to see.

But another thing Karloff doesn't mention to anyone—and even less to himself—is how he has seen it from both sides. How he has been the beneficiary of bending the law, twisting it, manipulating it, escaping it, but how he has also been a victim of it.

How his encounter with the Bulgarian court system as a child murderer was not his first legal encounter.

How he was recruited as a murderer in the first place because of a court mix-up involving his birth mother and birth father, and lost paperwork, and incompetent representation, and payoffs, and subsequent inept administration and foster care, how he slipped through the cracks, and how he was recruited by a gang because he had nowhere else to go.

How their expert procurers, their human snares, were hanging around at the courthouse with cash and treats, and snatched little Karloff and others like him right out of the criminal justice system. Broken homes, domestic disturbance cases, abandoned children—they were there to scoop up this human detritus, to train them and put them to work.

He was six. Six years old.

And he learned in the ensuing years in Bulgaria, growing and hardening into a professional criminal, about the collusion, the bribery, the trafficking system between the lawyers and the court officers and, worst, the judges. Symbols of probity. Symbols of corruption.

He will never forget the judge's name in his own mixed-up custody case or his physical appearance, although his memory has gone hazy in the intervening lifetime.

Surprisingly young, he remembers. Boyish black bangs hanging to his wire-rim glasses. A hawk nose. And most of all, the young judge's high-and-mighty attitude.

Applying the law to his struggling, troubled parents, only dimly remembered now.

Handing the six-year-old—unwittingly? knowingly?—into a life of crime.

The father of the dark path of his life.

Litvinov.

58.

ZACK KEEPS THINKING about that phone Joey is carrying.

If it's a remote trigger, presumably it works when you enter a certain numerical sequence. A certain code. A code that sends a radio signal to the bomb. Or maybe it's simply triggered when a call is received from a certain number and the phone is answered? Zack shudders.

So what if, when that number comes up or when the code is sent, Joey simply doesn't answer? Or doesn't enter the code he's instructed to? Wouldn't that foil it? Wouldn't that end the risk right there?

But likely if he doesn't answer or enter the code, there's some kind of backup trigger too. Some kind of feedback loop on a timer? His bosses have probably figured that Joey might get himself into position but then—suddenly suspicious, suddenly nervous—he might not follow through. So maybe there's a trigger regardless.

Figure it out.

Oh, easy.

It's just a matter of figuring out who Joey is supposed to blow up. And where. And when. And figuring it out without blowing up the phone—and both of them—in the process.

Zack tries to push the phone out of his mind. It's an impossible puzzle. But it won't leave him.

A phone that detonates itself? Itself and Joey? Zack can understand the rude merciless justice of it. Making Joey pay for his mistake. Making him pay for his sloppiness. For getting caught, ending up in court, and creating a potential path of evidence to his bosses.

And if it's not self-detonating and it is a remote trigger, then the relevant question is, where is the bomb?

59.

"SOMETHING'S UP WITH you," says Emily. "You're suddenly so distant."

Zack doesn't answer.

"But I think I know what's up," she says quietly.

Zack remains silent. Preparing himself. His mind careening in a thousand directions…

"It's obviously the stress of this guy being out," says Emily. "It's bringing it all back, isn't it? It's having its effect. This is when we need to be there even more for each other," she says. "When we have to be more supportive than ever. Watching each other's backs. Not just physically. Emotionally too."

She looks at him. "What do you say? Can we be there for each other?"

He is about to tell her, about to say something, to say everything, but he knows how devastating it will be, the betrayal it will feel like.

"Are we there for each other?"

He says nothing. Can bring himself to say nothing. So he just reaches for her and pulls her close.

Which he knows will only ultimately make it worse.

It's going to be ugly, thinks Zack. *It's going to be so ugly.*

60.

NEED TO SEE you, Zack texts Steve. Right away. Pretty important.

He resists the urge to add, *A matter of life and death.* It might be, of course, for Joey Richter and for dozens of innocent people but Zack doesn't dare explain the specifics to Steve, and he's pretty sure the phrase alone might scare Steve off.

Too important for a text?

Yeah.

Wow. K. Come on up.

Zack sits in Steve's only chair. Steve is on the bed, cross-legged. No gun anymore. His gun is in the bowels of the 14th Precinct, or already melted down.

"What's up, pal?"

Zack pauses.

"You can tell me anything," says Steve. "Your friend from age ten, right?"

"I don't know…," says Zack cautiously.

"Hey, I know I've been a little fragile these last few months," Steve says with a smile. "But go ahead. Try me."

Zack knows Steve won't be smiling for long.

"Steve, I…I need you to tap into your engineering skills…"

"Shoot," says Steve.

"You're good with cell phones, right? Didn't you even rebuild yours a couple years ago?"

"You remember," says Steve with satisfaction. "Took it apart, replaced some of the software." He grins, blissful, child-like. "I don't ever pay a cell phone bill," he says. "Like I said, happy to rig yours someday."

Ever since their time at camp together, at ten years old, Steve had tinkered with electronics. He'd built intricate stuff, modified stuff, taken stuff apart and put it back together. Walkie-talkies, radios, musical components, model rockets, radio airplanes, even the earliest cell phones. Learning it all from the Internet.

Looking inside this cell phone? Zack honestly has no idea whether it's something Steve can do. But Steve's the only person Zack knows to ask.

"I need you to look at a phone that's been tampered with."

"What do you mean?"

"Someone's opened it up and done something to it, and I have no idea what."

"Your phone?" Steve asks.

Zack shakes his head.

Steve waits for more explanation.

"Someone who needs our help," says Zack. "Someone who has nowhere else to turn."

"Okay, then," says Steve, looking a little mystified by this oblique line of conversation from Zack. "Happy to try to help."

"That's nice, Steve. Really nice. You're a good guy."

Steve shrugs.

"I need to tell you whose phone it is."

Steve frowns.

"It's Joey Richter's."

Steve is silent. Seems to only partly comprehend.

Zack rushes into it. Hoping at least some of it sticks. At least some of it is clear. "He reached out to me."

"Wait. And you, what, you…you met with him?"

Zack nods. "He texted me. That's how desperate he is. He's got nowhere else to go. His bosses are getting ready to kill him, Steve. I know you probably have no problem with that. And, well, more people may be at risk. His phone's been altered to do something. And he doesn't—and I don't—have any idea what it is."

Steve is silent.

"He doesn't want to kill you. He doesn't want to kill me. He wants, he needs, our help. And if we give it, if we help him, we can put our fear of him aside forever."

Steve takes a deep breath and narrows his eyes.

"All you have to do is look at it, Steve."

Steve remains silent.

"As a favor to me," says Zack. *Your bunkmate. Your first,*

your oldest friend. He leaves it all unsaid but knows it arcs between them.

"When? Where?" Steve's eyes are still narrowed.

"If you want to, now."

"Where's this mysterious phone?"

"It's with him."

"And where is he?"

Zack takes a breath. "Right outside. Waiting for my call. For your permission to come in."

Steve freezes. His eyes go wide. He looks at the door. "I don't think I can do it, Zack."

"I think you can. I'm right here with you."

Steve looks around instinctively, anxiously. Wanting to grab the gun that isn't here anymore, Zack realizes. "Zack, he knows I tried to kill him."

"Obviously he's looking past that. Can you do the same?"

"No," says Steve. "How can I?" And he looks for another minute at the door. And then at Zack.

"I'm right here," says Zack, quietly again, a calming mantra. He looks at Steve, who is looking at the door again.

Confronting demons? Weighing a face-to-face encounter as either a resurgence of all his terror or a liberation from it?

"Let him in," says Steve.

Joey Richter stands in Steve Furman's apartment.

Again.

He nods but stays silent.

As does Steve.

They are not openly angry; they are not openly fearful, either one. Mostly, they seem mystified by being in this same room together, again. There is something otherworldly about it for Zack and, he imagines, for them too. It's another universe, in a way. And yet this weird other universe is one they all instantly share.

Silently, Joey holds out his phone.

Silently, Steve takes it.

Gradually, his interest is absorbed by the phone. He's no longer looking at Zack or Joey. He seems to grow more interested, more curious about the phone, seems to disappear into its problems, imagining its circuitry.

He looks closely at it. He goes into his desk, brings out a penlight, and shines the beam at it. He feels along the seams carefully.

In a few minutes, he looks up at Zack. He looks up at Joey. Directly. As he has never done before.

Zack can't quite read Steve's expression. But Steve seems to have come to some conclusion about the phone. Some final inference that, Zack suddenly senses, is reverberating more widely with Steve's past few weeks.

As if Steve sees this encounter with Joey Richter as the logical end point for what Steve has suffered, from life-threatening bullet wounds to unrelenting fear, and letting Joey Richter back into his apartment can provide some long-sought-after release.

Steve smiles a little. A crumpled, unreadable, noncommittal smile.

And blithely, almost peacefully, he pulls the back cover off the phone.

61.

AT CAMP, THEY made an odd couple, Zack knew. The most popular, most outgoing kid in the cabin and his nerdy sidekick. The athletic, upbeat redheaded guy, his hair like a beacon of fun, sociability, and adventure for the rest of the cabin, and his sedentary, brooding, incommunicative pal Furman.

Zack would always wonder if it was the simple "oppositeness," the unexpectedness and contrariness of the friendship, that appealed to him as a ten-year-old. The "otherness" that was so new to him.

But even as a ten-year-old, there was something more to it for Zack. If they could be friends (and they were), if they could connect (and they did), think what that said about the world beyond them, about the possibilities for the world, and Zack felt that this was always part of the appeal for him, and maybe for Steve too. In a way, Steve offered Zack nothing beyond his basic companionship, beyond his steady presence, but for Zack, for both of them, that was enough. That was plenty.

And maybe that's why, as they grew older and their lives had no natural intersection, their friendship continued.

Because there was no real expectation on it, no conditions on it, from the beginning. Like a kid brother. Like family. No real choice about it. Always there.

When it came to camp activities, Steve would barely even try things. Would never take risks. And then, out of nowhere, he would suddenly take a huge one.

Refusing to take swim lessons. Then jumping in the lake one evening and flailing and screaming and needing to be rescued.

Refusing to go camping with the rest of the bunk. Then one night grabbing a sleeping bag and heading off alone into the woods, going missing, and a search party had to be dispatched hours later.

Trying to suddenly prove something to everyone? To himself? This sudden self-destructiveness, this sudden personal disregard. It was easy to forget that part of Steve because he was so otherwise predictable in his steady, quiet, private way.

But what happened with Joey Richter over the past weeks—being shot, almost dying—would certainly unleash again his uncharacteristic behavior—jumping in without knowing how to swim, heading out into the woods alone, trying to suddenly prove something to yourself and the world—like suddenly grabbing your gun to hunt down an assassin. Wasn't that the same?

Or maybe Steve simply, suddenly, felt too trapped.

Too trapped by Joey being at the door.

Too trapped by Zack's insistent request for help.

Maybe Steve didn't really know anything about that cell phone.

Or maybe he didn't really care.

*　　*　　*

Zack's eyes go wide.

He gasps.

He falls back instinctively.

Oh Jesus, no!!!

Perfect last words. Expected, conventional, utter final shock.

Joey turns to lunge for the door.

Zack is about to lunge for the phone.

But in a moment Zack realizes he is standing there, staring at the open phone.

"If it was booby-trapped, you'd see a wire crossing right here," says Steve. "It would have to come from the battery, which is here. But I could see through the slot between the phone halves that there was no wire like that. Lucky for us, the phone's been opened and altered so I could see in past the opening seam. I wouldn't have tried it otherwise." Steve's beatific, frozen smile never falters.

"You were sure?" says Zack. Catching his breath. Recovering.

Steve shrugs. "Pretty sure." And then he gestures to Zack to come close. Zack is afraid to. Steve points and explains anyway.

"See this little silver sliver here? It's a tiny little transmitter that's been shoved in there pretty cleverly. A transmitter to set something off. And I don't think it's to turn on Christmas lights or the toaster. If you go to certain sites on the dark web, you see exactly this kind of transmitter in the instructions on rigging a detonator. It's set to detonate something, presumably a bomb, by dialing a certain code. That's how ISIS and Al-Qaeda were setting off lots of their IEDs in Iraq and Afghanistan. With old cell phones." He turns the open phone over carefully, almost reverently. "I bet they use one of those six-digit confirmation codes, like companies send you for security. That's typical for communicating device to device."

After his intense concentration on the electronic elements, Steve finally looks up. "So where's the bomb?" A pause. "And what's the code?" The two key questions.

But Zack has a simpler question. "You've got the thing open, Steve. Isn't there a way to disarm it right now?"

"If there is"—Steve frowns—"I unfortunately don't know it. See, if I snip this wire here, which I *think* would disarm it, it might also set off the bomb…depending on the range of the signal and wherever the bomb is right now. Two big unknowns." He slowly, gently leans away from the open phone on the bed. "It could be waiting in the trunk of some bad guy's car in the middle of nowhere but it could also be hidden next to a hundred innocent people."

They all look at the open phone.

"And here's the other thing."

What? There's more?

"If I cut this wire and somehow it *doesn't* set it off, I'm pretty sure whoever rigged this is going to know immediately it was tampered with. I think it sends a signal to some other phone somewhere that periodically checks the circuit. That's how it's usually done."

Just the kind of feedback loop Zack had been speculating about.

"In which case," says Joey, "they'll know I was messing with it and come kill me and find a new errand boy." He says it as plainly as that.

Steve squints at Joey. "And if you simply don't dial the code when they send it to you?"

"If I don't dial it, they kill me too," says Joey. Just as plainly.

But you're going to die when you dial it anyway. Zack keeps the thought to himself. He knows it's one they all share.

Steve carefully lines up the back cover of the phone and presses it together. Zack reaches out to take it from Steve, to hand back to Joey.

"If you could somehow find the bomb and set it off safely…beforehand…away from its target…"

But Zack knows—they all must know—that's just a fantasy.

"Of course, you'd have to know the code." Steve looks at Zack. A shrug, a grim smile. "Hey, you did it before, Zack. With a passcode. With a prison ID. Maybe somehow you can figure this number out too."

Knowing, as they all do, that's pretty much impossible.

Joey opens the door to leave Steve's apartment.

Emily is standing there.

She looks at Joey. At Zack.

Her whole body is shuddering. She shakes her head slowly side to side. Incredulity. Disappointment. Finality. All in that headshake.

She turns and lurches down the stairs.

Zack lurches after her.

He catches up with Emily on the street outside. Grabs her arm.

She shakes it away. "You lied to me, didn't you!" she says. "You lied to me and texted him back and got together with him. And you brought him to Steve's! How could you? What's wrong with you?"

"Emily, I—"

"You weren't working extra shifts at the GreenGirl. One more lie!"

She must have gone to the GreenGirl to meet him, and surprise, he wasn't there, and instead of sending him a text or calling him, she must have thought it was an emergency of some sort, which she knew was likely to somehow involve Steve, so she'd come straight here.

"You showed me how you erased the text from him. You showed me your phone. Another lie. Your lie phone."

There is nothing he can say. He feels the street, the world, spinning around him faster…

"You weren't here helping Steve. You were here helping Joey. Helping a killer! Setting Steve back, I'm sure. Terrifying Steve…" Emily is shaking her head vigorously, as if to shake him out of her view. "You're crazy, Zack. *Stupid* crazy. And you knew you were risking our relationship, risking everything we had, and that's why you wouldn't tell me anything, but you went ahead and did it anyway. Which shows how much you care about this relationship. About us."

She looks at him, hard-eyed. "You knew it was Joey or me. And you chose Joey."

She turns away. "Don't come back to the apartment. Ever. We're done."

Her arm goes up for a cab. "Stay with Joey. Your friend Joey Richter."

For once, a cab is right there. She gets in. Slams the door.

Emily Lane is gone.

62.

ZACK'S DESPERATE RUSH down the stairwell to catch
Emily leaves Steve and Joey suddenly alone in Steve's
apartment.

Neither one looks at the other.

Joey is thinking about the last time he was here. He figures
Steve is too.

"I'll...I'll get out of your way," Joey mumbles.

Steve manages to nod.

As Joey backs away, he says, "Pretty cool how you opened
that phone. Pretty brave."

"Pretty dumb," says Steve.

"Pretty smart," says Joey.

Steve shrugs.

Joey stops and turns. "I'm going to jail, Steve. I'm either
going to die in jail or die before I get there."

Steve says nothing.

"I'm going to die soon, and you're not, Steve." A simple
fact, a simple formula, he wants Steve to remember.

Joey feels an urge to say more. But he knows how absurd, how inane an apology would be, or offering something philosophical or heartfelt or even some nervous random chatter.

So, wordlessly, Joey exits and gently closes the door.

63.

THAT WENT ABOUT as badly as it could have, thinks Zack.

No. Worse.

Emily seeing them together. Seeing Joey in Steve's apartment.

Hearing their three voices, no doubt, as she stood outside. Shaking with fury, with confusion, with an overwhelming sense of betrayal, in the dark hallway outside Steve's dingy apartment. About to turn and walk away, no doubt, when the door opened, and there they were:

Zack, Steve, and the assassin who'd been ready to kill her. Kill them both. Kill them all.

Imagining it from Emily's point of view, it would hardly appear as if Zack was there to save lives. Joey's, yes. But maybe others too.

More likely, it would appear that he'd lost his mind. And, well, had he?

Because he knew Emily would react like this. Because her feelings, her grounding, were so clear. That's something he loved about her, the clarity of her feelings, her convictions, her loyalties, her stances. And he went ahead and did it anyway—lied to her, went behind her back.

There is something self-destructive in him. His own Steve-like night stroll into the woods and jump into the lake. His own ticking time bomb, deep in his psyche, that he can't keep from going off. From going off repeatedly in his life, probably, in quiet ways sometimes, detonating sometimes so quietly that he doesn't even notice. But this one wasn't quiet.

But he needs me. There's no one else to help him. What crazy moral code, what weird compass, had him jeopardizing his relationship for that?

Innocent people might be in danger. Might be killed. This possibility only half understood from a strange, brief, tense conversation with an assassin—an isolated, disconnected, peripheral character—who may have easily misinterpreted the over-the-phone hints and insinuations of a mysterious, absent boss.

When Zack had stumbled into heroism by outwitting a professional killer, did he also stumble into a permanent hero complex? Is he twisting things around, seeing things in a certain light, to let himself be a hero again? Somewhere deep in him, does he miss the heroism? Is he looking to rekindle it? To the detriment and willful ignorance of all else?

Is Emily lost to him? The best thing that has ever happened to him, that came so forcefully, so paradoxically, out of the worst thing that ever happened to him, and he has abandoned it, cast if off, tossed it to the side of the road.

It couldn't get any worse, could it?

64.

OKAY, A DETONATION of some sort.

"It's in the courthouse," Joey had said. *"Inside the courtroom,"* Karloff had told Joey.

That's all they know. Or kind of know.

Presumably, Zack is guessing, inside the courtroom where Joey will be on trial.

He's trying to focus. Trying not to think about Emily. Using the riddle of the cell phone detonator and the bomb to push aside, to tamp down, all his unleashed emotions about losing her. Her pulling away in that cab. The image scorching his mind.

Concentrate. How on earth could they ever get a bomb in there with all that security?

"But they got this guy Will inside my jail cell," Joey had told Zack, describing Karloff and his techie sidekick Will, once they discovered the phone had been tampered with.

So Karloff could pull off more than anyone might think.

So many questions. So much speculation…

251

Steve had talked about the detonator's range as a big unknown. But if the bomb detonates via a radio signal from the phone, wouldn't it have enough range to trigger the explosion from outside that courtroom? So why put Joey inside the courtroom? Because you want or need him to die too? Or do you need Joey to first confirm that some target is indeed in there? Or do certain courtroom or courthouse walls block a radio signal, so Joey has to be inside?

And who *is* the target in that courtroom?

If it's a single target—a certain witness, a certain prosecutor—you wouldn't have to use a bomb in a courtroom. Karloff could just have them assassinated at their home, right? Or coming from or going to work? A shocking but totally conventional hit. Which would bring the full focus of law enforcement, but which Karloff, with his network, could probably survive. Hell, he could have hired Joey for the job.

But he's choosing the courtroom. To take out the prosecutors, the judge, the jury, the defendant, all at once? To take out the system, in a way?

Yes, the system will be disrupted. It will be bedlam. A tragedy covered relentlessly for weeks in the national news. But eventually the system goes on. Certainly Karloff knows that.

So, then, is it to simply *demonstrate* something to the system? Which means it's symbolic, to some degree. It's something beyond just the practical matter of Karloff maintaining his crime syndicate.

And let's say it *is* symbolic. Not just to get a job done, but to teach Joey a lesson as well. Joey's phone—first causing the problem, now solving the problem. There would be a perverse satisfaction in that for Karloff.

And if it is symbolic, then the code Karloff picked for it might be symbolic too.

Like, let's say, the prosecution's case number. Or Joey's prison number again. Or any of a thousand numbers.

Or maybe just a random number. Thought up by Will Shale, the tech guy who probably did the programming himself, and who seems quite comfortable, quite at home, in a random, lawless universe.

As Steve said, when he looked up at them: *So where's the bomb, and what's the code?*

Zack has stumbled on the right numerals before.

With a lucky glance, when he looked over at Joey's phone.

With a clever guess, when he came up with Joey's prisoner number.

Could he, against all odds, do it a third time?

Because wouldn't knowing the code presumably give Zack, with Steve's assistance, some control over the bomb? Either to disarm it, or if necessary to set it off before it gets inside the courtroom?

For now, Zack senses—simply, deeply, taking it on faith—that if he can somehow discover the code, the code will somehow, in some way, prove worth knowing.

"What can you tell me about Karloff?" Zack had asked Joey when they sat together in the GreenGirl at that first anxious meeting, once Joey showed Zack his phone.

"That's the point," Joey had said. "Nothing. No one knows anything."

But Zack now sees a different point. A deeper point. If no one can tell you anything about Karloff, then there must be a point to Karloff keeping it that way.

He's not a blank slate, as much as he might cultivate that. He has a history. He has a past.

And Zack will try to find out who and what he is.

Where's the bomb, and what's the code?

Maybe Karloff's past is Zack's only real chance at guessing.

65.

ZACK SPENDS THE night on Steve's floor. He has nowhere else to go. It's as if they're back at camp. As if they're both ten years old again and his life hasn't progressed at all.

He tosses and turns for several hours, can barely sleep at all. In exhaustion, he finally dozes off.

He opens his eyes to a sudden bright light that Steve must have switched on. Like a sudden, unscheduled interrogation.

He finds Steve staring at him. His friend's expression unreadable. But unprecedented for Zack.

Zack glances instinctively at his phone: 3:00 a.m.

"I've been lying here, not sleeping," says Steve quietly. "Watching you sleep, Zack. Lying here awake, thinking, replaying things."

Zack nods with sympathy, understanding, shifting on the floor.

"Joey, here in the apartment. I can't get it out of my mind," Steve says, "and the other thing I can't get out of my mind, Zack, is what I did with that phone."

"But you knew what you were doing, right? You were pretty sure it was safe?"

"It was something I told myself, Zack, because in that moment with Joey here, I didn't care what happened to me. If something happened, it would have been a kind of justice. Put myself out of my misery and finish Joey off, and you, Zack." He looks at him. "It might have been the right thing to do, for the way you've treated your oldest friend…"

"Now wait a second, Steve. You said you were willing to help."

"Zack, you gave me about fifteen seconds to think about it, with a killer waiting for my answer outside my door. You think that really lets me answer?"

"But Stevie. You didn't—"

"I was ready to kill myself with that phone, Zack. Do you know that? I was perfectly willing to kill myself with that phone."

"Steve, I wouldn't have brought it, I would never have asked, if I knew that."

"What kind of choice did you give me, Zack? Making me feel like our friendship hinged on my helping you. Making me feel like a tool, a piece of technology here to do what you needed. Coming to me 'cause I'm a nerdy electronics guy. Looking for my knowledge, for my brain, with no thought to how I would feel, to what it would do to me."

"Now wait, of course I was—"

"But this is what you do. Not just to me. This is what you did to Emily. You lied to her, kept her in the dark. It was obvious in her expression and her reaction. So it's not me, Zack. It's you. That's what I've been lying here thinking about—how you've shown who and what you really are."

Zack feels his chest clench.

"I need you out of here, Zack. You can't stay here. I'm learning from Emily. Learning a little late, but learning. Get the hell out of here…"

It couldn't get worse, Zack thought. But it did.

66.

"CAN YOU GIVE me extra shifts?" Zack asks his new manager, Dennis.

"I'll see what I can do."

"I'd prefer nights. Closing."

"Really? That's the worst shift…"

"That's okay," he says, figuring the subtext is clear. *I need the money.*

When the real subtext is slightly different.

At one in the morning, Zack sweeps up, wipes down the counters, and finishes the last of the cleanup tasks.

They are within minutes of closing, and he knows the routine by now. "Is it okay if I take off?" asks Zack.

Dennis has worked the late shift too. He looks around. "Place looks good. Sure, go ahead." Dennis is starting to look for his keys.

Zack heads out the door, waving good night to Dennis. He waits outside for a moment while his boss locks the door and heads into the back room.

Zack then uses his newly made copy of Dennis's key to slip back into the GreenGirl. He slides silently into the women's bathroom, leaving the bathroom dead bolt unlocked to indicate that it's unoccupied, and waits silently until he hears Dennis exit.

Zack then emerges into the darkened GreenGirl. He leaves the lights off, heads into the back room, lays out rags and aprons into a bed, and settles in to sleep.

67.

"WHAT CAN YOU *tell me about Karloff?"*

"That's the point. Nothing. No one knows anything."

Oh yeah?

Not so long ago, Zack would have headed up the giant stone staircase between the lion sculptures and into the giant high-vaulted main reading room of the New York Public Library, ready to attack the vast card catalogue.

But today, he simply flips open the cover of his old beat-up college laptop, still covered with rock band and soccer team and fraternity decals, he taps a couple keys, and he is suddenly connected to the world's information. To all its answers.

But his first answer will require a helping hand, and once again, he knows only one place to find it.

He digs out the card. He takes a deep breath. Dials.

"Hello?"

"Detective Lopez? It's Zack Yellin again."

"Zack! Always good to hear your voice."

Zack knows he's about to disappoint the detective once

again. Complicate the moment. Bring it down. Zack wishes he could disappear. Shrink away from this. But he sees no other way. "Um, I, uh, need a little hand again, sir. Might need you to pull a couple of strings…"

"You're not getting into any trouble, are you, Zack?"

They both know Lopez has heard by now about the close call between Steve and Joey Richter. About Zack's less publicized, second brush with heroism.

"No, no, sir…it's…just research."

"Mmmm. Research. Go ahead." Lopez sounds skeptical.

"I just need someone to look into the real name and identity of this guy whose street name is Karloff."

There is a pause until Lopez says sternly, "We both know you should not be doing this."

Zack says nothing.

"You're fooling around where you shouldn't…"

Zack is silent.

Out on his porch overlooking the potato fields of Long Island, Detective Lopez sighs and takes a deep breath.

The kid is really smart. He's proven himself before.

Lopez is retired. Has no actual obligations at this point, except to his own ethics and morality. No responsibilities, except to himself and his own instincts. So he could ask this kid exactly what he's up to. Or give free rein to the kid's curiosity and intuition.

"I've still got my guys at the Eleventh. I'll get you that right away."

*　　*　　*

Sure enough, Zack's phone rings with the return call in ten minutes.

"Real name: Demetri Calunius," says Lopez. "Born Bulgaria, 1958. Arrived in the US in 1969. A couple of arrests here on minor charges but no convictions."

"Thank you, Detective. I can take it from here…"

"And get this. Immigration records indicate he arrived here unaccompanied. No parents or relatives with him. Alone, at eleven years old."

"Huh."

"One more thing to know. International police forces now link a lot of old stored national data. So there might be a way to get information about him growing up in Bulgaria, even though he was only a kid."

"Huh. Interesting. But I can't be asking you or them for more research favors. And obviously my looking would require access and permissions and—"

Lopez cuts him off. "Ready? Your password is RLopez 5570890. It's still active."

Emily hates him. Steve hates him. Chris, the GreenGirl manager, fired him. Dennis, his new GreenGirl manager, tolerates him—for now. But Detective Lopez, retired, living somewhere on eastern Long Island, for whatever mysterious reason, still believes blindly in him.

68.

ZACK DIGS IN.

He works on his laptop in a corner of the GreenGirl before his shift. Sits there all day, in fact. Fueled by free coffee.

At six, he folds up his laptop, stows it in the back, and works his shift. Then pulls his stunt once more for camping in the GreenGirl storeroom.

Once Dennis leaves and Zack emerges from the women's bathroom (he figures this might be the last time he can use this trick), he doesn't want to risk anyone seeing the laptop's glow so he works in the back room with the door closed. He barely even notices. He is not in a supply room in a GreenGirl in midtown Manhattan. He is instead immersed in confusing, terrifying Bulgaria in the 1950s and '60s, thanks to a chain of research links and the help of an extant police password and the wonders of Google Translate.

By morning, he is deep into the history of Bulgaria's child adoption and foster care system, and 1960s criminal procedure in Sofia, its largest city.

Zack soon understands what he's looking at. A wake of chaos and collapse, judicial and otherwise, in a repressive postwar Soviet satellite. Laws and rules are in flux, opportunists prevail. But some ingrained systems of the old repressive Soviet regime seem to still be in place, and the judicial clerks, steeped in their ways, knowing nothing else, seem to have kept on dutifully, blindly, making notes and records.

Zack had the worst luck in exchanging phones with an assassin.

Then having that assassin inadvertently bring a detonator to a meeting over coffee.

Will his luck change with Bulgarian police and civil court records from a half century ago? He shakes his head and suppresses a laugh.

He comes across several references to a gang that recruits children to do their dirty work, because children are treated so mildly by the law. Was this the beginning of Karloff's life of crime? Is this somehow how and why Karloff arrived here alone? If so, it's suddenly clear to Zack how early, how deeply, Karloff must have been adopted into the life he leads.

These child criminals must have really been a problem. He reads the recommendations of the prosecutor's office that are harsh, stern, unforgiving. He reads several rulings from one judge—someone named Litvinov—and sees that they are phrased so similarly that the judge must have been overwhelmed with his case load of these child criminals, or simply couldn't be bothered to distinguish between them.

And all the time Zack is looking to stumble across the unusual name Demetri Calunius but he never does. Calunius—Greek-sounding—immigrants from neighboring Greece to

Bulgaria? No way to know. The child criminals' names are generally not in the records, Zack notices. They're referred to as "Offender 134—9" or "Offender 392—12," and Zack quickly enough realizes that the final digits in the sequence are their ages. The anonymity is presumably to protect them as juveniles. But for Zack, the absence of the name Demetri Calunius adds credence to his theory that Karloff began life as one of these child criminals. Only if, however, Karloff had been one at all.

And he keeps his eyes open for any number that might have been resurrected from Karloff's past to become a detonation code, six digits or not. He jots down the Offender numbers. He jots down case numbers and file numbers. But he has no way of knowing which ones, if any, refer to Demetri Calunius.

He knows it's an insane search. But he feels he has to try.

Zack digs in and keeps exploring but in the end, he turns up nothing that will alter Joey's fate, or the fate of innocent dozens in one of twenty possible courtrooms. Or if he has, he doesn't know it.

He's discovered everything he can about Karloff's past.

Yet he's found nothing.

Karloff. A ghost right from childhood.

69.

SOME OF THE other GreenGirl employees must have grown suspicious. They must have seen small things pilfered, supplies missing, and reported it to Dennis, who must have put two and two together about his employee who always requested the late shift.

Zack is fired. He's not allowed into a GreenGirl again. Any GreenGirl.

He has nowhere to go. Nowhere to stay. A few dollars to spend on a cheap room but he's reluctant to use it for that.

In different circumstances, he could crash with Joey. He thinks about that. If the cops watching Joey see Zack go in there, so what? It'll seem strange to them, it'll certainly unnerve them, if they know who Zack is, but it won't be illegal. It will only mean they'll keep an even closer eye on Joey.

But he and Joey can't risk Will or Karloff somehow learning that Joey and Zack have connected, or that Joey has reached out to Zack for help. It would signal to them that Joey probably understands more about his phone and his final assignment than he's let on.

Zack realizes how alike they are right now, he and Joey. How weirdly alike and how weirdly allied.

Both alone. Both with no place to go.

But Joey has an excuse. Good reasons. Joey has a desperate life, a broken home, an upbringing on the streets.

What is Zack's excuse? None. His own stupidity. His own aimlessness. His own carelessness.

Of course, Zack is not truly alone. He can take his cheap disposable out of his pocket and dial his parents at any moment. He can be rescued. They can send money or anything he wants. But something in him won't permit him to involve them. Won't even entertain it. It's the same impulse that won't let him abandon Joey. Some deep, weird sense of responsibility and commitment that must have been learned from his parents although nothing was ever explicitly said.

It's the same sense of responsibility and commitment he feels to dozens of innocent people in an imagined courtroom. *Imagined* people, after all. *Fantasized* people. Faceless dozens, for whom he has betrayed and abandoned his girlfriend and then his best friend, both of whom are all too real. Right now, this sense of responsibility and commitment is clearly ruining his life. But it's apparently part of who he is.

So it's not that they're alike, exactly, he and Joey. It's just that Zack has managed to sink to Joey's level from the lofty perch of local hero, and he's pulled off his descent all by himself, with no one else to blame.

They can't be seen in each other's presence. They can only text. And there's a text he needs to send to Joey. He needs to alert him. But he doesn't have it in him to admit it to Joey and he can barely admit it to himself.

I've found nothing.

70.

ONCE EVERY THREE months, Hi-Alert Medical Systems has to check on the wall-mounted defibrillators and other emergency medical supplies that are part of their maintenance contract with the state of New York. They're a regional sub-contractor, servicing literally hundreds of the wall-mounted box units in movie theater lobbies, mall restrooms, public schools, municipal office buildings, administrative buildings, and courthouses throughout the region.

So this morning, Richard Galossi, their regional service rep, is checking the units in the courthouse. All standard servicing is done in off-hours when court is not in session.

Galossi, in his Hi-Alert uniform, shows his lanyard ID and brings in his test equipment. It turns out that he actually needs to replace one of the courtroom units with a newer model that will hold its charge longer.

When he's done, Galossi locks the wall unit that is in the courtroom. Which anyone watching might find unusual be-cause you can't get access to the defibrillator in an emergency.

But as far as Galossi knows, no one has ever reached for that defibrillator or the emergency supplies. In fact, if there ever was a real health emergency in that courtroom, Galossi would bet they'd simply call an ambulance. He's pretty sure no one even looks at the wall unit.

In fact, this courtroom unit is the only one Richard Galossi maintains.

"All set," says Richard Galossi to himself. Entering a little check mark and a date and some notes onto his clipboard.

All set, thinks Will Shale, wearing his Hi-Alert uniform with the Richard Galossi name tag, slipping out the courtroom door.

It's actually the same uniform he wore for his ATM machine "repair" scam but with a new arm patch. Waste not, want not.

People love a man in uniform.

And the irony of a bomb disguised as lifesaving equipment earns no more than a quick smile from Will Shale.

In case of emergency, it says on the side.

There's an emergency in that case, all right.

71.

IT HAPPENS WITHOUT ceremony one bright morning. A morning otherwise like any other.

A police cruiser pulls quietly to the curb outside Rooms4Rent. Two cops uncurl out of the vehicle. The two surveillance cops in the unmarked car across the street get out of their sedan, too, and head toward the Rooms4Rent entrance.

Joey has been watching. Expecting it for days.

It would be so easy to escape them, he thinks. Duck into the back way that he discovered through the old plumber. Slip out of the city, start over, take his chances.

He could even grab the Ruger hidden in the custodial closet on the way out. He's rehearsed it in his head. He'd have the time. And he'd always have a way to shoot out of a corner—or to shoot himself, if the corner turned too dark.

Yes, he could escape them. But he can't escape Karloff. Karloff will not tolerate that. Karloff will have him chased down and eliminated, like it was nothing. He thinks his chances are better in front of a judge, inside the system, because he won't be betraying Karloff.

He decided days ago. The Ruger will stay hidden in the custodial closet, maybe forever. Like a favorite toy that at some point must be left on the shelf. When you finally give up, finally accept, the changed conditions of your life.

He has time to send one text, he figures. One short text. He doesn't really know what will happen to him or his cell phone after that.

He hopes they take it away so he can't do what Karloff wants.

He hopes they don't take it away so he can do what Karloff wants.

Joey isn't at all surprised by the police cruiser's appearance. But one thing does surprise him. That he got no heads-up from Will or Karloff. No text. No communication at all.

Is it simply that they don't want to risk a text being intercepted? Maybe the risk has increased with the surveillance being so persistent over the days and weeks that have passed as a new court date approached.

Or is it just further proof that they're done with him? That they don't care. That they have this last assignment for him, and he's written off after that.

That there's nothing more to say to him.

The one person he could reach out to is Zack. Joey pulls out the phone. But what's the point? Time's up. Whatever the kid has been trying to figure out for Joey, it hasn't worked. He slips the phone back in his pocket.

You're too fuckin late, Zack, Joey thinks bitterly. *I'm on my way to court. I'm a dead man.*

*   *   *

In the backseat of the cruiser on the way to Lower Manhattan, Joey imagines the lesser charges that the state must be proceeding with. He knows all about them from years of prison. Manslaughter. Criminal possession of a weapon. Felony assault. Battery. A conviction on any of these, he knows, will give a judge wide latitude with sentencing.

He's a little confused when the police cruiser glides past the criminal court building where he had his first trial.

"What…what's goin' on?" he asks from the backseat.

"We're headed over to the Supreme Court Civil Branch building," says the cop in the passenger seat.

The Supreme Court Civil Branch is for civil cases. Lawsuits, fines, financial settlements, monetary damages.

"I don't understand. What am I being charged with?"

"Your lawyer didn't tell you? Wrongful death," says the cop over his shoulder. "Must be one of the families coming after you."

Joey is now very confused. A civil suit? He's pretty sure wrongful death means a lower standard of proof. He knows that from prison too. Is that why they're charging him with it?

And what lawyer is this? Why wasn't he told? Maybe the evidence from the criminal case can be used in the civil case so they don't even need to talk to him? Or was he not told because of what they've already argued about his mental capacities? Being left out of his own defense, like in his criminal case before. This is all so weird to him. But he's starting to sense the shadow of Karloff in it.

"If it's a civil suit, why am I being brought there in a police cruiser?"

"Oh, we're just doing a favor to the court and the lawyers. Just making sure you show up, Joey."

The cop now turns to face him. Joey can read his badge. *Patrick O'Connor.* "I wouldn't get too excited, Joey. I'm sure the state is going to retry you. They're probably just dotting their *i*'s and crossing their *t*'s to make sure we get it right this time. But I guess they didn't want to hold up some grieving family from at least suing your ass." O'Connor leans toward him. "Where'd you stash all the money, Joey?"

"I don't have any money."

"Yeah. Right."

"I don't!"

"Well someone must think you do, because that's what they're coming after."

Joey has nothing. A few hundred bucks left from what his parents gave him. That's what some family wants from him? What a fucking waste of everyone's time. If they're so hurt and angry that they're now trying to get their own justice, they'll just feel worse when they discover he has nothing.

Hell, he'll give them the few hundred and save them the trouble. Here, take it, you poor schmucks. What's the point of a wrongful death suit?

But then he suddenly realizes the point of this wrongful death suit.

It puts him inside a courtroom.

And the impression, the theory that he has money stashed away from all his hits? He'd bet that fairy tale has somehow come from Karloff.

* * *

Joey figures the police were hoping to drop him off at the courthouse before the press and the news outlets were even awake. Probably hoped it would be routine, quick, unnoticed.

But it apparently leaked so quickly and spread so fast that Joey sees reporters already, eager beavers, outside the courthouse as they pull up.

And smartphones set to get pushes and alerts from news sources soon say it: JOEY RICHTER TO STAND TRIAL ON CIVIL CHARGES. ALLEGED HIT MAN FACES WRONGFUL DEATH SUIT.

Emily Lane's iPhone gets such a notification. *What does this mean for Zack's insane obsession*, she wonders.

Steve Furman's iPhone gets a notification too. *Wrongful death*, Steve thinks. *Some interim justice while the state puts together something stronger. They won't screw up again.*

Zack Yellin's primitive disposable phone gets nothing like that. But he'll find out on his own. Very directly. Very soon.

72.

LAST TIME, JOEY Richter came straight from jail so he was brought in the prisoner entrance at the back of the courthouse and didn't have to deal with the crush of reporters. This time, he'll be escorted from the police cruiser at the front curb, where wooden blue police barricades create a path to the front door.

Reporters will probably gesture to him and try to wave him over like he's on a red carpet and they want a comment. But just as the police cruiser pulls up, a balding guy in a baggy gray suit pulls open the passenger door and says, "Follow me." He takes Joey's arm, to help him navigate past the reporters to the courthouse entrance.

"Who are you?"

"Nat Becker. I'm your lawyer."

"Like a public defender or something?"

"No, Joey, you don't have a guaranteed right to a lawyer in a civil case."

"So somebody's paying you."

"Yes."

"Who?"

Becker leans in toward Joey, whispers in his ear. "Somebody who wants you to have representation and is willing to pay, and that's good enough for me."

Joey looks at Becker's fraying suit and scuffed-up shoes. This is no flashy Darwin Cope or Len Carter. This is someone who could use the money.

It's as if the scene from weeks ago is now running in reverse. Joey is being reeled back into a courthouse, instead of being released from it. The sense of the same scene running in reverse is enhanced by the situation's same surreal, otherworldly quality.

He is ushered through the courthouse doors accompanied by Becker alone. Three uniformed guards man the trays and the single metal detector. "Keys and cell phones and metal belts into the tray, laptops out, step through one at a time."

Joey puts his disposable phone into the tray, steps through the metal detector, retrieves the phone from the tray on the other side.

He sees the guards look a little more closely at Becker's laptop. The keys and phones, they don't even give a second glance.

In a criminal case, a defendant can't bring anything into the courtroom. In a civil case, it seems there's nothing you can't bring in. No weapons, of course. But cell phones, sure.

"So you can bring a cell phone into a courtroom?" asks Joey.

"At the judge's discretion. As long as it's kept off," says Becker, retrieving his laptop.

Karloff and Will have obviously thought this through.

Joey would admire it, if he didn't think they were about to kill him.

He scoops up his cell phone and shoves it into his pocket.

Truth is, Joey's been reluctant to even look at the thing ever since Steve showed him the shiny new components inside it. He doesn't like looking at it or feeling it in his pocket. It's a reminder of his fate, of doom, of inevitability.

He glances at Becker, who is trying to shove his laptop back into his beat-up bag. To someone like Karloff, this guy Becker must be disposable, where Cope and Carter may not be. Is Becker as disposable as Joey? As disposable as the phone in Joey's pocket?

If there really is a bomb in the courtroom, Karloff is saving not only on an assassin's final contract price but also on significant legal fees. Cope and Carter, Joey is sure, are on ski vacations, at beach houses, at children's soccer games or dance recitals. While bald, money-hungry, baggy-suited Nat Becker is shuffling into the courtroom alongside Joey. *You may be a lawyer but you're as stupid as I am*, thinks Joey.

Getting a cell phone detonator into the courtroom. Is this somehow what the whole civil suit is really about? Joey can barely get his head around the idea. And certainly can't begin to answer the even bigger question: why?

73.

ZACK STOPS INTO a GreenGirl.

A different one. One where no one knows him. One where he's never worked, never been seen. There are hundreds of them, practically interchangeable, and once again, he's glad it's a chain.

For whatever conscious or unconscious reasons, he relives his previous life for a few moments. Buys a Café Americano—this one from a surly, downbeat barista with a black crewcut and beard—treats himself to a cranberry muffin, and settles onto a stool at the counter by the window.

Is he trying to rekindle—with the right setting, the right props—his earlier life in some way? Does he expect Steve or Emily will magically appear in the window as if coming to meet him?

Emily and Steve aren't speaking to him. So he knows they're not forwarding any online news to his cheap, feature-less, app-less phone. So he flips open his old laptop, connects to the GreenGirl Wi-Fi, starts scrolling through some local news sites, and sees it. Joey Richter to Stand Trial on Civil Charges.

He still has his password from Lopez. He takes a sip of coffee and, with a few clicks, starts to scroll through the state of New York legal docket.

And there it is.

Civil trials, Part 231, *State of NY v. Joey Richter*, Judge J. Litvinov presiding.

Wait a second. Something echoes in Zack Yellin's head. Some reverberation of recognition, of mild familiarity, turning sharper, electric, in his mind.

Litvinov. Is it possible?

He momentarily forgets the coffee and muffin. He types furiously. Finds his way back through the links he'd explored previously. In a moment, he is back in Bulgaria in the 1960s, immersed as if he never left it.

Josepho Litvinov. Zack's heart jumps.

He dives in deeper, starts digging through more records, uses Lopez's old police password to get into immigration records, googles the judge's name in America, and New York district court records, but he already knows:

Josepho Litvinov, at some point in the turmoil of that collapsing judicial system, escaped Bulgaria, made his way to America, studied American civil law, took the New York bar, and sits today in Supreme Court, Civil Term.

The same Josepho Litvinov who sentenced those little child criminals? Who sent them into the circle of abusive foster care, or released them to be recruited again by the gangs, starved to toughen them up, all the stuff he'd been reading about?

Was Demetri Calunius one of those kids? And he wants

revenge? Has waited for revenge. Waited until a case went to civil court? To Litvinov's docket and Litvinov's courtroom? Is that possible? Has Karloff had the patience for that? Or did Karloff somehow steer the case to that docket and that courtroom?

Zack's mind is going a thousand miles an hour. He asks himself again: Why not simply have the judge shot at his home? Getting into or out of his car. Safe, anonymous, done all the time to judges and officials, in dozens of countries around the globe.

He can only surmise that Karloff is set on some larger vengeance. Vengeance on the entire justice system. Prosecutors. Attorneys. Clerks. Press. Bystanders. Everyone all at once. A statement of some sort. Hence the bomb.

And surmising more: that the quiet, stealthy, professional, exceedingly patient thug isn't totally without ego. He needs this statement, after all these years of anonymity. Something like that. Hence the bomb.

Here at the counter in a GreenGirl, Zack may have finally solved the puzzle. Figured out the true target. Not just Josepho Litvinov, but the justice system he represents. The corrupt, inept, dysfunctional justice system itself, as Karloff sees it, gathered conveniently together for him. Means, motive, and opportunity. All together in that courtroom.

But another possibility occurs to Zack. One that helps explain how Karloff continues to operate with apparent impunity year in, year out, and continues to elude the justice system. A possibility that explains Will getting into Joey's jail cell. One that explains a lot. That Litvinov and Karloff have been functioning as partners from the old country—distant, careful, so no one can put it together—and Litvinov has worked from inside the system to keep Karloff operating. Has Litvinov now somehow crossed him, or has Karloff just come to believe that Litvinov has crossed him, and the relationship must end—with a bang?

Litvinov and Karloff. Maybe a relationship that defies escape, defies resolution. A relationship fated to destroy what's around it.

Like that of Zack and Joey.

74.

"ALL RISE. THE Honorable Josepho Litvinov presiding."

Josepho Litvinov, from post-Stalinist Bulgaria, who has traveled cultures and continents to this courtroom.

Josepho Litvinov, whose ghostly fellow traveler may or may not be why this trial is convened.

Josepho Litvinov, who is stooped, white-haired, in his eighties, but there's no mandatory retirement for judges, and he is one of those civil servants who is proud to still serve, to still contribute.

Josepho Litvinov ascends slowly onto the bench.

All rise.

Emily Lane rises. It's her first assignment in her new role. The promotion she's waited for and worked so long for. Tinged now with mixed feelings. Extremely mixed. She should have known it wouldn't be clear and clean. She should have known a step into adulthood would be rife with ambiguity.

She's finally made the leap from content aggregator—finding, sorting, and repackaging existing news content—to actual reporting. Journalism—real journalism—her dream, her goal. This had always been the purpose of the crummy freelance "content-gathering" jobs. Always gathering other reporters' stories. *Any* other stories. None that were her own.

Her employer knew of her connection to the case because they had come across her name in the press accounts, and so they asked her if she would cover it to get an interesting personal angle. *Of course, you can say no,* her boss said. *If it's still too traumatic.* Holding his breath. Looking at her anxiously. She couldn't say no. Because he really didn't want her to say no. And for it to be her first real assignment made perfect sense.

This is her opportunity. And it's as if a life lesson is aimed at her—how opportunity comes at a price. Comes with strings attached.

It's the last place she wants to be, this courtroom, but maybe this will bring some kind of resolution so she can finally put it behind her, to see Joey Richter convicted. To stare at him from this side of justice.

She knows it's quite possible she'll see Zack in the course of this. That he may be called to testify in the civil case. She doesn't know how a wrongful death case like this works, exactly. And she's asked herself, how much is the possibility of seeing Zack part of her agreeing to take this assignment?

*   *   *

Detective Lopez rises. Back in the city. He still can't get over what happened in the criminal trial. He wants to see what happens in the civil trial. As if his being there will bring a conviction. Then again, his being there prevented Joey Richter from murdering Zack and Emily. His being there meant the EMTs got to Steve fast enough to save him. His being there prevented Steve from killing Joey and earning a prison sentence for himself. Lopez is not particularly superstitious, although he's not particularly *un*superstitious either. And this is better than sitting on his porch gazing out at potato fields. And, well, maybe in some way, for some reason, he's *supposed* to be here. If that's pure superstition, so what?

He notices that he's a few seats away from Emily, Zack's girlfriend, whom he last saw in that highly charged moment on the sidewalk when Joey drew his gun and Lopez came up behind him.

Lopez doesn't initially say anything to her—it would break the silence and decorum of the courtroom—but he nods briefly and amiably to her, and she nods back with a small smile, and he feels a wave of memory and gratitude pass between them.

Zack assumes that by now the bomb is in place. If Karloff's people can get a prisoner into Joey's jail cell with him, they can probably get a bomb into a courthouse, maybe even into the courtroom itself. Likely the courtroom is periodically swept but there's probably a schedule to it, and he'd bet Karloff's people know the schedule.

Or maybe the bomb was placed much earlier. During construction? Renovation? If this is a long-simmering revenge, maybe Karloff planned it a while ago. And, if planned and placed long ago, presumably they can arm it remotely. But if so, then couldn't they also detonate it remotely? They wouldn't need Joey at all.

So maybe the point of doing the hit like this is so the remnants of the explosion, certain to be searched by a police forensics team, can never trace back to Karloff. Would only trace to Joey's detonator phone, and Joey. Crazy, spiteful Joey, back in court, angry at the world.

Zack knows Karloff might send Joey a text at any moment. The text telling Joey what code to enter.

They don't know that Joey knows what the code represents. That Joey knows his disposable cell phone is more than a disposable cell phone.

But Zack has come to understand that if Joey gets the code, he might very well choose to enter it. Zack has come to understand how cornered, how trapped, Joey feels. How at the end of the line he feels.

Even in the short, tense time spent with him at the Green-Girl and at Steve's apartment, he's seen Joey become steadily more morose. More depressed. He's been starting to sense that Joey might really *want* to die. And to sense how Joey feels he owes Karloff for fucking up, for letting Karloff down.

Once Joey understood what he was holding in his hands, that he could control his own death and therefore his own destiny, Zack could see that some part of Joey wanted to enter the code when it came. He was ready to. Was willing to. And over the past few days, that part of him has seemed to grow.

A professional hit man, taking his last shot. Finishing his last job. Fulfilling the assignment. Maybe Karloff knew that some part of Joey would see it that way.

He came to Zack for help but in the end, Zack's help only clarified the grim reality Joey is facing. Making it concrete, putting it in front of him. And staring at that fate, Joey sees there is no helping him.

Zack will know the precise moment when Joey receives the text. He'll even know the code.

He'll know it because he switched phones with Joey. When they were in Steve's apartment. After Steve was done examining Joey's phone and carefully replaced its back cover and handed the phone back to Zack, who handed it back to Joey.

But in fact, Zack had pocketed it and handed his own phone to Joey. Identical-looking, after all, if you didn't see them side by side.

When Steve said the phone wasn't booby-trapped, that was good enough for Zack. He swapped the phones. Joey's phone still functions as a phone after all. And Zack figured he'd work out his next move on the fly. Once he had a minute to think about it. Which he never got, with Emily suddenly at Steve's apartment door.

He couldn't risk Joey entering the correct code, listening to Karloff and being the good soldier. Zack couldn't risk so many innocent people dying.

If Joey was desperate enough to turn to Zack, he was desperate enough to dial the code and be done with his desperation forever.

If Joey didn't dial the code, he would likely be killed by Karloff for his disobedience. But one assassin dying was better than dozens of innocent bystanders. It wasn't a pleasant calculus. But it was one Zack felt he had to make.

Zack knows the courtroom this morning is filled with people. Innocent people. And he knows the text might be sent to Joey at any moment.

He doesn't know when or whether Joey will look closely at the phone in his pocket as time passes in the courtroom. As the trial goes on around him, as no text comes in while he sits at the defendant's table.

And Zack doesn't know exactly what he's going to do, what his next move will be, when the code comes to him.

All of those thoughts are swirling in his head when the phone in Zack's pocket buzzes with a text.

Unknown number. This must be it. The text from Karloff, who thinks he's sending it to Joey.

The text contains just a six-digit number: 777548.

With the bland-seeming instructions:

Enter it and hit send.

75.

SITTING AT THE defense table, Joey Richter gets a text.

He feels it buzz in his pocket. He's afraid to even look at it.

But what choice does he have? He's decided. He will do what he's been told. What he's agreed. He's been a fuckup all his life. This is one thing he's not going to fuck up. So against courtroom policy, he has turned on the phone in his pocket to await the text. The defense table blocks anyone from seeing his lap. His lawyer, Nat Becker, is busy taking notes.

Joey glances down at the screen nervously, focuses on the text.

666745. Enter it and hit send.

The civil case goes on around him. He's barely even listening. He doesn't care. It's a fog of words, of motions, of countermotions. He glanced over just once at the victim's family at the prosecution table when he sat down. Long enough to realize he has no idea which victim it is. Whose family are they? It only confuses and depresses him further.

He's been confused all his life. It's *always* been a fog around him. And this code, this phone, is no clearer.

Zack's and Steve's speculations on what this number is about. Where it's detonating. *If* it's detonating. Even that is still unclear too. Part of him still doesn't understand, doesn't believe, that Karloff would go through all this trouble. Would put it all on Joey. It makes no sense. Part of him thinks, is sure, this code isn't really about an explosion at all. It's just a test of loyalty. Or for something else entirely. The idea of a detonation? That just came from two imaginative slacker kids, after all, and from his own reading of Karloff. And he knows better than anyone that he almost always reads things wrong.

But regardless of all this, and in light of all this, he's ready.

He thinks.

Can he do it? Can he finally prove himself to Karloff? Can he prove himself to his parents, who despise him?

Can he finally show a self that is truly selfless? Can he prove himself to himself?

He enters the number nervously.

Pauses at the last digit. Feels the courtroom around him retreat from his awareness. The droning legalese of judge and attorneys, the shifting of papers and shuffling of feet, the hum of air-conditioning, all fading back. The courtroom's brightness around him falls away, too, becoming merely a kind of bright shadow. There is only him and the phone in his palm.

Joey presses the last digit. Takes a deep breath. A last breath. A cleansing breath.

Hits send.

Ready to die. Ready to not exist.

And yet, he is still here. In the courtroom. At the defense table. Nothing happens.

Keeping it tucked in his lap, he looks at the phone and now sees texts to Steve, to Emily, to Zack's parents. He looks at the number the text came from. Wait. It's his own number.

Joey is shocked. Confused. But in the next second he understands utterly, completely and absorbs it in a moment.

Zack switched phones on me. He took my phone away.

Joey doesn't know what will happen next. With Will, with Karloff. They don't know he has the wrong phone.

But he realizes quickly that if he texts from Zack's phone to Will and tells them Zack switched phones on him, they'll know he was in contact with Zack. They'll know he knows about the phone. They'll kill him for sure.

He realizes in the next second that Zack, wherever he is with Joey's phone, is going to receive the actual code from Karloff. What's he going to do with it? Joey doesn't know. But one thing he's pretty sure about—Zack is never going to punch it in.

Joey's not sure yet—it's still so confusing—how or why he received this code to dial. If it's coming from Zack, who got it from Karloff, why would Zack forward it to this phone? Why would he want Joey to enter it?

But for now, Joey is alive. The courtroom around him is focused on his case. They're probably going to convict him.

Entering the code did nothing.

But Joey can't help but smile.

Zack wouldn't let me kill myself.

That crazy redheaded kid apparently cared enough about Joey to save him from himself.

76.

777548.

Zack still doesn't know what the number signifies or how it was chosen.

But he knows exactly what it is. What it will do.

Not just if he enters it.

He's afraid that even if he merely clicks on it, the dumb disposable phone might cheerfully, cooperatively send the six digits for him. He still doesn't know anything about signal range. Maybe he has to be inside the courtroom for the signal to be received. Maybe he doesn't.

Carefully, so carefully, he navigates away from the text.

Will Karloff or his tech guy Will figure out that Joey is holding the wrong phone? Presumably they'd have to see Joey's phone up close to know.

Zack's only power in holding *this* phone is the ability to blow a courtroom of innocent people to kingdom come.

That's a lot of power. And of course, no power at all. No leverage at all. Because a blown-up courtroom is exactly what Karloff wants.

Last time Zack had Joey's phone, he had numbers, photos, evidence of a dark life. This time, now, he just has a six-digit code.

A pretty forceful and formidable one.

There's not much else to find on the rest of Joey's phone. He's already searched it. And now he doesn't want to fool around with the phone any more than necessary.

Although one bit of fooling around is necessary.

He carefully, very carefully, sends a text to his own phone. To Joey.

A text with a different number, just to be safe. A totally made-up six-digit number. Instructing Joey to dial it. Because Zack has the feeling, the reasonable feeling, that Karloff may have someone in the courtroom watching Joey. Someone unaware they could soon be splattered against the courtroom walls. Someone reporting back to Karloff.

And if they report seeing Joey dutifully, earnestly entering a number and nothing happens, maybe Karloff and his people will think there's a glitch. A failure of technology. And not a failure of Joey. And maybe that is a way to buy a little time, while Zack tries to think of something better.

He sends the text and then sets Joey's phone down carefully.

It was impulsive, Zack switching the phones. The same impulsiveness that had him looking around a stranger's phone and getting into the original fix.

He didn't really have a plan for it. Still doesn't. And what if Joey, seeing that the phone he's holding has never been opened and realizing what Zack has pulled on him, is either so pissed off or so terrified of failing in his assignment or still wants to prove himself the good soldier, so he caves in and admits to Karloff or Will or their crew what happened?

Then what?

First, Zack was running from a killer for hire.

Now, he'll be running from a whole criminal network. A cartel.

Joey had made mistakes. Not being careful. Grabbing the wrong phone in the GreenGirl.

Not accepting Zack's dead-phone deal and coming after Zack to kill him.

Not paying attention. Letting his phone get switched in Steve's apartment.

But this guy Karloff. He isn't a guy who makes mistakes. You don't get to be where he is by making mistakes.

Zack might be on the run again.

This time with no Emily. No Steve. No plan.

No Joey, even.

Where would he go? Where would he hide? How long could he hold out?

And the courtroom of innocent people he imagines he's saving? Is he really saving them? Or are they still in a danger that he doesn't understand?

He knows he can't run again. It's time to turn to help. Time to turn to the one person who's saved him before.

Who saved him from getting shot in the street. Who saved his friend Steve by providing Joey's address. Who even saved Zack hours of time by giving Zack the password to search police databases.

The guy who's always been there for him.

He didn't want to bother Detective Lopez without real evidence, when it was just a crazy assassin with a harebrained story. But now it's time to reach out to him.

Zack searches once more for Lopez's card in his wallet.

It's not there.

He looks through his wallet again carefully. Then frantically. Nothing. Did he lose it when he dialed him last? He was concentrating on the police database password that Lopez was providing—RLopez5570890—trying to commit it to memory. Did he leave the card somewhere on that GreenGirl table? Is it buried somewhere in the messy GreenGirl storage closet?

He needs the card because, being super cautious with Joey's phone and not really knowing where it might end up, he's been immediately deleting any calls he makes from the phone's call log—including the previous call to Lopez.

Lopez's number is still on Zack's own dumb disposable phone, of course. Which does Zack no good. Since his own phone is now in Joey's hands.

Emily doesn't have Lopez's number. Neither does Steve. So it does no good to reach out to them, if they would even respond to Zack. Lopez is retired so Zack can't reach him through a general police department number either. And they're hardly going to give Lopez's personal number to Zack if he calls the precinct. He'd have to show up in person, explain, persuade, prove he's who he says.

He stares at the phone, trying to think through some solution, some way to reach Lopez.

Figure it out. Joey's hopeful plea comes back to him.

But it turns out time's up for figuring it out.

And there will be no running or hiding. In fact, quite the opposite.

"Zack Yellin?"

He looks up from where he's been sitting in the back of a GreenGirl, staring at Joey's useless phone.

A kid Zack's age in a white button-down shirt and a thin black tie is hovering over him with a toothy smile.

"Yeah?" says Zack cautiously. Is this a deranged fan? Someone who recognizes him from the news six months ago?

The toothy grin gets toothier. The kid slaps a printed document in front of Zack. "Part two-thirty-one, state of New York versus Joey Richter. Summons to appear tomorrow morning."

Zack stares at the summons.

"You're a tough guy to find, Zack Yellin. No known address. I've been looking for you in GreenGirls for days."

77.

DETECTIVE LOPEZ IS in the gallery of the courtroom.

He sees the defendant texting on his phone.

You're not supposed to use your phone.

And who the hell would you be texting when you're on trial for wrongful death?

Emily is a few seats away from Lopez.

She, too, sees the defendant looking down at his phone.

It occurs to her that Zack could be texting him. A shiver runs down her spine.

The Zack she no longer knows. Why would he do that?

She sees Joey smiling a little. Why?

The assassin—sitting there, smiling.

She dutifully records it in her notes. Reporting on the behavior of the defendant. He's smiling.

She feels like retching.

78.

WILL GETS A text from Karloff. What the fuck?

Followed by a phone call before Will can even respond. "What the fuck?"

A live call from Karloff is always a bad sign.

"What?" Will sits up. He hears the trouble in Karloff's voice.

"Nothing happened," says Karloff.

"How do you know?"

"You hear me? Nothing's happened."

Someone must be watching for Karloff, thinks Will. Someone in the courtroom. Someone else who's going to be killed and doesn't know it.

"He's looking at the phone. He dials a number, for fuck's sake, and nothing happens. Why the fuck not? A glitch in the technology?"

It's a glitch. But not in the technology, thinks Will. It was as dumb and direct a wireless technology as you could use. And there'd be no signal decay, given the range of just a few yards. For Will, it was totally straightforward work.

The problem was human error, he was sure. Entering the digits wrong? But much more likely *not* entering them, because Joey has figured it out. How could he though? It was pretty much impossible someone would just *see* it, Will is sure of that, especially someone like Joey, and from what Will has just heard from Karloff, the guy was still *using* his phone. Or trying to. So clearly he has no idea.

"Is there any other way to detonate it?"

Will shrugs. "I can build another one," he says.

"How long will that take?"

"Buy the phone. Wire it. Just a few hours. Ready for day two of the trial tomorrow morning."

"Great." Relief, enthusiasm, energy. Will hears all three.

"But someone has to get close enough to sync it." Will is immediately sorry he brought up this solution, this line of thinking.

"How close is that?"

Will's stomach sinks. "It means getting into the courtroom somehow."

"Then do it somehow," says Karloff. And hangs up.

And suddenly Will is going to be in the one place he doesn't want to be. He's the one person besides Karloff who knows not to be there...and he's just been selected.

79.

"THE COURT CALLS Zack Yellin to the stand."

Zack strides to the front of the packed courtroom.

With a phone in his pocket that can, as far as he knows, blow them all to oblivion, if and when he presses the six digits. Hardly a feeling of power. A feeling of terror, of disorientation. The end of the world in his pocket. *Is that the end of the world in your pocket or are you just unhappy to see us?*

Just like the switching of phones has repeated itself, the trial is a repetition too. Playing out again, as if reality is some kind of inescapable loop.

But it's not just a switching of phones, Zack realizes. More than switching phones, they're switching roles.

Because Joey was supposed to be the one with the detonator in his pocket.

And instead, Zack has it. For the opposite reason, of course. The explosive phone is there in his pocket so it *doesn't* go off.

"State your name and address, for the record."

"Zack Yellin," and he pauses, doesn't know what to give as an address. "No current address," he says.

"Do you promise to tell the truth, the whole truth…"

He scans the packed courtroom. *Imagined dozens.* And here they are. Quite real.

He scans the gallery of the courtroom and sees Emily and Detective Lopez a few seats from each other. He sits up straight, startled by both.

Lopez. Not on Long Island but here in the courtroom. Just yards away. And yet Zack can't reach him. Can't call or text him. Can't tell him anything about the switched phones or a suspected bomb or a detonator in his pocket. Unless he blurts it out and causes a stampede, a riot, pandemonium. *Hey, Detective Lopez. See this? I think it's a detonator.*

And Emily. Confusion, longing, fear for her safety, all tumble within Zack, unsortable. *What is she doing here?*

Lopez. Emily. The past is repeating. Reorganizing itself. In some manner he doesn't really understand.

"Mr. Yellin, do you recognize the defendant?"

"Yes."

Joey and Zack lock eyes and exchange looks blankly, un-readably, giving nothing away. An exchange of looks observed by several dozen in the courtroom.

Exchanging looks with the only other person in the court-room who knows what is in Zack's pocket.

You took my phone, Zack.

Yes, I took your phone, Joey.

To save innocent people, Zack? Or to save me from myself?

"Can you describe the circumstances under which you first met Mr. Richter?"

Zack knows the standard of proof is much lower in a civil action. He can already detect the slightly different phrasings and framings of the attorneys. He knows that wrongful death is usually about restitution but Joey barely has a dime. So what's the point here? Just the satisfaction of hearing a guilty verdict? Or has the family been told that Joey has money stashed away? Or is this suit about something else entirely? Like Zack's suspicion that it's been somehow helped along by Karloff.

It occurs to Zack once again, looking at Joey, how Joey truly had nothing, nowhere to turn, no one to turn to, when he texted Zack Yellin.

And now, on the stand, Zack understands—Emily leaving him, Steve tossing him out, his GreenGirl jobs all lost after bedding down in a supply closet. He understands Joey's feeling of nowhere to turn, nowhere to go.

But it is Joey's reaching out and Zack's responding that has led to this moment. Which has put a potential explosion in Zack's pocket.

Zack tells the story to a packed courtroom again—the switched phones, the assassin's phone filled with photos, being lured to a rendezvous he figured he might not survive, being chased on the city streets, the assassination attempt on the street corner.

He wonders: Is this all he'll ever be known for? This story? This bizarre event? Will his life be stopped, held forever, in this tale?

"And you expect us to believe you two switched phones like that? And you came up with the other phone's code?" The same question that Darwin Cope had asked, but this time asked sympathetically by the prosecution, inviting Zack to explain, to help the judge accept the strangeness of the universe.

Because this is a civil trial, argued before a judge without a jury. This elderly judge with the strange name—Josepho Litvinov—with his strange, vague, unidentifiable accent, whose origins Zack imagines only he knows.

"That's what happened. I wish it didn't," Zack says to the courtroom. "I wish none of this was happening," he says, looking at Joey.

And certainly no one in the courtroom would believe that he and the defendant have switched phones *again*, and as a result he has a remote trigger in his pocket.

He feels time ticking, the bomb ticking, in a way, at a pace he doesn't understand, but he also has the strong sense of time looping somehow because he is giving the same testimony, looking at the same defendant.

Suddenly time compresses acutely, rears up disruptively.

Zack sees Karloff enter the back of the courtroom. He barely recognizes him from a single arrest-record photo on one of the police databases, but it's him. Hair white now. Decades older. But same jutting cheeks, same small, piercing eyes.

Is it the first courtroom the criminal mastermind Karloff has been in since he was a child in Bulgaria?

In front of Josepho Litvinov?

This judge? Once again?

Zack looks over to Litvinov. Did he notice Karloff enter? Does he have any inkling who it is?

The possibilities, the permutations, run through Zack's head immediately.

Karloff is here, risking being seen and identified.

Is he here to somehow frighten Joey into doing it? Into following through? Presumably, he doesn't yet know Joey *can't* do it.

Or is he carrying a cell phone detonator of his own? To use when? Where? How?

If Zack got into this courtroom with his altered phone, then no problem, certainly Karloff could too.

Are both Zack and Karloff equally empowered? Equally destructive?

Or has the code been changed? And Joey's phone in Zack's pocket is as powerless now as Zack's phone is in Joey's pocket. And only Karloff can detonate and destroy.

Now Litvinov can see Karloff. A figure materializing out of the past. Litvinov presumably wouldn't recognize him. If Zack is guessing correctly about their shared past, Litvinov hasn't laid eyes on him since Karloff was a child. He might know of Karloff's presence in the city. Maybe the small Bulgarian expatriate community has made them aware of each other, too few degrees of separation. Or has Karloff stayed so invisible, so underground, that Litvinov has no idea? "Karloff" is a criminal whose real name only surfaced through research, after all. And Litvinov is a *civil* court judge, nothing higher.

Maybe Litvinov didn't know until this moment? Until looking past the white hair, catching something familiar, something dimly recognizable, from across the world, from across time? Zack doesn't know. But nobody in the courtroom is physically closer to Judge Litvinov than Zack, here on the witness stand. He looks for a flickering light of recognition to cross Litvinov's eyes, but sees nothing.

Zack has continually wrestled with it: if Karloff—Demetri Calunius—wanted vengeance on Litvinov, why not hire an assassin like Joey to simply kill him?

But from up here on the witness stand, looking out over

the courtroom, Zack understands vividly. It makes a certain sense.

Because Karloff wanted this.

A courtroom. Justice. Coming full circle.

And now, even more than that. Even better. Worth the risk to Karloff. To *see* Litvinov. To have Litvinov *see him.*

Which only the courtroom could provide. For both of them, for others, to bear witness.

To make the justice system—at last, for one final, compelling, overwhelming moment—work for *him.* For Karloff.

Before the old judge leaves the bench. Before it is too late.

Obviously he's planned for it to happen anonymously, to just have Joey set the whole place ablaze, but maybe Joey's failure has offered Karloff a glimpse of what he really wants. To be face-to-face for some kind of settlement, some kind of accounting, with his past. To have Litvinov see him, to have Litvinov know, in his final moments.

What good is revenge if the victim doesn't know? Revenge, if the victim doesn't know, is no revenge at all.

Revenge is not a stab in the back. It's a stab in the front. Eye to eye. Knife to heart.

Zack looks at Karloff, the set of his jaw and his proud, deliberate movement. Zack is sure Karloff wouldn't come into the courtroom unless he has the power. Unless he has control.

He must have a cell phone detonator in his pocket. A new detonator. Replacing Joey's, which is in Zack's pocket.

But he's not going to blow *himself* up.

"And is this testimony, to the best of your recollection, entirely consistent with the testimony you gave in Joey Richter's criminal court trial several weeks ago?"

"Yes, Your Honor."

Karloff's eyes on him.

Emily's eyes on him.

Lopez's eyes on him.

His own eyes not leaving Karloff.

What's he doing? What's his plan?

80.

WHEN DETECTIVE LOPEZ—*ex*-Detective Lopez—sees Karloff enter the courtroom, he goes on high alert. He sits up. His traditional, easygoing, slothful style gets sloughed off, abandoned. He's like a lounging mammal who's suddenly roused, ready, transformed at a moment's notice in a rush of adrenaline that courses through his considerable frame.

Lopez assumes he's the only one in the courtroom who knows who Karloff is, besides Zack.

He knows what Karloff looks like only because he researched it on some police databases with his old password.

He researched it on the police databases only because Zack Yellin had asked about Karloff in passing, trying to be casual and informal and breezy about what he was up to. But Lopez knew that, whatever Zack was looking into, it was not casual and informal.

He knew Zack could be getting himself into trouble. Again. The kid has a proven knack for that.

Lopez's hunch was that it could be the kind of trouble

where maybe Lopez should come back to the city to make sure things unfolded smoothly and predictably with no further drama. Maybe he'd come and sit in the courtroom—just like a typical old, fat, retired cop, glad to be done with the case work but missing it too.

But there was also something in Lopez that hadn't wanted to stop Zack. That's why he'd given Zack access to the police database. He wanted to give the kid the free rein he needed. Because, well, he thought the kid might find something they'd all missed.

He'd noticed how suddenly nervous, how uncomfortable Zack looked up there on the stand when Karloff came in. Well, if the kid was in trouble, Lopez's number was still in Zack's phone, right? Smart, brave kid like Zack, he could dispense with courtroom etiquette and just text Lopez in an emergency.

Now, seeing Karloff in the courtroom—*voluntarily* in a courtroom of the state of New York—Lopez is sure his instinct is right. Something is up, and he bets it involves Zack.

Why? Why is Karloff here?

81.

"**AND CAN YOU** recount, one more time, what happened in the GreenGirl when you sat down across from the defendant and Emily Lane, who was effectively the defendant's hostage at that moment?"

Zack continues testifying.

He tells of immersing the two phones in the two coffees. He was hoping to make that the end of it, he explains. Hoping to convince the defendant to let this GreenGirl meeting be their last.

He looks across the courtroom at Emily. Can't help it. A rush of affection, of sorrow, of wistfulness, of desire, sweeps over him. Is any similar rush of feeling happening in her? Of course, she was the one who asked him to leave. Furiously. Impulsively. But there's the deep reservoir of what they had, isn't there? It doesn't evaporate overnight, does it? And he's never wavered in his feelings for her—and she knows it. Somewhere, she knows it.

After all, she is here.

Here while the cell phone detonator has been safely in Zack's pocket.

But now she is here while Karloff stands only a few feet away from her—with, very likely, a new detonator in *his* pocket. As if, in a magic trick, it has switched pockets.

If so, what can Zack do?

Can he yell it out? *There's a bomb in the courtroom and that man has the detonator!*

There'd be panic. Pandemonium. Or else, stunned paralysis. In the brief, confusing moment before all their existences ceased.

No, not a good option.

82.

ZACK, ON THE witness stand, is indeed witnessing everything. The only one, besides the judge, facing the right way to observe the whole courtroom.

And that's when Zack sees it. A young, wiry guy with tattoos handing a cell phone to Karloff.

They're in the back row of the gallery. Only Zack sees it.

Wiry, tattoos. It must be the guy Joey described. The tech guy, Will.

Handing Karloff a cell phone. And then, silently, unobtrusively, exiting the courtroom.

Zack watches Karloff take the new phone and slip his old one into his pocket. The old one is an iPhone, Zack can see. How many crimes, how many murders, have originated from it? The ultimate diePhone, Zack thinks.

He sees Karloff step back toward the courtroom door.

He sees Karloff stand there at the door a moment, survey the room, and then look down at the new cell phone he was handed.

A cheap disposable—Zack can see from here. *Oh my God…*

If the numbers of the code *are* significant, would Karloff keep the same code?

Or in the wiring, in the syncing, did it *need* to be the same? Could it *not* be changed?

Zack doesn't know, of course. He probably won't ever know.

Because he sees Karloff start to type. Deliberately. Digit by digit.

What to do? How to stop him?

Think. Figure it out.

Beneath the rim of the witness box, Zack scrolls through the few texts on Joey's phone and calls the last one back.

A phone rings at the back of the courtroom. Heads turn, looking.

It keeps ringing. Karloff has little choice but to take it out of his pocket. Distracting him from the disposable he is holding.

He is now holding two phones. Which draws some attention from a few of those around him. Including an overweight Hispanic man seated near him.

Who gets up. Seems to be heading toward Karloff, toward the ringing.

But there are still lots of people, lots of bodies, between Lopez and Karloff.

Karloff doesn't answer the phone. Instead, he fumbles with it to stop its ringing.

How else can Zack confuse Karloff? Delay him? Give Lopez a few more precious seconds to get to him?

He only has time to send a short text.

He sends a text with just six digits.

777549.

Changing just the last digit of the code. So he doesn't blow them all sky high. Taking the risk. The risk of a single digit.

Zack still doesn't know what *777548* means. But he assumes it means *something*.

And meaning something, and receiving it from Joey's phone just slightly wrong, could be just enough to baffle Karloff for a moment.

Karloff looks down at the number on his iPhone. Looks up, confused.

He looks at Zack. Who looks back blankly. No phone in Zack's hand. It's back in his pocket.

Karloff looks at his iPhone again. And then back at the disposable.

He is backing out of the room now, focused on the disposable as he begins to type once more, when a big, overweight Hispanic guy approaches him.

And brushes past him.

Zack watches helplessly as Lopez passes Karloff, exiting the courtroom.

To become the only survivor, Zack realizes, of whatever Karloff is about to unleash.

Damn. Lopez has proven himself highly skilled. Highly intuitive. But he's not magical. He's not superhuman. How would Lopez even know what Karloff looks like—a master criminal known for his low profile, his invisibility?

And then, in a motion so unexpected in the realm of normal, hushed, formal courtroom etiquette that no one sees it coming, Lopez—just a fat Hispanic guy who brushed past Karloff in the doorway—turns back and grabs Karloff's disposable phone out of his hand.

Now the phone is in Lopez's hands. Just like that.

And Karloff—who'd been looking down, typing something, hardly even aware of the big Hispanic guy—is apparently so confused, so unnerved that he doesn't even reach to grab it back, but instead backs out of the room, turns, and disappears.

Lopez would go after him but there's something more pressing to do.

Detective Lopez reenters the courtroom. Holding the disposable phone up for Zack to see.

And holding up his badge—his old detective badge—high over his head, displaying it to the entire courtroom.

Litvinov halts the proceedings. "Everything okay, Detective?"

"I'm so sorry, Your Honor, but we need to clear the courtroom."

Groans of annoyance and skepticism rise from the gallery. "Some kind of scare called in, Detective?"

"Yes, Your Honor. Something like that."

"Is it really necessary, Detective?"

"I'm afraid it is."

In an abundance of caution and amid continued grumbling, the courtroom is cleared immediately. Judge Litvinov, in his still-detectable Slavic accent, instructs participating attorneys for both the prosecution and the defense, as well as the current witness, Zack Yellin, and the other witnesses slated to appear after Mr. Yellin, to please stand by. Two court officers will stand with Mr. Richter and his attorney, Nat Becker, and will permit no verbal exchange of any kind with the defendant. All trial participants are instructed to remain in the entrance plaza outside the courthouse until further notice.

"How did you know?" Zack asks Lopez, rushing up to him as soon as Lopez emerges onto the bright plaza with the rest of them, after helping to direct the dogs and bomb squad inside the courthouse. "How did you put it together?"

Lopez looks confused. "What do you mean?"

A man holding two phones? How could Lopez guess about a detonator just from that? No one could be that smart. Not even Lopez.

"How did you know?" Zack asks again.

Lopez still appears puzzled. "From your text, Zack."

He takes out his phone and spins the screen so Zack can see it.

Don't let Karloff send a text from that phone.

A message from Zack Yellin.

Or, at least, from Zack's phone.

Zack looks over to Joey, across the plaza, surrounded by court officers. Joey, who is smiling.

He'd done exactly what Zack had. Brought up the most recent calls and texts in Zack's phone. Saw a call to a Raymond Lopez and sent him a text.

Pretty quick thinking, Joey. Pretty damn impressive, thinks Zack.

Pretty quick thinking for anyone.

83.

WAITING. WAITING IN the plaza.

Waiting for the civil case to continue. To conclude.

And waiting for my life to move on, thinks Zack. To get past this event, this never-ending story that keeps repeating itself, holding Zack tenaciously in its grip, caught in its net forever.

Waiting. Still waiting. That is his thought as he stares, inevitably, confused, across the plaza at Emily. What is she doing here exactly? Does she have the same feeling as Zack? That she too is tied to this event? Does she wonder if, in the same way they can't shake this event, they can't shake each other? That their fates are tied to each other, and that maybe this is the silver lining of this cloud of inescapability?

Maybe the waiting—the literal and symbolic waiting to resume—is bothering her too, bothering her in the same way, and she can't stand it either because in a minute, while they wait, she crosses the plaza toward him.

*　　*　　*

Police dogs and bomb personnel sweep their sensitive equipment under the courtroom benches and around the raised witness box and the judge's dais and along the courtroom walls.

Beneath the emergency defibrillator case mounted on the back wall that is required in every courtroom by state law, the dogs begin to bark.

The bomb squad's search devices simultaneously start to beep and ping.

A remote-controlled robot is called in.

The device is removed. Placed inside a specially equipped armor-plated vehicle waiting in the parking lot behind the building. Dismantled inside the vehicle by another remotely operated robot.

It all takes time. It all requires waiting.

Detective Lopez is still standing with Zack when Emily approaches.

"I'm covering the trial for my new job," she explains, apparently reading his puzzled expression from across the plaza. "I'm a reporter now. For an online news group. They figured I could bring some special insight, considering…" She trails off with a shrug.

It's what she wanted, he knows. A real journalism job. He immediately sees the irony that it was her connection to him, to the story, that finally gave her the chance to have it. That it probably wouldn't have happened so soon otherwise. But so what? It's a great result for her. "Congratulations on the new gig," he says. And then goes mute. He has no idea what to say next.

He knows that this is a safe place for her to see him. At a safe remove. On the witness stand. But now, unpredictably, they're out here, all of them milling in the plaza. Of course, she can simply turn and go. She didn't have to come over to see him. Or is she there at the trial partly to see him again? It is a question she won't have to answer directly for herself, he realizes. She can hide it from herself, inside this one-time chance to advance her career.

She looks awkwardly down and around. Avoiding looking at him, Zack notices.

Lopez smiles sadly, realizing immediately, from their awkwardness together, their uneasy silences and uncomfortable shifting, that they're no longer seeing each other. That, like this waiting outside the courthouse, their relationship is on hold too. Waiting to resume? Waiting for a verdict? By each, by both of them?

"How are you, Emily?" Lopez asks neutrally, pretending not to notice anything amiss and not wanting to get between them.

"Not bad, Detective."

"Congratulations on the new job." He adds his sentiments to Zack's. "And if you've wandered over here looking to ask the old detective for some scoop about this bomb scare, let me save you the trouble: no comment."

She smiles slowly. "Hey, my first 'no comment' as a reporter."

Lopez can't help smiling back. He leans toward her and says, more quietly, "But I can give you a little exclusive."

He puts a hand loosely on Zack's shoulder. "Your boy Zack just saved dozens of innocent lives." Lopez looks at her meaningfully. "Including yours."

Emily steps back a little, looking startled by this. Lopez can tell that she, like many out here, must have thought it was just precautionary. Not real. A phoned-in, idle threat.

"I can't tell you more right now. I'm not authorized to discuss details. But Zack can, if he wants. There's nothing stopping him from telling you."

And Lopez backs away, leaving them. And while Zack tries to figure out what to say, some place to begin, he loses his chance. Because seconds later, Litvinov appears in the plaza with several police officials. In his slight Slavic accent: "Civil case docket 231 will now resume." And they begin to flow back into the courtroom.

As they do, Emily looks at Zack, and her surprise seems to drop away. "Still playing the hero, huh?" Unsmiling but wry. "Hero is not a viable career choice, Zack," she says, mock-sternly. "But you do seem to have a weird talent for it."

Admiration, frustration, acceptance, and annoyance seem to all be rolled together in her response.

He shrugs.

She shakes her head and can't resist a smile. "As talents go, I guess it's a good one."

She heads to her seat in the gallery, and he heads, as

directed, back to the witness stand, and Joey and Nat Becker head back to the defense table.

As if nothing has happened in the last hour.

And in one way, nothing has. Thank God.

And in another way, everything has.

84.

JOEY RICHTER IS convicted in the wrongful death suit. The evidence is so plentiful and irrefutable that Joey's lawyer, Nat Becker, barely even tries to dispute it, according to numerous press reports, including the firsthand coverage from a reporter named Emily Lane.

But as for any penalty or punishment beyond the guilty verdict itself, a civil suit never entails a prison sentence, and it turns out the defendant has no money for wrongful death compensation. A court-ordered search of bank records for Joseph Richter turns up nothing. The impression of Joey having stashed unspent funds from his life of crime turns out to have originated with a jailhouse informant who communicated that to the prosecution team from the criminal trial. The previous prosecutors provided the name of the informant, Will Shale, but he had been released some time ago, and no one can locate him now to follow up.

Nat Becker is never compensated by the party that retained him beyond a small initial down payment for taking the case. When it becomes clear that Joey Richter has no resources,

Becker is questioned by the court and the press about who actually hired him. He avoids answering directly. He seems embarrassed to have accepted the case.

Judge Litvinov's sentence provides for the garnishment of all future earnings from the defendant. It's all Litvinov can do, really. Zack, Steve, and Emily assume—and, ironically, hope—that it will amount to only a few dollars a week, taken from Joey's prison earnings because, even before the civil case verdict from Litvinov has been delivered, the state files its new criminal case against Joey Richter on lesser criminal charges. Assault, conspiracy, manslaughter, criminal possession of a weapon, attempted murder. All viable charges to get Joey Richter off the street.

In the end, the Civil Part 231 proceedings are overshadowed by what happened—or what hadn't happened, thankfully—inside that courtroom.

Ending not with a bang but a whimper, thinks Zack. And in this case, a whimper is better.

The details of that day, of the plan and of the device, are eventually made clear to Litvinov. He realizes how close he came to dying and that this was not just another empty bomb threat deserving only groans and eye-rolls.

He is asked whether he recognized Karloff. A fellow Bulgarian immigrant. He shakes his head. No, sorry.

"I did notice the man you're talking about at the back of the gallery," Litvinov says. "Maybe something was vaguely familiar about him. But I can't place it. It must be too far, too dimly in the past."

85.

THE HUNT FOR Karloff soon involves much of the department.

Because now he's been seen. He's no longer a shadowy half-figure. Now there are current photos to go with the name, and a real name—Demetri Calunius—not merely a street name. Now his image is enhanced in multiple angles from multiple courthouse cameras. Entering. Exiting in a panicked hurry.

The shadowy portrait finally fills in. Racketeering, armed robbery, burglary, weapons charges, pornography, and prostitution.

The boy assassin who'd made his way to America. To the American underworld, where he established and administered a long-running criminal enterprise.

For a while, Karloff can't be found. No trace. It's assumed he's abandoned the area—deserted his local empire, to be dismantled by the police department piece by piece—to resurface with some new identity somewhere. After all, he's demonstrated the skills to pull that off before.

But months later, in an abandoned warehouse, he is reportedly cornered, trapped.

The police close in.

A dozen squad cars, two SWAT teams, command-and-control vehicles. A perimeter is established.

Shots are fired.

None, however, by the police.

Three shots, Zack is told.

Self-inflicted, Zack is told.

One after the other.

Why? Why would this criminal mastermind, so adept at survival, voluntarily sacrifice his survival instinct in the end?

It occurs to Zack Yellin that he alone might know the real reason.

Karloff's singular, deep abhorrence at the idea of appearing in a courtroom to be judged. A courtroom like the one in Sofia that had shaped his life. Echoing with merciless judgments on child custody, foster care, and a life of childhood crime? Zack feels sure of it. Karloff sought to destroy a courtroom, after all. It clearly had some symbolic, weighted meaning for him.

Zack wonders if Karloff ever realized that, had he not showed up in that courtroom himself, he might never have been caught. He might have continued in his criminal life, unstopped and unstoppable.

But if he had never been in that first courtroom in Bulgaria, he would have never been on the path he was on.

Three shots, Zack is told.

As if it took three shots to kill himself. Three shots, even self-inflicted, to kill a man like Karloff. That's how strong his survival instinct was. The survival instinct that he knew he had to overcome to successfully kill himself.

Two shots into his own torso first before a final shot to the head, apparently. To self-inflict pain first? To fully experience his own destruction? To be absolutely sure of getting the job done right?

Three shots. Further expanding the myth of Karloff.

Or shots fired by someone else? Shots that he commanded someone to fire? An underling or underlings so obedient to him that they'd do whatever they were told? A theory that furthered the myth as well.

Three shots. As if to finish off superhuman evil.

But Zack knew it wasn't superhuman evil. Merely too-human evil. Unwilling to end up in a courtroom again. Unwilling for his life to circle back to that.

Three shots. Playing on the public's imagination. And on Zack's. What kind of a person can do something like that to himself? What does it take? Can that really even happen?

*   *   *

Zack ponders those questions in the days that follow. They play at the back of his mind even as he and Emily—tentatively at first, but fully and unambivalently very soon—start to see each other again.

The questions keep turning over in his head—repeatedly, insistently—as they settle back into their lives and into their relationship, as the tensions of the trial ebb into memory, into just a news story, covered by Emily Lane.

Which is why Zack is both utterly stunned, and not surprised at all, to enter their apartment one evening two weeks later, switch on the overhead light, and find Karloff sitting on their bed with a gun and silencer pointed straight at Zack.

86.

KARLOFF USES THE gun muzzle to motion Zack to sit. He stares at Zack silently. Zack looks back blankly. His mind has shut off completely.

"It helps to be a myth," Karloff says at last—accent harsh, brusque, but his words seem measured, chosen carefully. "It keeps the police off the trail of reality."

Zack can hear the words. The accent. But he is aware of only the gun. Everything else recedes. The familiar apartment around him, its familiar objects—lamps, coats, dishtowels—becoming distant.

"I fooled them for now," says Karloff, "but I can't fool them forever." He shakes his head side to side, almost gently, as if still trying to take in the turn of events. "My network is ruined. So I go back now to Bulgaria. Where I come from. Where I can still disappear."

Karloff furrows his brow and casually inspects the end of the black silencer. A tradesman checking a tool. "You fooled me," he says, his irritation still strong. "Your little phone trick…you fooled me, didn't you?"

The last weeks come circling back to Zack. A whirl of circumstance. A roller coaster coiling tightly through switchbacks of terror and tension and victory and love.

He knows how the world has always seen him—as a child of luck and lightness, of air and smiles and fun, of cleverness and ingenuity, who has always somehow managed to dodge the darkness. But now the darkness has found him. He is cornered by it. It is, in the end, apparently inescapable.

Something in him should have known it would end this way. Something in him has always known it would.

His breath, his final breaths, come short, pained, tight now. Each is a conscious struggle. He is already heading toward nothing. His existence is already ceasing. His body and his mind are preparing together, shutting down.

Karloff points to the silencer. "With this, no one will hear it, even in this building. No one will know till I am long gone." He twists the silencer firmly against the barrel until there is a click.

The gun. Its oiled black muzzle. It's all Zack can see, all he can focus on or think about.

Only dimly, numbly aware now…It's sensation as much as thought…

The last moment of my life. The worst moment of my life.

Yet the moment manages to become far worse.

A key jangles in the door. Emily steps in. Drops her heavy purse to the floor, kicks off her boots, and only then looks up to see Zack, and Karloff, and the pointed gun.

"Perfect!" says Karloff, the word particularly rich in his accent, thick with satisfaction, final-sounding, joyful, and he smiles.

Emily screams.

Zack hangs his head, closes his eyes…Numb, defeated, prepared…

Karloff fires.

Three shots. Exactly like the myth.

But the myth of Karloff's end had been wrong. So wrong.

Three shots. Almost casually. Almost an afterthought.

Three shots. Exactly where Karloff—where Demetri Calunius—must have been envisioning for days. Imagining for weeks.

Exactly where they would powerfully make their point.

Into the middle of Zack and Emily's mattress.

He looks up at Zack and Emily. The message clear: *I can kill you right now. I can kill you anytime.*

"You fooled me," Karloff repeats, "and I fooled you."

The implication: *We're even.*

"And if you tell anyone I'm alive, I still have just enough network left, and their visit to you will be very different from mine." The hint of a smile. He heads for the door.

And Zack and Emily will never say a word.

87.

ZACK SITS ACROSS from Steve in a GreenGirl near Steve's apartment.

"Hey," Zack says warily.

"Hey."

Zack has no idea why Steve has texted to invite him. But he assumes it would take something important. Something that could somehow surmount Steve's feelings about Zack's betrayal.

Both of them know Zack wants to mend the relationship. Will do whatever he can to piece it back together.

Steve looks at him. Somberly, cautiously, and then—slowly, unable to stop himself or resist—he smiles. "I solved it."

Zack is utterly confused. "What do you mean?"

"I solved it," Steve says again. "And I had to show you."

Show me what? Zack doesn't understand.

"Seven-seven-seven-five-four-eight," Steve says.

The number of the detonation code sent to Joey's phone in Zack's pocket.

The number Steve had challenged Zack to try to find. To

figure out a code one more time, like Joey's phone code and his Apple ID. And Zack never could.

"I was following the trial," Steve says. "I mean, how could I not? Following it every day online. Including Emily's coverage."

Steve spins his laptop. He shows Zack photos and video from the civil trial coverage—mostly participants entering and exiting the courtroom. No video or photos allowed in the courtroom, of course.

"Seven-seven-seven-five-four-eight," says Steve again, still smiling.

Zack is sitting up. Alert. Eager.

Steve shows Zack footage of Litvinov heading to his car in the special gated judicial parking lot.

Getting into his car. A totally nondescript Toyota Avalon.

Zack watches Litvinov pull out and pass the news camera.

And sees it immediately.

State of New York judicial license plate number: *777548*.

He looks at Steve. He understands instantly.

The original plan for the bomb must have been to blow up that Toyota, with Litvinov in it. Maybe Karloff's assignment for Joey, dumb Joey. Untrustworthy, inept Joey. Because how could you screw that up? Enter the number that you see on the license plate into your phone, Joey, and *kaboom*. Simple. Foolproof.

But Karloff must have decided, somewhere along the way, he wanted *more*. More elaborate. More interesting. More lives. More damage. So a bigger plan was hatched. A plan to get inside Litvinov's courtroom. A plan that involved a victim's family, and a lawsuit, and a gullible lawyer, and a jailhouse informant, and a lot of patience. A plan that in the end was too ambitious.

If he'd kept to his low profile, his invisibility, Karloff could have gone on forever—stealthy, effective, terrifying, unknown. But he hungered for a larger "justice."

A larger justice that eluded him.

777548. At last Zack knows what it signifies. Karloff's hubris. His arrogance.

But more than that, his darkness.

Why didn't he simply kill Zack and Emily? *"You fooled me, and I fooled you,"* he had said. Implying that *we're even.* And what good is getting even, what good is revenge, if no one's there to see it?

The courtroom revenge drama he'd planned had been ruined. So did all that pent-up drama need to go elsewhere?

And a drama needs an audience. Even a small audience. And, well, a *live* audience. Karloff's hubris. His arrogance. Maybe, strangely, it had saved them.

"I could have texted you but I wanted to see your face," says Steve.

"Well, you can see I'm pretty impressed."

"I solved it," says Steve. Leaning back from the laptop. Lifting his coffee cup to Zack in the gesture of a toast.

And Zack is thinking about that phrase: *solved it.* Because he suspects that Steve is fully aware that he's here solving something else too. Restoring their friendship. Putting the pain behind them.

"Yeah," agrees Zack, reading between the lines, dropping his wariness, smiling at his old friend at last, "looks like you solved it."

SIX MORE MONTHS LATER

88.

ZACK SITS WAITING for Joey Richter.

Visiting hours are Fridays, 2:00 to 4:00.

Joey shuffles out in his loose prison grays, smiling. Smiling to see Zack.

"Hey," says Joey brightly.

"Hey," says Zack.

He watches Joey settle into the folding chair on the other side of the clear plastic divider. ·

"I've never been inside a prison," says Zack.

Joey looks at him. "I've never really been anywhere else."

Zack notices immediately. Joey seems calm. Untroubled. His drawn, haggard appearance, his air of desperation as he begged for Zack's help, the mixed terror and fury of a cornered animal—all seemingly gone.

In Joey Richter's trial for manslaughter, criminal possession of a weapon, and conspiracy to commit murder, the evidence was overwhelming. The state made no missteps. The prosecutors went light on Cloud technology and didn't rely on the gruesome photographs. They focused instead on hard evidence that a jury could easily understand. Like the Ruger recovered from a custodial closet at the Rooms4Rent where Joey Richter had been staying and that firearm's brutal history.

Best of all, Zack didn't have to take the stand. The case against Joey Richter no longer revolved around Zack's testimony. The prosecutors decided that Zack was too risky as a witness. If he told his whole story on the stand—mistakenly swapping iPhones with an assassin, *then* swapping matching disposable phones, a bomb planted in a courtroom, helping to foil its detonation from the witness stand—it would sound unbelievable to a jury. It would create significant doubt. The prosecutors couldn't take that chance.

The jury deliberated for only a day. According to statutes, the judge had significant leeway in sentencing. Joey got thirty years.

"They treating you okay here?" Zack asks.

"They always have," says Joey.

"Well, I wanted to see you, check on you, and well, say thanks for helping to save everyone's life," says Zack.

"A professional killer. Who took lives for money," says Joey. "And then saved them for free." Obviously it was a moment Joey had thought about.

Zack leans forward toward the divider. "And why *did* you?" he asks. He's been wondering about it for weeks. Because Joey Richter would not have suddenly been interested in saving lives. He would not have suddenly gotten religion or worried about meeting his maker, none of that.

Joey smiles thinly. "I didn't care about saving those people.

All those clerks and guards and justice system jerks. All those media leeches. Lopez. Your girlfriend. I didn't give a shit about any of them. I didn't even care about saving myself. I'd be just as happy to blow us all up." He looks hard, unsmiling at Zack. *You know it's true.*

"Then why?"

He shrugs. "I wanted to show you how smart I am, that's all."

Zack looks at him.

"Prove it to you," Joey says. Adding, more quietly, "Prove it to myself."

"Well, I've got to admit it…you proved it," Zack says. "That was some quick thinking."

Quick thinking by both of them, Zack knows. Quick, accidental teamwork.

Lives saved by a couple of texts. A misleading, confusing, merely numerical one from Zack to Karloff. A truthful, direct one from Joey to Lopez.

"So listen," says Joey, "since we're talking about why. Now it's my turn to ask. You were willing to see me, to help me, when I reached out to you. Why?"

Zack shrugs. "You had no one else."

"You lost your girlfriend, you lost your best friend, to reach out and help a killer?"

Zack has no answer for that. There is nothing to say, no good defense, for the absurdity of Zack's choice.

"So who's the crazy one, Zack? Really. Who's the crazy one?"

They sit there a little longer with nothing more to say to each other. With nothing ever to say to each other, not really.

They regard each other through the divider. For what, Zack knows, will be the last time. Probably Joey knows it too.

A divide, too, of culture, upbringing, circumstance, and opportunity that could hardly be any greater.

Joey Richter. Zack Yellin.

One, a killer who coldly, brutally cut lives short.

While together, they saved lives by the dozen.

89.

AT THE END of the visit, Zack exits the prison. A pat-down, an interview, that echoes, bookends, the procedures of his entrance.

Exiting the prison—merely as a visitor—he is embarrassed to experience a sense of liberation. He knows how lucky he is that the prison behind him is merely symbolic for him. That he can walk away.

Exiting the prison of the story. The prison of events. Emerging from the insanity into the light. Finishing out, at last, his own weird sentence in the spotlight, in the crosshairs. In certain ways an unbearably long sentence. In certain ways a mercifully brief one.

As he heads out to the parking lot, he texts Emily.

She pulls their rented car up to the curb.

Emily, who drove here to upstate New York with him. Who's been waiting for him patiently while he visits Joey. Pulling up now to the prison lot curb like she's picking Zack up from an errand. Like an elderly couple that always does their errands together.

This is something he had to do, this visit.

And she never questioned it. She understood.

"Now, unfortunately, it's the long drive back," Zack says.

"GPS says three hours forty minutes," says Emily, turning the car toward the exit gate.

"I could definitely use some coffee," says Zack. "Didn't we pass a GreenGirl a few miles back?"

Emily smiles. "Sure did."

"What do you say?"

"I say absolutely." Emily looks over now from the driver's seat, grinning. "But only if you promise to hang on to your phone in there."

A month ago, Zack finally got rid of the disposable and got another iPhone. He looks down at it now. All its possibilities. All its coiled, compressed power. Staring back up at him.

This mute, inanimate object that is anything but mute and inanimate. That is the opposite of mute and inanimate.

It's a liePhone, Zack thinks cynically.

It's a slyPhone.

A cryPhone.

A sighPhone.

A lastgoodbyePhone.

A onemoretryPhone.

A neverknowwhyPhone.

But at least, presumably, no longer a diePhone.

"It stays in my pocket," Zack says. "I promise."

ABOUT THE AUTHOR

Jonathan Stone is the author of the Julian Palmer mystery series, which was hailed as "stunning" and "risk-taking" in starred reviews from *Publishers Weekly* and as "bone-chilling" by the *New York Times*. His biggest bestseller *Moving Day*, and his novels *Days of Night* and *Parting Shot*, have been optioned for film. His short stories have been anthologized in two Mystery Writers of America annual collections as well as *Best American Mystery Stories 2016*. A graduate of Yale, Jon is married, has a son and daughter, and lives in Connecticut.